Lessons I Learned from Nick Nack

Also by Padgett Gerler

GETTING THE IMPORTANT THINGS RIGHT

Lessons I Learned from Nick Nack

PADGETT GERLER

ISBN 978-1-4961-8300-2

DISCLAIMER

This book is a work of fiction. Names, characters, places, and incidents are either products of the author's imagination or are used fictitiously. Any resemblance to actual events or persons, living or dead, is entirely coincidental.

DEDICATED TO THE SPECIAL WOMEN IN MY LIFE WHO HAVE SURVIVED AND THRIVED WITH GRACE AND ATTITUDE

Mary Helen Grimes
Cathy Hofknecht
Mary Emily Pow
Helen Wallace

ACKNOWLEDGMENTS

Mary Helen, my thanks to you for sharing your journey with me and for showing us all how to live life with grace, love, and faith.

Cathy S., thank you for your professional and medical guidance. Your insight helped me understand Rowdy and Nick Nack's journey.

Mama, thank you for nurturing me with unconditional love and for insisting I learn the difference between the subjective and objective cases.

Ed, thank you for being my first, my last, and my always reader.

And special thanks to my family, my friends, and my readers who love me and encourage me daily to be a better writer, a better friend, a better person. Your support touches me.

Lessons I Learned
from
Nick Nack

Prologue

"**N**o! Absolutely not!"

"But Mom!"

"Alexandra, quit whining. I said, 'No', and that means 'No way, no how, never!'"

My daughter ran from the kitchen, stomped up the stairs, and slammed her bedroom door, rattling the windows.

"Come on, Rowdy. Don't be so selfish."

"Selfish? How can you say that, Mark? You know how I feel about dogs. I don't want one, and I'm not going to have one. And that's that!"

"But don't Alex and I get a say-so?"

"You get *bitten* by a dog and then let me know how you feel about *having* a dog. Only then do you get a say-so."

"But, Rowdy, that was a long time ago, and it was an isolated incident."

"Don't minimize it, Mark! How many kids get bitten in the neck by a dog? It was terrifying."

"Rowdy, we wouldn't get a full grown Rottweiler or Pit Bull. We'd get a gentle little puppy—one that would grow up with Alex and become a family member."

"My family members aren't covered with shedding hair, and they don't pee on the carpet. *And they don't bite me in the neck!*"

For weeks my husband and daughter whined and cried and begged and behaved like brats, but still I would not budge. I was not

1

having a neck-biting monster in my home.

Then Mark played his trump card: "Rowdy, Alex is an only child. You don't want more children. She needs a companion. We owe it to her."

Then *I* stormed out of the kitchen, stomped up the stairs, and slammed *my* bedroom door, rattling the windows. I flopped on the bed, pounded my pillow, and kicked my feet like a tantrum-throwing child. Once I'd recovered from my lapse from maturity, I returned to the kitchen.

Fuming, I said through clenched teeth, "I will not feed a dog. I will not bathe a dog. I will not be a poop collector for a dog. I will not walk a dog. I will ignore a dog's existence. Most of all, I will not allow a dog to come into this house. It will live in a dog house in the back yard where it can't possibly get at my neck."

Squealing and jumping up and down, both Mark and Alex agreed to my terms.

In preparation for the adoption, my husband and daughter went to Home Depot where they found a home for their new furry child. Large enough for a family of four, it came in seven hundred pieces with assembly instructions in Chinese. I had been thinking plywood lean-to.

Nick Nack, named for *nick nack paddy whack give a dog a bone*, came from a local shelter to live with us. I was pleased that Mark and Alex were willing to take a dog that no one else wanted, but their adoption of a waif pooch did not change my mind. I still did not want a dog; I'd just agreed to tolerating their dog ownership.

Nick Nack arrived when she was eight weeks old and was, at that age, too young to stay outside alone in her doghouse-mansion. And since I would not allow my child to move into the back-yard mansion to keep the dog company, Nick Nack would live in a cardboard box in Alex's room until she was old enough to graduate to her large, expensive, outdoor home. And, I figured, at her age she was too young to get at my neck.

"Oh, Mom, isn't she adorable?"

Well, of course, all tiny puppies are adorable, and Nick Nack was no exception. She was a little ball of black fuzz, romping and yipping like some wind-up toy. But I wasn't getting sucked in. That little black ball of fuzz was going to grow into a large, black, snarling, hairy beast.

As one would guess, by the time Nick Nack was old enough to move to her large, expensive home, she had become so accustomed to the *really* big house that she couldn't have been coaxed into the *merely* big house in the back yard with a sixteen-ounce Porterhouse, a futon, and a plasma TV.

By her projected relocation date, Alex and Mark's dog was no longer a cute ball of black fluff. Part Chow and part Lab, she had become tall, with stick legs and a long snout like a Lab. Like a Chow, she had a black tongue, pointy ears, and a huge, fluffy black coat and tail. She wasn't menacing looking—just comical, as if she were made up of some mismatched canine parts someone found lying around. Even if I were amused by her odd appearance, I still didn't like her and wanted absolutely nothing to do with her. But I couldn't have pried her out of the Big House with a shoe horn.

"Okay, she can stay in the house, but she is *not* to put one paw on the furniture. Understand?"

"Yes, we understand."

"And you are to keep her away from me."

"Got it."

�✥✥

Mark and Alex *loved* Nick Nack.

Nick Nack loved—you guess it—*me!*

Why? Who knows? Because I certainly did not love her and made that quite clear. True to my word, I did not feed, bathe, walk, clean up after, or pay attention to Mark and Alex's dog. But she adored me and hovered relentlessly.

Per our agreement, my family kept Nick Nack off the furniture and tried to keep her away from me. Their attempts at the latter failed. As soon as Mark or Alex turned their backs, Nick Nack would appear at my side and stare up at me with adoring eyes.

Each day I'd return home from running errands to find her waiting at the door for me with a where-have-you-been-I-was-so-worried-I'm-so-glad-you're-home look in her eyes. It didn't matter whether I came in the front door or back door, she seemed to intuit where I'd appear. I could have crept through the dining room window, and, somehow, she'd have known and would have been there to greet me. If the dog had had opposable thumbs, she'd have met me with a martini and my slippers.

Nick Nack's adoration baffled me. I clearly wanted nothing to do with her, but she stubbornly refused to get my message. No matter how I tried to ignore her or screamed at her to leave me alone, she remained my shadow. She just wanted to be nearby. Out of exasperation, I eventually admitted defeat, gave up, and grudgingly abided her presence.

And she demanded nothing of me in payment for her adoration: no treats, no hugs, no kisses—no attention whatsoever.

One

"Mama, if the world was flat, could we see Africa from here?" I was taken aback by my daughter's question. When I was about eight, the same age as Alex, I asked my mother that very question, sitting in the same spot. We were on the beach in front of our family cottage at Emerald Isle, staring out to sea. I thought I was the only person who had ever thought of seeing Africa from the coast of North Carolina. But Alex is so like me in every way. The first time I held her in my arms, I was amazed at how much she looked like my baby pictures. Since I'm Rowdy Alexander Murphy, I named my so-like-me little girl Alexandra Rowdy Murphy.

Most of all, like her mother, she adores her daddy, Mark—the first and only man I have ever loved.

Eight-year olds don't understand that weather conditions and visual limitations would prevent her from seeing Africa from North Carolina, even if the world were as flat as a pancake. But I wasn't as patient as my mother and was in no mood to explain why seeing Africa from North Carolina would be impossible, under any circumstance. In fact, I wasn't in the mood to answer any questions at all.

I had more pressing issues on my mind.

The day before I was at home in Raleigh, tending a pot roast and halfway watching some afternoon talk show on my tiny kitchen countertop TV when Mark pulled into the driveway. Usually when he got out of his car, he'd smile and wave at me through the kitchen window. But that day he didn't look my way; instead, he just ducked

5

his head, crammed his fists into his jacket pockets, and slouched to the back door.

"Uh oh, bad day on campus," I said to Nick Nack, now my constant shadow.

I immediately lost interest in Jerry who had become Jerri by way of a sex change. I gave the TV a click with the remote so that I could focus my attention on my apparently-troubled husband. I dropped the meat fork in the sink, rinsed and dried my hands, and turned to get my afternoon peck on the lips.

Mark came through the kitchen door but didn't shed his jacket and hang it on the hook, as he normally did. He also didn't give me my afternoon peck on the lips. I reached to hug him, but he didn't respond, his hands remaining deep in his pockets.

Mark still made my pulse quicken and my heart beat a little faster. The shock of blond hair that he'd had when I first met him still fell casually over his forehead, begging me to lovingly coax it back into place.

I reached out my hand, but before I could touch his hair, he said, "I want out."

It really was bad. The campus politics had taken their toll on Mark, and he was sleeping poorly and eating little. I had fixed a pot roast, his favorite, in hopes of enticing him to eat something. The kitchen was full of its aroma, but the promise of pot roast didn't seem to be softening Mark at all.

"Out? Do you mean out of a class? Out of a committee? Or do you mean out of your teaching career altogether?"

"No, Rowdy, I want out. Out of our marriage. I want a divorce."

I've heard women say that when their husbands tell them, "I want a divorce," it is as if they are speaking a foreign language, one they'd never heard and, of course, didn't understand or speak.

Mark and I stood and stared at each another in silence.

Finally, he said, "Say something, Rowdy."

My first thought—and it escaped my lips before I could catch it—was, "Who is she?"

Mark had never given me reason to doubt his fidelity. He was an attractive, middle-aged college professor who had female, and sometimes male, students who adored him and threw themselves at him. Most professors, attractive *or* unattractive, have students who worship them. I had worshipped a few myself. Mark had never, to

6

my knowledge, responded to any of his students' advances.

But, then, he had never asked for a divorce.

Then he tossed his head in an unnatural way, shaking his shock of hair into place without my help, let out a nervous laugh, and said, "Oh, Rowdy, don't be silly; there's no one."

It took only three days to confirm what I already knew to be true: he was lying.

Her name was Tawni. Tawni, with an *I*, for god's sake. All right, I get the irony. But Rowdy is a family name, not a pony's name or a teddy bear's name. And it doesn't end with an *I*.

"I'm so sorry, Rowdy. I wouldn't hurt you for the world."

"Then why are you hurting me?"

"We tried to fight it. Honestly, we did. But it was just bigger than the two of us."

Mark was a brilliant man, a scholar, a college professor. When in the hell had he started talking like a bad made-for-TV movie? Probably about the time twenty-four-year-old Tawni waved her man-made D cups in his face and told him what a brilliant scholar he was.

She was a student—not his student, just a student he had seen on campus. She'd seen him, too, and had made a point of being where he'd be as often as she could. And she came on to him in a big way. But he'd had many students come on to him. I believe she just came on at the right time: graying temples, the merest sign of a jowl, slightly expanding waistline. Mid-life crisis. It was either Tawni or a red sports car.

I could have competed with the red sports car. Tawni, though, was out of my league with her flowing golden mane, her longer-than-should-be-allowed legs, her drum-tight abs, and those man-made D cups.

"But I do love you, Rowdy..."

"Stop right there, Mark. If you dare finish that sentence with 'like a sister,' I swear to god I'll slap the crap out of you."

So he just shrugged his shoulders and pinched his lips tight and broke my heart—again.

As soon as Mark packed his bags and walked out of my life, I headed with Alexandra for the coast, thinking it was the only place I'd find comfort and solace. I had loved our family cottage at Emerald Isle, North Carolina and had spent summer vacations there since Daddy had bought the place when I was seven years old.

Mark and Alexandra treasured the cottage as much as I did, and we made new memories with each visit. When I returned after Mark's departure, the evidence of those memories was everywhere: shells and driftwood we had collected along the shore, pictures we had taken, journals we had kept. The commemoration of Mark's July birthdays, Alexandra's hand-made birthday cards to her daddy, all fashioned lovingly during our summer vacations, danced across the refrigerator. Each was adorned with sand and shells and seaweed and her little-girl hand writing. Knowing that the three of us would never again make memories in our beach home broke my heart. My trip to my beloved island hadn't given me the comfort I was looking for. All I'd gotten were painful memories and questions from an eight-year old that I couldn't or couldn't be bothered to answer.

But, god, I loved this place.

I felt a lump rise in my throat as I stared out at My Ocean. Yes, *My* Ocean. I had claimed it as mine the day Daddy bought the house.

"Mine, all mine!" I'd screamed, pulling away from Mama as she tried to slather me with Coppertone so that my fair, freckled skin wouldn't blister.

But I was too impatient for sun screen. I wanted to feel My Ocean on my body, wanted the raging surf to fling me about. Although I was only seven years old, Daddy had taught me to swim and maneuver the powerful surf in this very ocean when I was just five. I raced into the water, fearless, and threw myself into the towering waves. I loved the way the roiling breakers made me twirl and spin and turn somersaults, holding me down, dragging me backward and forward, making my lungs hurt from holding my breath, finally hurtling me to shore. I'd stand on wobbly legs and pause just long enough to take a deep breath and pull my sand-laden bathing suit out of my butt crack before racing back for more.

While I entertained myself in the surf, Mama would corral my four little brothers on the sand, amusing them with snacks and juice and sand buckets and shovels. When they tired, she'd line them up like little soldiers on a blanket under the beach umbrella and let the rumbling surf lull them to sleep. Daddy would stand calf-deep in the water, fishing and keeping an eye on me as I tumbled for hours in My Ocean.

When I became exhausted from my surf tumbling, I was content to sit on the sand, wrapped in my beach towel, staring out to sea, wondering what secrets the ocean floor held, asking Mama if I would be able to see Africa if the world were flat. Once I wondered what the ocean would look like if it were drained—like a bathtub with its plug pulled. The image of sunken ships and human skeletons and whales and sharks and other frightening sea life piled up to the horizon scared me so badly that I quickly re-plugged my ocean and filled it back up, never to drain it again.

I smiled at the memory but still shuddered at the thought of an empty ocean.

Each summer, the day after school ended, my father would pack the station wagon to overflowing and head for the coast. He would strap his old army foot locker to a rack on the top of the car and fill it with our bath supplies and all the staples Mama would need in the kitchen at our beach home. The inside of the station wagon held our clothes and beach toys and seven family members and two dozen Krispy Kreme donuts. The car groaned and rocked from the weight of its load.

Once outside Raleigh we drove through rich, green farmland where the tobacco fields were waiting for harvest and the corn was beginning to tassel. Occasionally we'd come upon a farmer dressed in denim overalls, perched high atop his tractor, bouncing up and down in his seat, driving slowly along the highway from one field to the next. We were all anxious to get to the beach, but those slow rides behind overall-clad farmers driving tractors were an integral part of our trip. The closer we drew to the coast, the more animated and anxious we became. We'd giggle and chatter and sound as if we were sucking helium.

When we'd arrive at our cottage on Emerald Isle, we'd unfold our tightly packed limbs and tumble out, like Shriners emerging from a stunt car in a Labor Day parade. Once we'd stretched ourselves back into shape, we'd clamber up the rickety stairs that would take us to our beloved home for the summer.

The cottage was—and still is—a bare-bones home, just the essentials to house a family of seven lucky enough to spend each summer at the beach. There were three bedrooms and one bathroom, as well as a combination room that served as living room, dining room, and kitchen. Best of all, our home stood on stilts and peeked over the dunes, directly out to My Ocean.

There was no air conditioning; it wasn't necessary with the mild sea breeze that blew through the open windows and massive live oaks that shielded our home from the blazing summer sun. There was a large porch that stretched across the back of the house, where seven rattan-bottomed rockers tilted back and forth with the gentle currents of air.

At the end of our days of playing on the beach and frolicking in the ocean, Daddy would cook our supper on his charcoal grill. If he'd caught fish in the surf that day, he'd grill fish. If not, we were content with hamburgers or hot dogs. Sometimes he'd barbecue chicken or roast oysters or grill shrimp. It didn't matter what we ate; anything tasted good after a day in the salty sea air. After supper, while Mama washed the dishes and Daddy cleaned the grill, my brothers and I would put on our seersucker pajamas, the only thing that didn't irritate our freshly-pinked shoulders. Then we'd sit in our rockers on the back porch, Mama rubbing Noxzema on our sunburns and humming some song that she and daddy loved. From there we'd watch the day disappear.

Sometimes Daddy would say, "What y'all say we ride down to DQ and get us a Dilly Bar?"

At the mention of DQ, my brothers and I would squeal and scurry for the station wagon, wearing only our pajamas and rubber flip flops. I'd climb into the middle seat, and one of the twins, usually Sam, would hop into my lap. He'd always smell like little-boy sweat as he'd lean back against me and stick his thumb in his mouth. The other three boys, Will, Greg, and Kevin, would pile in the far seat that faced the back window. They'd hope that a car would follow so they could stretch their smiles wide with their fingers and waggle their tongues at the passengers.

The Dairy Queen, just a few miles down the beach, was a favorite hang-out for parents eager to settle beach-wired, pajama-clad, sunburned children. Finding a booth for the seven of us usually took a wait, but we didn't mind. My brothers would hop and twirl their energy away, and Mama would comb my long, red, tangled-by-the-sea-breeze hair with her fingers—it felt so good—until Daddy claimed us a spot, got us settled, and brought our Dilly Bars to us.

And as we made chocolate rings around our mouths, Mama would say, "I spy with my green eyes something blue and white and sorta round."

And we'd each want to be the one to guess the thing that Mama was spying.

Once she said, "I spy with my green eyes something long and red with a yellow stripe."

After many incorrect guesses, Will jumped up and screamed, "It's Rowdy's hair with her yellow hair band."

And he was right.

I reached up and wiped my sleeve across my weepy eyes as I remembered how happy my little brother had been for guessing that Mama was spying his big sister's long red hair.

When we'd get home from DQ, Mama would say, "Now, y'all run wash the chocolate off your faces and brush your teeth. And don't forget to dust the sand off your feet before you get into bed. You don't want to be sleeping on sandy sheets. Daddy and I'll be in in a minute to hear your prayers. Now scoot."

And while we were getting ready for bed, Daddy would put a record on the stereo—usually Marvin Gaye or Sam Cooke or Johnny Mathis—and then he'd take our mama in his arms and slow dance her around. I would hear the floor boards creaking as they held on and swayed, the sand making gritty sounds as their feet slid back and forth. I'd know that Mama's head was on Daddy's shoulder. I'd know their eyes were closed as they listened to Sam Cooke croon, *"Yoooouuu send me. My darling, yoooouuu send me, honest you do."* [1]

All parents should slow dance. It makes their children happy. It makes their children feel safe.

But sometimes Daddy'd have to leave us to go tend to business back in Raleigh. He owned an insurance company which he could pretty much run from Emerald Isle, with the help of Mrs. Gresham, his secretary, and Mr. Hines, who was an agent, like Daddy.

Every once in a while, though, he'd say, "Better head on to Raleigh and give John and Betty a hand."

We'd beg him not to go and would hang onto him as he'd head for the car, but he would smile and hug us all and pat us on our backs and say, "Gotta go, Kiddos, but I'll be back soon. Now, y'all be sweet, you hear, and take good care of Mama till I get back."

We knew he had to go and that begging him to stay wouldn't change a thing. But we just wanted him to know that we loved him and would miss him. We also wanted to hear him call us *Kiddos* and tell us to be sweet and to take good care of our mama.

He'd be gone for days, or maybe a week. Mama would be lonely and we'd miss our sweet daddy, but we were always in a glee when he'd return to watch us twirl in the ocean and grill our fish and take us for a Dilly Bar.

And dance with our mama.

Two

Year after year we'd be drawn back by the music of our beach. Even as we went away to college, Mama and Daddy would open the house at the beginning of summer, the two of them spending the season there and waiting for the precious times when their children could join them.

As my brothers and I married and our family grew, our cottage became cramped. That didn't bother us. We'd just drag out inflatable mattresses and sleeping bags to cover the floor as we bedded down. We'd whisper and chat to whomever lay beside us until the sound of the pounding waves rocked us to sleep.

The summer before the twins were to return to college for their senior year, the entire family met at Emerald Isle to spend one last week and help Mama and Daddy close up the cottage for the winter. I remember it as our most precious time together.

Alex was a toddler, the only grandchild and the darling of her uncles. My brothers passed her around for a week, her feet never touching the floor. They fed her, bathed her, played with her on the beach, and, as Will said, put kiss bruises on her.

Daddy taught Mark how to fish that summer. As they stood calf-deep in the surf, Daddy told Mark about the insurance business, and Mark told Daddy about teaching at State. They'd always been cordial but never really close. That summer, though, they discovered just how much they cared for each other.

And with the boys occupied, that left us girls to shop and gossip and relax on the beach. Will and Marilyn had been married two years.

Marilyn was a piano teacher who taught lessons in her and Will's home. She was quiet and shy but so sweet and kind. She didn't laugh loudly and joke the way our family did, but we loved her; and even though she was a little stand-offish, she seemed to enjoy her time with us that summer. She and Will told us that last week we were together at Emerald Isle that they were expecting their first child. Mama and Daddy were beside themselves with excitement.

Greg and Sandy had been married just a little over a year, but Sandy took to our family right away. Petite with long, dark hair, she was a dynamo. She was take-charge and could blow up inflatable mattresses, as well as fry the best chicken I've ever tasted. She could also tackle a wave as well as I could and beat all my brothers at beach volleyball. She was a third-grade teacher, and I could imagine her running her class like a loveable drill sergeant. She fawned over Alex and wouldn't let Marilyn lift a finger because of her pregnancy. I came to adore Sandy that precious time we spent together at the beach, helping Mama and Daddy say good-bye to Emerald Isle for the summer.

When our week came to a close, we stood on the porch and chatted for a good while, putting off our leaving, knowing that this would be the last time that all of us would be together at the beach until Mama and Daddy opened the cottage for us the following summer season. Finally all of us kids hugged each other and then hugged and kissed our parents good-bye before climbing into our cars to go our separate ways. We left Mama and Daddy standing there on the porch, their arms around each other, waving to us until we turned and disappeared from their sight. They would make one last sweep of the house to be sure we'd turned off the faucets, stored the beach chairs and umbrellas, taken all our possessions with us, and locked the downstairs storage room. Then they'd pull the curtains, lock the door, and climb into their car to head back to Raleigh.

Summer was officially over for the Alexanders.

They were on a country road about two hours outside Raleigh. A truck driver, drunk from a night of partying, ignored the stop sign. The coroner said my parents were gone in an instant, didn't even know they'd been hit.

There are no words to describe my siblings' and my devastation and grief. We were inconsolable. Our parents had been our rock, the glue that had held us all together. My nights were sleepless and so gut-wrenchingly painful, I was certain I couldn't survive the loss. By day I lay on the sofa and sobbed; by night I lay in my bed and sobbed. Mark was wonderful during my grief, comforting me and taking over Alex's care.

But only when I was able to envision the last hour of my parents' life could I stop crying and move forward. Imagining their deaths did not diminish my sorrow, but I was comforted by the certainty that my parents loved each other to the end and left this world happy in each other's company. Had one gone first, surely the other would have soon died of a broken heart.

After seeing their children off and closing the beach house at season's end, Mama and Daddy would have climbed into their car, and Daddy would have said one last time, "Think we got everything, Mama?"

And my mother would have smiled, patted his hand, and said as she always did, "I believe so, Darlin', but if we've missed something, we can get it when we come back."

At first they'd chat:

"I think Will has put on a little weight. Don't you think he looks good?"

"Isn't Alexandra a darling? She's the spittin' image of Rowdy. I could just take a bite out of her."

"I just love Sandy. I'm so glad that Greg found her. She's a doll."

"Can you believe the twins will be graduating next year? The last of our babies, college graduates."

Once they'd talked about all their children, they'd fall silent.

Then Daddy would say, "How about a little music?"

"Good idea. Let's listen to Johnny. We haven't heard from him in a while," Mama would say.

So Daddy would pull down his sun visor, take out a Johnny Mathis CD, and slip it into the slot. About an hour from Emerald Isle, *Wonderful, Wonderful* [2] would begin:

> *Sometimes we walk hand in hand by the sea,*
> *And we breathe in the cool, salty air.*
> *You turn to me with a kiss in your eyes,*
> *And my heart feels a thrill beyond compare.*
> *Then your lips cling to mine*
> *It's wonderful, wonderful*
> *Oh, so wonderful, my love.*

Daddy would look over at Mama and smile, and then he'd reach for her hand. I know, for certain, they'd be holding hands.

My brothers and I moved through the days following our parents' deaths like zombies. We planned and attended a funeral, and we chose to have our parents cremated so that we could scatter their ashes in the ocean in front of their beloved home at Emerald Isle. When the time came, we siblings elected to go to the island alone; our spouses understood. We gathered at my house at daybreak and set off for the coast.

At first we rambled about nonsense, trying to smother the pain that was filling the car; but by the time we reached the outskirts of Raleigh, we were wearied from the weight of the ache and just stopped trying. I slipped one of Mama and Daddy's favorite CD's in, I believe it was Jackie Wilson, but by the time *Lonely Teardrops*[3] started, we were all weeping loudly. I ejected the CD and returned it to its case as we chose to ride the remainder of the trip in silence.

When we reached our beach house, we didn't go inside but kicked off our shoes and headed directly to the ocean. It wasn't a conscious decision; we just somehow knew that being in the home that our parents had created for us would be too painful on a wound that was still so new and raw.

As we crested the dunes, we scanned the shore. It was nearly deserted, just as we had hoped. Only a lone survivor tossed a stick for his dog. It was late afternoon, Mama and Daddy's favorite time on the island. The swimmers and sunbathers had called it a day, had headed back to their houses, as if they had known we'd need the beach all to ourselves.

We walked hand-in-hand to the water's edge, Will and Greg each carrying an urn. Before we released our parents' ashes to the sea, we began talking about Mama and Daddy and our memories of them here on their beloved Emerald Isle.

"Do y'all remember how Mama and Daddy used to dance?" I said. "We could hear them from our beds. I'd fall asleep to their feet making scratching noises on the sandy floor. That's my favorite memory."

Will said, "I liked it when we'd play Eye Spy while we ate Dilly Bars at DQ. Mama could always spy the neatest things that none of the rest of us could see."

"I always hated it when Daddy had to go back to Raleigh to

work," said Greg. "Mama was always so sad and lonely without him."

"That's right," said Sam, "but aren't you glad that she was sad instead of glad?"

Kevin, Sam's twin, said, "Sam and I always loved it when y'all would run off and leave us. We'd whine and pretend we cared, but we knew we'd have Mama all to ourselves."

Without saying a word, Sam smiled and put his arm around Kevin's shoulders, pulling him close as the tears streamed down his brother's face. Seeing their closeness and knowing they shared something of our mother that I knew nothing about made me jealous. I so desperately wanted her back so that I could make one last memory with her. No matter how many memories I already had, I would always want one more.

When it appeared that we had talked ourselves out and had put off the inevitable for as long as we could, I said, "All right, guys, are y'all ready?"

With that we stepped forward into the surf, where Will and Greg lifted the lids from our parents' urns and handed them to the twins. Then the two of them released our mama and daddy's ashes. We watched them catch the currents of air and twirl high into the sky before raining down and nestling on the surface of the sea. We stood silently and motionless until they completely disappeared beneath the water. Only then did we turn and walk slowly to the car.

As we returned to Raleigh, we attempted to joke and be our normal selves, but we had Mama-and-Daddy-sized holes in our hearts, and we soon buckled under the weight of trying to keep it together. Intermittently we cried, sobbed, sniffled all the way home. By the time we reached my house, we could barely look at one another, as if the evidence of our parents' love for each other was more than we could endure. We shared perfunctory hugs, careful not to make eye contact, for fear of losing it again. The boys climbed into their cars, and I watched as they drove out of sight, none of them waving, tooting, or looking back.

My heart told me that we'd never truly recover from our loss and that the five of us would never be the five of us again. Oh, we'd try out of love and respect for one other and our parents, but we all sensed that the Alexander family had died with Mama and Daddy.

As the oldest I'd called and written and even arranged beach vacations. One by one my brothers dropped out, saying it just wasn't the same without Mama and Daddy, that it hurt too much. Though I missed our parents as much as my brothers did, I had a passion for Emerald Isle and our beach home that the boys never seemed to have or understand. I could love our cottage and My Ocean without Mama and Daddy. I could love it with my own family, Mark and Alex. Over time, my brothers simply relinquished their ownership to me.

So when Mark left, I rushed back to that place I loved, hoping to ease my pain. But, for the first time, the place felt empty and so very lonely: no Mama and Daddy, no brothers, no Mark. The emptiness was just more than I could bear.

So without fanfare or a proper good-bye, I packed the car, locked the cottage, and returned to Raleigh, feeling as though I'd never come back to my wonderful Emerald Isle.

Three

I returned from the beach to find that Mark had come back to the house to collect the remainder of his belongings. How can one's heart be broken over and over? You'd think that once it was broken, it couldn't be broken again. Wrong!

I wandered throughout the first floor, smelling his cologne, feeling his presence that was no longer there. I discovered empty spaces, spaces that once held our joint possessions, possessions Mark had felt compelled to return to the house to retrieve: two throw pillows bearing the NC State logo; an omelet pan and Crockpot, though he'd never cooked a meal in his life; a blue-and-green throw rug that had been in my childhood bedroom; two lawn chairs; all the towels from the downstairs powder room; a wooden seagull on a stick that we had purchased one summer at the coast. His choices baffled me. He'd never shown interest in such things. Perhaps I didn't know Mark as well as I'd thought.

I trudged up the stairs to our bedroom to find that the bottom three drawers of our dresser were empty, as was half of our walk-in closet. My side was still in order, blouses color-coordinated and neatly lining the top rod, slacks and jeans marching along the bottom, shoes standing at attention on their rack. Mark's side was naked; even the hangers were missing. With all the weight on one side of the closet, I wondered what kept it from tipping over.

I walked into our bathroom and opened the medicine cabinet. It, too, was half empty; missing were Mark's toothbrush, his Colgate toothpaste (My Crest remained.), his Old Spice deodorant, his Hugo

Boss aftershave, his Nyquil, his Advil PM, and his litany of vitamins and minerals and age-rejuvenation supplements. This half-empty existence didn't make sense to me, didn't seem real, until I returned to our bedroom. I reached for the bedside-table drawer on Mark's side of the bed, pulling it out slowly, putting off the agony as long as I could. I knew what I'd find: the condoms were gone.

My breath escaped in a raspy croak, and I grabbed the table for support. Only then did I see the note:

Rowdy,

I have taken my personal effects and have enlisted the services of an attorney to assist my sorting out the particulars of our separation. I suggest you do likewise. Once you let me know the name of your attorney, I shall pass the information to my counsel so that he can iron out the details of the property settlement. In the meantime, I shall pick up Alexandra on alternate Friday afternoons for weekends with me. You can reach me on my cell or at 919-848-3333.

Mark

That's when I knew, beyond a doubt, that this was real.

I had so hoped that he'd just go play house with Tawni for a few weeks to get the middle-age craziness out of his system before returning home to tell me how stupid he'd been, that he really loved me and me alone, and that this was all a foolish mistake. Short of his profession of total stupidity, I felt he owed me a chance to reason with him, a chance to beg him not to leave, to convince him that our marriage was worth salvaging. Only when I was certain that wasn't going to happen did I allow myself to dissolve. Still grasping the empty drawer, I sank to the hardwood floor and let the tears flow.

How had this happened? Mark and I had been so in love. Oh, sure, our marriage had gotten routine after a decade, but don't all marriages? And once Alex arrived, our focus turned to her. Aren't new parents supposed to divert all their attention, all their energies to their little ones? Don't they behave as though life hadn't existed before their babies arrived? We did. We were so giddy over our love for Alex that we forgot to be giddy over our love for each other. I just couldn't remember when we decided that our coupledom was no longer important, that it should take a back seat to our parenting. After Alex came into our lives, our intimate, lingering candle-light dinners in the dining room morphed into garishly-lit rushed packaged meals in the kitchen with strained carrots in Alex's hair. We even stopped observing Saturday date night, an event that was always special and, without exception, culminated in yummy, unhurried sex.

Yes, the sex: it, too, had become routine, perfunctory, almost an obligation. There wasn't a great deal of passion in our love making any more, but we managed to have sex the standard 2.3 times per week. Or is 2.3 the number of children we were supposed to have? I forget, but I do know that our sex had become routine, formulaic, and hurried.

But it hadn't always been that way.

Our attraction had been instantaneous. We met in line at Starbucks in Cameron Village. I know that's so cliché, but we really did have one of those meet-cutes in Starbucks. I felt as though we were starring in a Nora Ephron movie, and I half expected Jimmy Durante to appear and begin singing *Make Someone Happy*.[4]

We were standing in line. He tapped me on the shoulder.

When I turned to face him, he said, "Your hair is beautiful," and I blushed.

My hair really was beautiful. I'd always gotten compliments. Red with coppered sun streaks shot throughout from my summers at the beach, I wore it long and naturally wavy. I was so glad I'd washed it that morning and let it dry naturally.

"Your eyes, too, they're stunning," he said, and I blushed deeper, batting my emerald green eyes, another target of many compliments.

Then I laughed as he said, "Now it's your turn to say something nice about me."

So I said, "You have great taste."

By week's end we were in his bed, my beautiful copper-streaked red hair damp and clinging to my face and his. We were so good together. Oh, god, so good. I'm tall for a woman, Mark somewhat short for a man. Our bodies fit perfectly, like adjacent puzzle pieces, which made for beautiful, luscious sex.

We couldn't keep our hands to ourselves. When we were with friends, we virtually ignored them. We just couldn't get enough of each other.

We lost count of the times others said, "Get a room!"

We were married before the year was out. We wanted to be a couple, wanted to announce to the world that we loved each other, cherished each other, and didn't want to wait another minute to begin sharing the rest of our lives together.

We carried our passion into our marriage, and for a time we made love with abandon. He adored my lean swimmer's body, my milky— he called it translucent—skin dusted with pink freckles. He'd known it so intimately, had kissed every inch, and I had let him explore me without a shred of embarrassment or self-consciousness.

His body was firm, muscular, tan; and he had that sexy shock of blond hair that always fell over his forehead. I loved that shock of hair, that shock of hair that matched the hair that ran down his abs and disappeared into the waist of the khakis that rode low on his hips. I would always love his blond hair, just as I loved his firm, muscular body.

I tried to remember when, why it had fizzled. I just didn't know, but I knew that we'd waited too long to rekindle our flame. We'd somehow snuffed it out.

Stale. That's the word I was looking for. We'd gotten stale.

As I grieved the demise of our luscious sex, I sobbed. I remember the sobbing, but I don't remember falling asleep from exhaustion. I awoke to a dark room and Alexandra shaking me.

"Mama, are you okay?"

Even in my drowsiness my first concern was Alexandra. Mark had vamoosed, and I was all Alex had left, except, of course, on alternate weekends. I needed to be strong and calm for her. But how could I do that when my heart was broken, my insides were jelly, and my life looked totally screwed? Well, I was an adult, and I'd just have to figure it out as I went along.

And as I was hoisting myself from the floor, trying to figure out how to behave like the adult, Alex said, "Mama, Nick Nack peed on the living room rug."

I'd figure out later how to be strong for Alex. I crumbled to the floor and bawled my eyes out.

Four

True to his word, Mark picked up Alex on alternate weekends to begin a two-day play date. Our child was seeing our separation as an adventure with new friends, new toys, and new surprises every time she left me to be with her dad and Tawni. At eight she was too young to understand the complications, the suffering, the ramifications of divorce. And the permanence of the situation had not yet sunk in.

I didn't like the arrangement one bit, but what choice did I have? Mark's leaving me did not negate his being Alex's father. He still had the right to see her, even if it were on his self-designated alternate weekends. I'd just have to accept it.

The thing I was having a really difficult time dealing with was Tawni—tall, young, beautiful, blonde, busty Tawni. I wanted Alex to love her father. I just didn't want her to love Tawni. I didn't think that was too much to wish for, but I also knew that I had no control over my child's feelings. Just wishing she wouldn't love Tawni couldn't keep it from happening. I also knew I couldn't keep her away from Tawni, as much as the thought appealed to me. As heartsick as I was, I didn't want to be the bitchy, spurned ex who made unreasonable demands and used her child for leverage or revenge, placing her in the center of the turmoil.

As I was nursing my hurting heart, trying to behave like a mature parent, Alex came bounding down the stairs, dragging the pink-flowered duffel bag Tawni had given her for play weekends—not to be confused with the *work* weekends she spent with me.

"Hey, Sweetness," I chirped cheerily, "are you ready to roll?"

"Yes, ma'am," she said.

But when I reached to hug her, her mood suddenly changed: "Mama, I miss you when I go to Daddy's."

Her remark took me by surprise. I knew my daughter loved me, but I'd thought she was so consumed with fun that she hadn't had time to think of me when she was with Mark.

"I miss you, too, Alex. But I always know that you'll be back in just two days."

"Why did Daddy go away?"

It appeared out of the blue, but I should have known it was coming. Why hadn't I prepared my speech? But what was my speech? Mid-life crisis? Stale marriage? New hottie? Boring wife?

So I gave what I thought was the appropriate stock answer: "Honey, people just change. They want different things. Daddy and I still care for each other very much, but we just can't live together anymore. But you know, Alex, that we will always love you more than anything else in the world."

"I know, Mama, but I miss Daddy when he's not here."

"I'm sorry, Alex. I miss him, too."

There, I'd said it. It was true. I missed Mark, and our daughter needed to know.

"Are you okay, Mama?"

"Sure, Honey, I'm okay, but I get sad sometimes."

And she also needed to know that I was sad. But she needed to think that I was okay with her alternate weekends with her dad, that bonding with Tawni was all right, and that her mother would be fine.

Even if that were a stretch.

"Tawni's nice," was all she said.

Was she feeling guilty? Disloyal? Perhaps she wanted me to tell her that it was all right to like Daddy's new friend, but I wasn't ready to sing Tawni's praises or give my blessing to her bonding with Alex. Maybe I'd misjudged her. Perhaps she was, at only eight, beginning to recognize the fall-out of divorce.

To lighten the mood as she prepared to leave for another weekend, I said, "Well, she'd better be nice to my sweetie, or I'll just have to pinch her real, real hard," and I reached over and playfully pinched Alex's nose.

She put her arms around my neck and laid her head on my

shoulder and said, "But she's not as nice as you."

I held her close and rubbed her back.

"Anybody home?"

It was so like Mark to spoil a moment. Or a life. He strolled in without knocking, all smiles and glowing with new love, ready to whisk Alex away from me.

"Hi, Daddy!" she crowed, releasing me and sailing into him arms.

Even though I'd just assured Alex that I was fine with her alternate weekends away, her delight at seeing the father who had abandoned her and her mother broke my heart again.

See there, it's never ending.

But I smiled cordially, prepared to send my child off to play in Mark's new fun world.

After he had cleared out his share of the drawers and his half of the medicine cabinet and closet, he set up housekeeping in Tawni's one-bedroom garage apartment.

When Alex returned home from her first visit with her father, she flung her arms wide with excitement and crowed, "Oh, Mom, it's so adorable! Tawni and Daddy live up over where Tawni parks her car. She and Daddy get the bedroom, and I get to sleep on the fold-out sofa in the living room. During the day we just fold it back up, and you'd never even know there was a bedroom there. It's *so* cool! And the kitchen is so cute—right in the corner of the living room. It's teeny-tiny, but you can do anything you do in a regular kitchen. The refrigerator is really little, too, and it doesn't hold much food, so we have to go out and shop for supper every day. It's neat! We just decide what we want to eat, and then we go get it. Oh, Mom, you'd just love it. It's just like playing house."

Playing house. That's just what I thought, too.

But, I would *not* love it.

And while Alex was spending alternate weekends at the play house with Mark and Tawni, I was stuck at the real house with a damn dog I didn't ask for, didn't want, and resented the hell out of. That just wasn't working for me, and things were about to change. Nick Nack was going to find a new home with the fun folks in the play house.

So I said, "Alex, before you and Daddy leave, will you please take Nick Nack out back. I think she needs to pee."

"Sure," she said and screamed, "come on, Nick Nack, let's go!"

And the two of them crashed out the back door.

When our daughter was out of earshot, I said, "Mark, you have to take Nick Nack."

Mark put his hands on his hips, pursed his lips, and shook his head in exasperation as he said, "Rowdy, don't be unreasonable. There's just no room for a dog. It's a one-bedroom apartment, for heaven's sake. And there's no fenced yard for her to run."

"But, Mark, you promised I wouldn't have to take care of a dog if I agreed to let you and Alex have Nick Nack."

"But things have changed since we made that agreement, Rowdy."

"They sure have! But *I* didn't change them. Why should I have to suffer *all* of the consequences of your dumping me? You get to skip off to start a new life, leaving me with a broken heart, a broken marriage, an empty house, a confused child, and a damn dog I never wanted in the first place."

Knitting his brow, trying to look pitiful, he said, "Do you think I haven't suffered, Rowdy? I wouldn't have hurt you for anything. It just happened."

Oh, that again. That old saw just wasn't part of this particular issue, and I wasn't having it for one minute.

Ignoring his response, I threatened, "Okay, then, if you won't take Nick Nack, the pound will. And, Mark, I *will* take her to the pound. Because *I'm not keeping a dog!* Got that?"

Mark stuck out his lip and said, "Now, Rowdy, how can you do that to our child? She's already lost so much. Nick Nack means stability to her. You wouldn't take that away, would you?"

Even though Alex missed her Daddy, she had yet to realize that she had suffered a great loss (what with the play weekends and toy apartment and fun, fun, fun!). But I went along with Mark's assertion that Alex had, indeed, lost something.

"Lost so much? Whose fault is that?"

Dropping the pity act, Mark said, "Okay, Rowdy, let's not go pointing fingers, shall we? There's enough blame to go around, but you don't see me pointing any fingers, do you?"

"Blame? What blame? I was home, minding my own business, cooking pot roast. How am I to blame?"

With the truth slapping him in the face, Mark softened and said, "I know, Rowdy, I'm sorry. But you have to understand that I can't take Nick Nack. There's just no room for her. And since Alex will be spending most of her time with you, I think her dog should stay here."

I knew no matter what I said, he was not changing his mind. So angry, I just clenched my jaw and stared at him.

After a prickly silence, Mark said, "I'm sorry, I'm just sorry," and hung his head. He crossed to the back door and called weakly, "Come on, Alex, time to go."

She rushed back in, Nick Nack close behind. She grabbed her bag, gave me a quick hug and a peck on the cheek, and, running for the front door, yelled, "Bye, Mama, I love you!"

Mark reached for my hand and gave it a squeeze. "I'm sorry, really I am," was all he said as he released me and strolled for the door.

I didn't follow. I heard the door click behind him.

I am not a violent person, but when Mark strolled out the door, taking the daughter I loved and refusing the take the dog I hated, the dog he couldn't live without, all of the pain and anger I'd been stuffing for the two months since his departure came boiling to the surface, erupting like a volcano. For the first time in my life, I wanted to physically hurt someone, and that someone was Mark. I wanted to rip his hair from his head and pound his face. But since he had already disappeared—again—and I wouldn't have struck him even if he had been still standing in my kitchen, I took my frustration out on the kitchen counter. As I screamed, I beat and pounded and pummeled until the pain of the Formica abuse reached my shoulder and a bruise began to appear on the ball of my fist. When I could no longer stand the pain and was exhausted from my tirade, I sank to the floor and wailed, cradling my wounded fist and arm in my good hand. I hate victims, but I wallowed in my victimhood, did the breast stroke in it, and dived in deep. Only when I was bathed in perspiration and hoarse from my fit, did I slow to a whimper.

That's when I noticed Nick Nack quaking in the corner of the kitchen. Her usually-alert ears were pressed firmly against her head, and her tail was between her legs. When I looked her way, she ducked her head and peered up at me with fear in her eyes. She somehow knew this outburst had something to do with her, and she also knew she'd be wise to stay out of my way.

As I pulled myself to a standing position with my unmaimed hand, I narrowed my eyes at her and said, "Don't look at me like that, you bitch."

And I wasn't using the doggie derivative of the word. Then I stormed out of the room, leaving her frightened and shivering.

I climbed the stairs, not knowing where to take my tantrum. I found myself in my bathroom, staring in the mirror at my ravaged image. My wet hair was plastered to my scalp in ringlets, and my face was tear-stained and splotched with red. My shoulder throbbed, the ball of my hand was swollen, and the bruising was already turning a deep purple. How had I allowed this to happen? Mark had, once again, skipped off smiling to his new life, his new toy apartment, and his new toy girlfriend, leaving me to maim myself while the dog I despised looked on in confusion.

I shed my damp clothes, turned on the shower, and stepped in.

As much as I hated the thought of Alexandra and Tawni bonding, I was grateful they were together, shopping or giggling or talking about Hello Kitty. Alex did not need to be witness to my meltdown, and I needed the time to myself to figure out how I was going to move forward, *without* the husband I loved and *with* the dog I loathed.

Once I'd rinsed my mayhem down the drain, I toweled dry and felt almost human again. I put on fresh jeans and tee shirt and shook my head so my hair could dry naturally. Then I padded down the stairs to fix myself a glass of iced tea.

When I got to the kitchen, Nick Nack hopped up from her puddle of fur by the back door and clicked across the tile until she was by my side. She leaned her heft into my thigh and licked my wounded hand, as if I'd never yelled at her, never called her a bitch. I was baffled. Regardless of what I did to her, she loved me and did not hold a grudge.

I knew there was a lesson in Nick Nack's behavior, but I was in no mood for a learning experience from a dog. Instead, I reached into the cupboard, grabbed a doggie biscuit, and flicked it on the floor.

As I opened the fridge to retrieve the pitcher of iced tea, I said, "You know, I really wasn't going to send you to the pound."

Nick Nack just gave me a satisfied smile and clicked across the floor to crunch on her treat.

I poured myself a glass of tea and sat at the kitchen table and watched the sun go down. When my butt got numb, I stood, stretched my stiff back and rubbed my behind back to life. Then I rinsed my glass and put it in the dish drainer to dry.

I opened the back door and said, "Okay, Nick Nack, run on out back and pee because I'm closing up early and hitting the sack."

Always obedient, she ran outside, marked her territory, trotted back in, and gave my bruised hand one last lick before curling up on her pallet. She looked up at me with loving eyes, but I was still so angry that I stubbornly refused to admit that she was a good girl. I clicked off the light and climbed the stairs.

I brushed my teeth and headed for my bedroom. I slipped into my nightgown and crawled into bed where I stared into the darkness and clutched my aching heart.

Five

I dozed off in the middle of the night but woke when I heard Nick Nack click up the stairs and creep into my bedroom, a room that was off limits to her. She stood just inside the threshold and whined quietly. I tried to ignore her, but she persisted. I looked at the clock. 8:00 a.m. I resented the dog, but I wasn't cruel and heartless. The poor creature needed to go outside.

I dragged myself out of bed, brushed by Nick Nack, and headed down the stairs saying, "Okay, come on. I'll let you out."

She followed me obediently down the stairs, to the back door, and out into the back yard. While she was outside, I filled her bowls with food and water, one of those things I swore I'd never do, and put the coffee on to drip. Nick Nack returned from the back yard, where she went straight to her breakfast. She ate and I drank my coffee in silence. When we were finished, I rinsed my coffee cup and put it back in the drainer, and Nick Nack returned to her pallet to stand guard over me and my home. I looked out the kitchen window. The back yard was bleak, the trees were bare, the temperature was hovering around freezing, and I was alone, except for a dog. Not a damn thing about the weekend said *fun*.

I dragged myself down the hall and opened the front door. A blast of cold air hit me as I stepped onto the frigid porch in my bare feet. I picked up the newspaper and took it to the living room, where I flopped onto the sofa. I didn't have the energy to remove the rubber band from the paper or the desire to read what was wrapped inside.

I sat motionless in my rumpled pajamas until around mid-afternoon when my stomach began to growl. I shuffled to the kitchen, where I rummaged in the pantry until I found a Three Musketeers bar. God only knew how old it was. I pulled a Coke from the fridge and returned to the living room, as I sat on the couch and ate my chocolate and carbonated lunch.

And that's pretty much how I spent the weekend, was spending most weekends when Alex was away, flopping from chair to sofa to bed, not brushing my teeth or showering, leaving the bed unmade, all the while side-stepping Nick Nack who felt it necessary to shadow me from kitchen to living room and back to kitchen. Then Sunday afternoon after yet another weekend of unproductive moping and playing the victim (I was getting too damn good at that.), I'd finally shower and make myself presentable for Alex's return.

She was all giggles and giddy excitement when she came skipping through the door. I was secure in my daughter's love for me, and even though she told me she missed me when she was away, she adored her play weekends with her dad and Tawni, especially Tawni. And why not? Tawni was more Alex's contemporary than she was Mark's. They watched mindless TV shows and went to the amusement park. And Tawni took Alex shopping and bought her cute, hip clothes because, "Mom, Tawni just knows *all* about fashion."

And I don't.

I'll admit I'm not a fashionista. I used to aspire to the latest trends when I was younger, but it just doesn't seem important—or comfortable—anymore. I've become a jeans and sweatshirt and tennis shoes sort of gal. I buy my clothes at Target: it's easy; it's cheap; Target jeans fit me. But Alex never seemed to notice I wasn't hip until Tawni came along and made it obvious.

And even though I'll admit to knowing little about current fashion, there's one thing I do know: toenails. That's right; I can give a mean pedicure. And Alex has always loved having me paint her toenails. That's why I invented toenail night. We'll sit on my bathroom floor in our matching pink terry cloth robes, cotton balls stuffed between our toes, and paint each other's toenails. It's when we're the closest. It's when we share our deepest secrets and do our best talking. It was during one such toenail night that my seven-year old daughter asked me what *sex* meant. Damn Internet! Damn TV! I wasn't ready for The Talk, but I was so grateful for toenail night.

Toenail night makes all our talks easier.

This particular Sunday afternoon Alex returned home from her play weekend sporting bright green toenails with glitter. We usually stick to pale pink.

In as lilting a voice as I could muster, I chirped, "Oh, I see you and Tawni had toenail night."

"Oh, *no,* Mom," she crowed, rocking back on the heels of new pink polka dot flip flops, looking down at her toes admiringly, "Tawni took me to a place where they do *real pedicures.*"

My heart hurt. It sounded as though my daughter was saying that my pedicures were fake. How could that be? She was only nine years old. Isn't nine too young to know the difference between real and fake? And, damn it, my pedicures are *not* fake! Okay, I don't know fashion, but I do know toenails. Why, I was the *inventor* of toenail night. I know that doesn't make me Madame Curie, but it's something. Something special. Please give me that.

She continued to prattle, "I sat in a great big chair with my feet in warm water while these balls rubbed up and down my back. It was so cool. And the lady sat on a stool and painted my toenails. And there were so many colors to choose from."

And green with glitter was the best color she could find.

"Tawni got her toenails painted green with glitter, too."

Of course, she did.

"So we could be toe twins!" Alex trilled.

I smiled through gritted teeth and, eager to change the subject, chirped cheerfully, "You hungry, Sweetie?"

"Guess so," she said, noncommittally.

At the end of play weekends, I waited for Alex with macaroni and cheese and applesauce, two of the few foods on her list of edibles. Alex seemed to be leaning toward vegetarianism. She didn't care for meat. She said she didn't like the texture, didn't like the way it felt spongy against her teeth. Now, occasionally I love a good steak or pork chop, but when Alex described meat's texture and sponginess, even I considered vegetarianism. In addition to disliking meat, Alex also disliked vegetables. So, technically, she could not be considered a vegetarian. It's crunchy. It's slimy. It's green. So she took her chewable vitamins and ate lots of macaroni and cheese and applesauce, supplemented by fruit smoothies masking protein powder.

As we ate our bland, boring supper, I would ask her in a casual, I-really-don't-want-to-know-I'm-just-being-polite sort of way about her play weekends with her dad and Tawni.

"Daddy and Tawni took me to the indoor water park. Tawni rode down the water slide on my mat with me until I wasn't scared to go down by myself. And Daddy was so funny, Mom. He made all sorts of silly faces at us when he went down the slide. And he's gotten so skinny that his bathing suit almost came right off. Tawni and I laughed so hard."

How dare that new woman laugh and make inside jokes with my daughter. That was my job. My right. My privilege.

Not hers.

"What did you have to eat this weekend?"

I wanted to know how Tawni was handling making macaroni and cheese and applesauce every night in her adorable little kitchen in the corner of the living room of the play house.

"Well, Friday night me and Daddy and Tawni..."

"Daddy and Tawni and I, Alex."

As soon as I said it, I regretted it. I was sure Tawni didn't correct Alex's grammar on play weekends. But as a former English major with a brief stint as an English teacher, I felt it my duty to make sure my child used proper grammar. But I didn't want to make her sorry to be back home by my finding fault. So what if she did use *me* in the subjective case at eight. She had time to learn.

"Sure, Mom, *Daddy* and *Tawni* and *I*," she said with sarcastic emphasis on each word, "went to the movie and had popcorn for supper. For dessert Tawni had Junior Mints; Daddy had Sugar Babies; I had Peanut M&M's."

While I was fuming over my child's father giving her popcorn and M&M's masquerading as a meal, she was on to Saturday's menu.

"Me and Tawni..."

I let it go. Grammar class had been dismissed for the day.

"...went shopping, and then we went to Snoopy's for a hot dog."

"Hot dog? Aren't you the one who can't stand the texture of meat?"

"But it's okay if they put chili on it. It sort of changes the way the hot dog feels against my teeth."

"Chili? Are you aware that chili has meat in it? You can eat meat on meat, but you can't eat meat alone?"

"Uh, guess so," she said, shrugging her shoulders dismissively.

Perhaps one meat cancels out the other meat, making the entire meat-meal null and void. I guess it's like drinking a Diet Coke with a candy bar. The diet part of the Diet Coke cancels out the calorie part of the candy bar. Or so we tell ourselves.

I was incredulous. For years I'd tried to force meat on my offspring, until I could no longer stand the tears and whining and pinched lips and turned-up nose. Yet in a matter of months, an outsider—yes, she was an outsider, an intruder, an interloper, an alien—had gotten Alex to eat meat on top of meat. Before I could recover, Alex was off to Sunday brunch at Pizza Hut. I kept my told-you-so smugness in check as she told me that she had refused to share Mark and Tawni's pepperoni pizza, insisting, instead, on a cheese pizza of her own.

She scooped the last morsel of macaroni and cheese onto her fork with her finger and shoved it into her mouth. Still chewing, she jumped up, grabbed her duffel bag, and headed for the kitchen door, ignoring her napkin and, instead, wiping her mouth on the back of her hand. Before she disappeared, she stopped, turned, and blew me a kiss.

Then she said, "That was good, Mama. Thanks."

And she ran upstairs to hang up her cute new clothes and admire her sparkly green toes.

Six

I allowed my life to become just one lonely day after the next. I spent my afternoons missing Mark but assuring Alex that, although I was sad sometimes, I was going to be just fine. I spent alternate weekends wallowing in my loneliness, missing Alex, begrudging her bonding with Tawni, and being livid that I'd been saddled with Nick Nack. I resented that she was here to stay and continued to ignore her as she shadowed my every move from sofa to chair to bed and to scream at her if she got too close.

When Mark left, taking his clothes, toiletries, and condoms, I also allowed him to take my energy, my enthusiasm, and my drive. But my life hadn't always been so directionless.

As the oldest child in my family, I was the leader, the classic overachiever. I excelled in school and knew from the third grade, when I first read Charlotte's Web, that I wanted to be a teacher—an English teacher. I wanted to teach students who loved reading just as much as I did. Not once did I have doubts about my chosen profession.

I never said, "Well, maybe I want to be a nurse or a fireman or The President of the United States," as all my classmates did.

"I want to be an English teacher," was what I'd say, should anyone ask.

I'd say it even if no one asked.

So it came as no surprise to anyone when I earned an academic scholarship to NC State, my daddy's alma mater, to study education with a concentration in English. I excelled at State, just as I had excelled in elementary, middle, and high school, and, at the beginning of my senior year of college, began my student teaching at Broughton High, the school I'd graduated from less than four years before.

I rocked student teaching. I knew I would. I was born to do the job. The school assigned me a class of brutally competitive, Ivy League-bound overachievers who practically gave themselves whiplash from flailing their arms furiously so as to be the first to be called upon to answer my questions. They all knew the answers, but each needed to prove to me and to one another that he or she knew the answers first and best. Their enthusiasm for learning was intoxicating, and I, of course, had the foolish notion that it was I who inspired their enthusiasm and curiously, when, in fact, they had been enthusiastic and curious from birth.

But being in that electrifying learning environment excited me so and assured me that I'd made a brilliant decision when I had decided way back in the third grade that I wanted to be an English teacher. I was so anxious to finish my senior year at State and become the real deal—a bona fide teacher, not just the student-teacher variety.

Upon graduation I received an offer to teach at a Raleigh high school which will forever remain nameless, as long as I'm the one talking about it. The school gave me three classes of literature students. Expecting a group identical to the precious geniuses I had student taught at Broughton, I was distraught to find that I had the sixty-four most underachieving adolescents in the entire school system, perhaps the entire universe. They were the I'm-here-only-because-my-parents-will-take-away-my-car-if-I-skip-class students. They weren't bad or stupid, just apathetic.

From day one they displayed a don't-even-bother attitude. I tried, oh lord, I tried, but it's impossible to excite apathetic students with Macbeth. They'd slouch or snooze or sigh and roll their eyes. They'd yawn audibly, displaying their gold-studded tongues.

When the classics failed to capture their imaginations, I'd turned to more current American authors. What teenagers don't love Holden Caulfield and Atticus Finch? Well, I know three whole classes of teenagers who didn't. So I gritted my teeth and succumbed to that brand new phenom, Harry Potter. Yet even Harry didn't work with these kids. They were the only sixty-four people on the planet who weren't mesmerized by the antics of Harry and his sidekicks, Hermione and Ron.

They'd wait for the movie.

And their attitude toward grammar was as dismissive as their attitude toward literature. How does one get to be sixteen years old and not know that *for he and I* is improper grammar?

Doesn't everyone have a mother who says, "Darlin', just because someone accompanies you doesn't mean you change the case."

Apparently not.

I'd ask, "You wouldn't say 'for he' and you wouldn't say 'for I', would you? Then why would you say 'for he and I?'"

The anti-grammarian would stare blankly at me, and I'd carry on, digging my hole deeper and deeper.

"The pronouns you should be using are in the objective case because they are the *objects* of the preposition *for*. *He* and *I* are subjective pronouns; *him* and *me* are the objective pronouns. So the proper usage is *for him and me*."

The perpetrator would sniff loudly, drawl, "Whatever," and turn to his neighbor and say, "dude, you got any gum?"

At the end of year one, I ran gleefully from my classroom, knowing that next year would be different because I'd never have to face those sixty-four literature-, grammar-, and attitude-challenged adolescents again. And to make sure of that, I'd passed them all.

I'll be damned if the school didn't dig up sixty-four identical teens for me to teach (and I use the term *teach* mockingly) the following year. Guess the administration figured since no one got shot and no one's parents sued me or the Wake County School Board that first year, I was a perfect fit for this crew.

I made an effort, but, not surprisingly, my students did not. Again, I tried Macbeth, then Holden and Atticus, then Harry. Don't know why I thought it would work the second time when it hadn't worked the first. Isn't that the definition of *insanity*?

I'd say, with less enthusiasm and little hope of affecting change, "It's *for him and me*, not *for he and I*."

And I'd get the same clueless stare or bored eye roll I'd gotten the year before.

At the end of year two, I filled a cardboard box with my red pencils, my pencil cup that said AUTHORS DO IT WRITE (I'd thought it was clever when I'd plunked down $12.50 in the Hallmark store.), my water bottle, my ceramic apple (which I bought for myself because I was certain no one else was ever going to gift me an apple), and my spare cardigan. I toted my belongings down the hall, stopped by the principal's office just long enough to drop off my resignation letter, and headed for my car.

I should have been devastated that my chosen profession had been rendered a bust, but, surprisingly, I was relieved to be out from under the weight of the disappointment. In two years not one student had smiled at me or directly addressed me by my name. And the more I tried to draw them out with my enthusiasm for literature, the more they let me know that they were there just for the car. I sought help from the administration, only to be told that they'd heard it all before.

So I drove out of the parking lot for the last time, never looking back, confident that I had done everything I could to educate those teens. The problem was them, not me. Oops! The problem was *they*, not *I*.

Ever the optimist, though, I said, "It's not the end of the world; I'll find something else."

Mark and I had been married a little over a year when my career imploded, so he had been witness to my teaching meltdown.

He was most sympathetic and comforted me, saying, "Take the summer to think about your options. There's no hurry. You deserve to sleep late, lie around the pool, decompress for a while. You've had two grueling years."

That first morning of freedom from apathy, I awoke at nine o'clock to find that Mark had already left for campus. He taught summer school and continued to advise students, so I'd have my days to myself. I sauntered to the kitchen in my pajamas, stretching out ten full delicious hours of sleep, to eat a leisurely bowl of Cheerios and read the paper—something I hadn't done since the previous summer. There I found on the kitchen table a note from Mark:

> Sweetheart,
> Take it easy today. You've earned a break. I'll be home around 6:00. Be thinking of some place special you'd like to eat dinner. Then who knows what could happen? (It just might involve that sexy negligee.)
>
> Love you so much!
> Mark

38

My heart hurt from the memory.

We'd been so in love. We treated each other with respect, cherished our time together, and didn't take each other for granted. And he bought me sexy negligees from Victoria's Secret.

We stoked the flame. We didn't allow our love to get stale.

That first morning of glorious summer, after eating my breakfast, I showered, even shaved my legs, made the bed so precisely and tightly I could have bounced a quarter on it, and dressed in comfy shorts and a tee shirt. I still had seven hours all to myself. I slipped my feet into my flip flops, grabbed my keys and my purse, and headed for my car. I was going to the library to get fluffy novels to read in the sun by our apartment complex swimming pool.

Fifteen minutes later I was perusing the stacks. Two hours later I was still in the library. I'd think I'd found the books I wanted, and then something else would catch my eye. I was trying to whittle down my pile of a dozen when a young woman wearing a yellow badge that read VOLUNTEER hanging from a lanyard around her neck pushed a cart into the stacks and began putting books on the shelves.

I didn't make it to the pool—that day or ever.

I went directly to the front desk and whispered to the librarian who was working feverishly and expressionless at a computer terminal, "Can I get some information about volunteering here in the library?"

Without a word she reached beneath the counter and pulled out an application for prospective volunteer helpers. She handed it to me, managed a semi-smile, and returned her attention to her computer screen. I went to the nearest study station, rummaged in my purse for a pen, and began planning my summer of library volunteerism.

Two days later I got up at seven, pulled on my jeans and polo shirt, slipped into my comfy New Balance shoes, and hung my yellow volunteer badge around my neck. I felt very official.

I loved it from the beginning. It wasn't rocket science, but there were books. Lots of books. Nothing but books. Five mornings a week it was my job to place returned library books back in the stacks where they belonged. I loved touching each book, knowing that the authors had spent years, perhaps decades, putting their hearts and souls into their words. Every writer thought his or her book was special, yet we would line them up, thousands of them, till they all looked identical. But I knew they weren't identical. I knew they were all unique. I loved them all, even the ones I didn't know personally.

When I finished returning the books to their proper identical slots, I would fill book club orders. As requests came in, I'd check the system to determine how many copies we had of the book they'd be reading. I'd gather as many as we had in stock and request the shortfall from the other local branches. Once all the books arrived at my branch and the order was full, I'd delight in calling the club coordinator to tell her she could pick up this month's selection. I wanted the club members to invite me to all their meetings, to read what they were reading, to find out what everyone thought of their selection, to let them know what I felt about the character development, the plot, the voice.

But they didn't know me; I was just a faceless voice from the library who whispered into their phones, "Your books are in. We'll hold them on the shelf by the information desk for you to pick up."

I wanted so badly to add, "Oh, you're just going to love this book. The author developed the protagonist so beautifully, and the plot twist at the end is going to make you laugh," or "Don't bother with this one. The characters are just so boring and one dimensional."

But I couldn't do that. It wasn't in my job description. Just call; don't critique.

As the end of summer neared, as much as I enjoyed my work at the library, I realized that I needed to begin thinking about what I was going to be now that my teaching profession was behind me.

Then Alex decided that for me.

When we discovered that I was pregnant, Mark and I were surprised but over the moon with happiness and excitement. I knew I wanted to be a mom; I just wasn't planning on it so soon. But Alex arrived and smiled and looked just like me and made me know that it had worked out just the way it was supposed to. So I'd be a full-time mom, and, much to my delight, I learned that I'd be able to continue my job at the library until her arrival.

Turns out her arrival barely interrupted my volunteerism. After a brief absence, I strapped my newborn to my chest with a sling and went back to volunteering. I didn't do much re-shelving in the beginning, but I was still able to fill book club orders. Once Alex was old enough, I'd drop her at the library daycare each morning, where a gentle grandmotherly volunteer looked after her and, in time, read to her.

From time to time I thought of getting a real job, one that would pay me, but I kept putting off the inevitable because the thought of leaving the library made me sad. Then Daddy died and made my decision easy. Because he owned an insurance company, he and Mama were heavily insured and heavily invested. Their hideous, devastating deaths left my brothers and me well cared for. I was able to buy for cash the house I still call home and invest the remainder— enough to keep me relatively comfortable for life.

I'd rather have had my daddy.

But because of my parents, I could keep my volunteer job at the library, surrounded by the books I loved, doing work I enjoyed, providing a service for my community. And once Alex began school, I was able to arrange my hours at the library so that I could be at home when she arrived in the afternoons.

After Mark's departure I continued to go to the library on weekday mornings, but the books no longer gave me the delight and comfort they once did. The library just couldn't fill that cavern of pain and loneliness that Mark had left behind. It ceased to be a joy.

And then there was the home Mark and I shared, the home I'd purchased with the proceeds from my parents' estate. True, the house was mine, but I'd never thought of it as just mine. Mark and I had lived in it together, had loved it together. I didn't want it to be mine, all mine. I wanted it always to be ours. Owning it was small consolation for the emptiness I felt. Just as the library had ceased to be a joy, so had my home.

Seven

I awoke to Nick Nack's chuff-chuff-chuffing. At some point she had just assumed the position on the rug beside my bed. I can't pinpoint when it had happened; I just realized one day that she was there. She'd follow me upstairs at night and trot into my bedroom, as if she were co-owner. And to be honest, an unwanted dog was better than nothing, as long as she kept her distance and showed no signs of wanting to get at my neck. One has to be awfully lonely to accept those terms as criteria for companionship.

I still hated self-pity and victimhood, but somehow I just couldn't help wallowing in it and feeling sorry for myself. As hard as I tried to prevent it, my heart ached to the point of debilitating pain, and I was the victim of Mark and Tawni's self-absorption. Mark's leaving had been excruciating, and I even felt the victim of Alex's cluelessness. My brain told me that she was just a child, a victim of the divorce herself, but my heart cried otherwise. But, in her defense, I had told her that I was okay and that I wanted her to be with her daddy.

Yet the loneliness was palpable, like a physical being. I had no one to turn to. I had never needed my parents so profoundly—not even as a child—yet they were both gone. My brothers were scattered; however, had they been living next door, they'd have offered little comfort. After Mama and Daddy's death, the gulf that separated the five of us just seemed to widen over time. When I'd called to tell them that Mark was leaving me, they all showed genuine concern but couldn't mask their discomfort from hearing my news and their eagerness to end the conversation. I had not heard from any of them since that call.

And my friends: they were gone, all of them. Most of my best friends from high school had left Raleigh for college, never to return, except to visit. Stephanie Cole and Patty Pelletier had gone to school somewhere in New England. After graduation Stephanie moved to New York where she got a job working with a modeling agency. I know she wasn't a model, but I'm not quite sure what she did at the agency. We tried staying in touch, but she was always off to a photo shoot in some interesting location. Maybe she was a photographer. When Patty graduated, she moved to California to try her hand at acting but, instead, had married the producer of a popular sitcom. They lived somewhere around LA—Hollywood, I think.

Katherine Peedin had gone to college with me at NC State and was still in North Carolina, but I couldn't remember where. High Point? Charlotte? And then there was sweet, giddy Sue Ellen McEachern. She'd gone to Appalachian State and was pregnant and married before the end of the first semester of our freshman year. She was living in Garner, right outside Raleigh, with her very nice, very placid, always-smiling husband, Seth. They had three semi-cute chinless children with straw-colored hair and close-set eyes. I'd run into her from time to time in the mall, wrestling with strollers and children and shopping bags, looking harried but happy.

But we hadn't made a concerted effort to keep in touch. It was no one's fault. We got busy. Our interests changed. Our circumstances changed. Our friends changed.

There was a time, though, when the five of us had been inseparable. We'd met in the sixth grade when we all joined the Raleigh Parks and Rec swim team. We stuck with our love of swimming and, four years later, became one-third of the Broughton High School girls' swim team. We spent seven years reeking of chlorine and brought home three state swimming titles for our efforts.

Weekends found us inseparable, as well: sleepovers, bacon cheeseburgers at Hardee's, shopping at Crabtree Valley Mall, movies at the Rialto Theatre. And we cruised Raleigh in Katherine's awesome red vintage '65 Mustang convertible, a bribe from her parents.

Katherine's eccentric, former-hippy mom and dad served as host parents to foreign exchange students, and over the years they had kids from India and South Korea and Germany and France living in their home for six weeks at a time. Katherine's Mustang was her incentive to play nice with them at school and to entertain them on the weekends. We joined her in her playing nice and entertaining but were so relieved when those kids went back to wherever they belonged so we could return to our normal life of being just Stephanie, Patty, Katherine, Sue Ellen, and Rowdy.

Then came the semester exchange student Peta Nordegren left Norway and twirled into our lives. No more than four feet eight, she had long, silky, pale yellow hair and eyes so shockingly blue they seemed to have a life of their own. She had a freckled nose and a constant smile, and she chattered non-stop. And she didn't walk; she skipped. We were in love. In fact, the entire student body of Broughton High was in love. Each of the girls wanted to be Peta's best friend, and all the boys wanted Peta to love them. But she was all ours.

During the six weeks Peta was with us, we cruised Raleigh in Katherine's Mustang, top down, hair flying, music blaring, so happy to be us. Though the five of us were addicted to Hardee's bacon cheeseburgers, Peta adored the southern fried chicken and green Jell-O at Balentine's Cafeteria in Cameron Village. So every Saturday, because we were all in love with Peta and wanted to please her, we'd head to Balentine's for a lunch of fried chicken and green Jell-O. Afterward we'd drive to Crabtree Valley Mall where we'd spend the afternoon trying on cute American clothes.

Though Peta spoke perfect English with just a hint of an accent, she had a hard time understanding us.

She'd scrunch up her precious little face and say, "Huh? I don't understand what you say."

We'd cry, "How can you not understand us? We're speaking English, our native tongue, the same language you're speaking!"

Finally, in exasperation, she threw her hands in the air and exclaimed, "Oh, I don't know. It's just that your words are so round."

"So round?" we screamed and collapsed in laughter.

We'd been told we drawled and twanged, but we'd never been told that our words were round.

On that day, the five of us, best friends forever, dubbed ourselves the Round Hounds.

At the end of Peta's six-week stay, we sobbed and held onto her as she hugged us all and told us how much she would miss her new friends with their round words.

We began addressing one other as Your Roundness and passed notes in class signed Roundly Yours. Soon the entire Broughton High student body knew us as the Round Hounds. Teachers quickly became annoyed with the moniker, and classmates lost interest. But we vowed we'd forever be the Round Hounds.

We left for college, promising to write weekly and to cruise and eat Hardee's bacon cheeseburgers when we all returned to Raleigh. We did write, for a time, always signing our notes Roundly Yours. Over Christmas holidays Katherine would collect us in her Mustang, and we'd visit all our old haunts, top down, radio blaring, teeth chattering. We continued to address one another as Your Roundness, and Peta always managed to find her way into our conversations.

But over time memories faded, and eventually new ones pushed them aside to take their places. Our notes became shorter and further apart as we acquired new tastes, graduated from college, began careers.

One Christmas I answered the phone to an unfamiliar voice saying, "Rowdy, let's get together for lunch."

"Who's speaking?"

"Rowdy, it's Patty. I just got home for the holidays."

"Oh, my gosh, Patty, I didn't recognize your voice. You sound so...foreign," I laughed.

"Well, I've worked hard to get rid of the drawl," she said, half joking, I'm sure, but breaking my heart nonetheless.

"Sure," I said, heart still aching, "lunch sounds great. How about fried chicken and green Jell-O at Balentine's?"

"Oh, gahd, that's disgusting. I haven't had meat in I-can't-remember-when." And when she had recovered from her meat revulsion, she chirped, "There's a trendy little bistro at Cameron Village. Mother and I had lunch there the last time I was home, and it was divine. Let's give that a go. You call Katherine and Sue Ellen and see if they are free tomorrow. I ran into Steph's mother yesterday. Steph isn't coming home this year. She's on some sort of photo shoot up in Montana. So it'll just be the four of us, if the others can make it. Well, ciao!" she cried and was gone.

First of all, *Mother?* We called our mothers Mama. And all in?

What's that about? And when did Stephanie become Steph? It sounded like a bacterial infection. And ciao! Whatever… Guess I'd find out what was going on the following day at the new trendy little bistro which, by the way, was so trendy that the lunch we ate there was just about the restaurant's last.

I called Sue Ellen's house and found her happy, yet still harried. I could hear children screaming in the background. She just talked louder in an effort to drown them out.

"Oh, sure, I'd love to come, Rowdy. See you tomorrow."

I found Katherine at her parents' house and learned that she was living in Asheville, not Winston Salem or Charlotte, as I had thought. She had become a ceramicist. I hadn't even known she had artistic talent. But, yes, she could meet us at Cameron Village, would love to see all of us.

I was so excited about getting together with the gang but was sorry that Stephanie wouldn't be able to make it. She was our comedian, the one who could make us double over in laughter like no one else could. Whenever a disruption broke out in class, the teacher could always rest assured that Stephanie was at the root of it. I'd so missed her humor. Katherine was our beauty, with her long, blonde hair and blue eyes. She had no idea how beautiful she was. She was also one of the kindest, most unselfish people I'd ever known. Guess her parents' good deeds rubbed off on her. Sue Ellen was the sweetest, most optimistic of us all. She could always find the good in people and refused to let us gossip. I was the brain, the studious one. I helped all the others with their homework and term papers. And then there was Patty, our leader. She was the one who held us all together. I was so glad she could make it home from California.

Katherine, Sue Ellen, and I arrived sharply at noon. Patty, the one who had arranged the luncheon, arrived fashionably late at 12:45. The three on-timers had forty-five minutes to memorize the pretentious, over-priced menu and to come to terms with the sad realization that we no longer had anything in common. Could Stephanie's humor have held us together? I doubt it.

Sweet Sue Ellen had hauled her youngest along so we could all marvel at the adorableness of her chinless, close-set-eyed, straw-haired youngin.

"Sorry about this, girls. Seth is a saint, but he can handle just two little ones at a time. Hope you don't mind."

We assured her we didn't.

She'd packed enough paraphernalia in her oversized pink flowered Vera Bradley bag for the child to survive in the wilderness for a month, should the need arise. And when the conversation lulled, as it often did, she'd twist her face at her little girl—I think it was a girl— and yelp, "Oh, yes you are! Oh, yes you are!" to the kid's utter disinterest. I had no idea what the mother was inferring the child was, but Sue Ellen was adamant that oh, yes, she was one.

Katherine was as beautiful as ever, her pale blonde hair still long and flowing, her eyes still crystal blue. She had moved to Asheville after college and had become an artist with a large local following. She seemed to be treading in her parents' hippie footsteps. She had not married or had children, and she appeared so at peace with her work and her life. She talked as if she were speaking through wind chimes—all soft and tinkly and musical. I loved her, always had, but she seemed to have become so other-worldly to me. I couldn't imagine her driving a vintage, red Mustang convertible.

Finally, at 12:45, when Patty came clicking in on her six-inch Louboutins, make-up just so, wrapped neck to ankle in fur in the unseasonably mild fifty-five degree North Carolina winter, I was so hungry I'd have given a vital organ for a bacon cheeseburger or even some green Jell-O. She shook her edgy, Rodeo Drive hairdo and air kissed us all near both cheeks.

"Oh, how European of you," I cattily hissed, but only inside my head.

"You must try the edamame, fennel, and arugula salad with the beet reduction," Patty huffed nasally through clenched, newly-veneered teeth, as she shed her mammoth coat and tossed it casually on the empty chair next to her.

Though I'd memorized the menu, I couldn't pronounce anything but the prices. So I did as Patty instructed and ordered the edamame, fennel, and arugula (so that's how you pronounce arugula...and edamame) salad with the beet reduction. We waited another thirty minutes for our salads to arrive. I couldn't imagine how it could take thirty minutes to throw together a salad. But I knew that no matter how that salad with the strange fixings tasted, it would be delicious, in light of the fact that I was teetering on the brink of starvation. I was wrong. Blech! And the $4.50 dandelion tea tasted like dirt. Who the hell puts dandelions in tea? Well, I'll answer that myself: a trendy little restaurant that is about to go out of business and wants to stiff four unsuspecting women before closing its doors for good!

The four of us had grown in such different directions that we sounded like we were a part of the Pentecost, speaking in unknown tongues. Unlike the participants of the actual Pentecost, though, we didn't understand one other. But I knew what could reel us back in, make us the friends we were in high school, make us understand each other, make us the Round Hounds once again.

I turned to Patty, our self-appointed leader, and said, "Your Roundness..."

But the look on her face made me freeze. It was fleeting, instantaneous, but I saw it. I wondered if the others had seen it, as well. It wasn't there, right on the tip of her memory; she had to dig through her recall file before she grabbed the card that read Round Hounds.

"Oh, yeah, Round Hounds. That was funny. What was her name? That exchange student?" she said in her unknown California tongue, snapping her well-manicured fingers, as her half-dozen gold bangles jangled on her wrist and her enormous canary-yellow diamond caught the overhead light and nearly blinded me.

Nice recovery, but it was too late. For me. I felt my breaking heart crumble a little more.

"Pia?" said Sue Ellen, while spooning cold baby peas into her youngin's mouth.

"No, no, not Pia. It was Tina, wasn't it?" said Katherine.

I let them argue about our precious, skipping friend's name, but when I was certain they'd never retrieve it from their atrophied memories, I said sadly, "Peta. Her name was Peta."

"Yeah, that's right, Peta," said Patty. "She was from Denmark, as I recall. You know, Ira and I went to Europe on our honeymoon. We went to Copenhagen to see some castle or other. Or maybe that was Stockholm. Anyway..."

No, it was Norway. Our precious Peta was from Norway. Not Denmark. Not Sweden. It was Norway. And we were never to forget that. To forget her. To forget us.

I was having a difficult time holding my breaking heart together, so when Patty paused to take a breath, I said, "Gotta run."

They fell silent and looked at me quizzically.

"It's been nice," I said, "but I really have to go. Let's do this again."

They all smiled semi-smiles, and their mouths said, "Yeah, let's do it again," while their eyes said, "Ain't happ'nen."

I drove home, my heart aching from the death of the Round Hounds. I tried to remain composed but was crying, tears dripping from my chin, by the time I reached the house.

"I don't understand," Mark said, his brow furrowed.

"Oh, of course you don't understand! You're a guy! What do you know about friends?"

Then I threw myself face down on the sofa and sobbed into a damask throw pillow.

As I suspected, we would not get together again.

"Hey, did you see Katherine when she was home? Y'all were pretty tight in high school, weren't you?" an acquaintance would ask in passing. "God, she's gorgeous!"

But I didn't see gorgeous Katherine or Patty or Stephanie or even Sue Ellen, who lived just fifteen miles away and shared my mall. I'm guessing they didn't see one another, either.

Alex came along, Mark got tenure, we became involved in campus activities, and my life just changed, like the rest of the Round Hounds' lives. The memories faded, as did the pain in my heart over the loss.

But Mark's leaving changed everything. I needed the comfort of the Round Hounds. I needed to cruise. I needed loud music. I needed to feel the wind in my hair. I needed to share a bacon cheeseburger. I needed to reconnect.

So I picked up the phone and called Patty's mother.

"Well, hello, Rowdy darling. So good to hear your voice. I was so sorry to hear..."

"Yes, thank you, Mrs. Pelletier. How's Patty doing?"

"Well, *Patricia* is doing fine. Loves living out there on the left coast. And she adores motherhood. Number five is on the way, you know."

"No, I didn't know. That's great news."

"She and the kids and the nanny are coming for Christmas. Don't know if Ira will be joining them. Well, he's Jewish, you know, so I guess Christmas isn't a big deal for him, even though Patricia celebrates with the children. But anyway..."

"Maybe I can drop by when Patty—Patricia—is in town."

"Oh, well, yes, let's see now... I'm not sure what her plans are, Dear. You know, lots of family... And all those kids... How 'bout I have Patricia give you a little buzz when she gets in? Sound good? Okay, Darlin', I hear someone at the door..."

Patricia never called.

So I dialed the Pelletiers' number. Patty answered the phone.

"Oh, hi, Rowdy. Merry Christmas. I'm so, so sorry about you and Mark."

"Thanks, Patty," I said, my voice trailing off, nowhere else to go.

"Hey, Patty, I thought maybe we could get together while you were home."

"I'd love to, Rowdy, really I would, but I just don't know what *Mother's* schedule is. You know, she has to be in control, and she's been barking orders like a drill sergeant ever since our plane touched down. Right now she's lining us all up in the living room for our family Christmas portrait. Have you ever tried to keep five kids clean and lined up all at once? Oh, shit, she's screaming for me. Gotta go. I'll try to get back with you, Rowdy, but I just don't promise."

She didn't. I let it go.

And the friends I had made after college had all been Mark's acquaintances. We had so many social commitments because of his University job, so the women I met were either colleagues of his or wives of his colleagues.

I tried calling them after the separation, but they all sounded intolerably uncomfortable talking with me. I guess they felt a loyalty to Mark since he had been there first, had been their friend before I entered the picture. I'd see them at Whole Foods or Quail Ridge Books or the wine and cheese shop. They'd stammer and fidget, cutting their eyes as if they were afraid someone might see them speaking with me. They'd promise to get in touch. They never did.

I guess Mark got custody of them.

Eight

Alex was with her dad, so Nick Nack's chuff-chuff-chuffing was my only companion. Yet her presence and her chuffing were growing on me. Even though I still wasn't comfortable letting down my guard around her, I did take some comfort in knowing she was there and that she wasn't going to leave me.

When Nick Nack says she is going to call, she calls.

Alone in my bed made for two, I rolled over and looked at the digital clock. 2:00 a.m. loomed green.

"Shit!" I spat and throttled the mattress with my fists.

Nick Nack stirred, smacked her lips, and settled back into her boneless puddle of fur. In seconds she had chuffed herself back to sleep. I longed for a dose of whatever she'd taken that had allowed her to drift off, carefree, in an instant. I knew, though, that I wouldn't be drifting off. 2:00 a.m. was my companion. And 3:00. And 4:00.

I sat up and dangled my feet over the edge of the bed, my toes grazing Nick Nack's fluffy coat. As she breathed in and out, her fur tickled the bottoms of my feet. I considered letting her tickle my feet for the rest of the night but felt I needed more.

I stepped over the heaving black mound onto the cold, hardwood floor and groped for my blue terrycloth slippers. Once I'd located them, I slid my feet in and headed for the door. As I slapped down the stairs, I could still hear Nick Nack's heavy breathing. My slipper slapping hadn't interrupted her slumber.

I pulled my heavy gray wool coat over my flannel pajamas and wrapped my long, red knit scarf—the one with the NC State logo, a gift from Mark—around my neck three times. I grabbed my purse, walked out the front door, my slippers flapping across the front porch, and headed for my car.

It had snowed earlier in the evening, a rarity in Raleigh. The snow had blanketed the lawns—a very thin blanket, but a blanket nonetheless. We'd all rushed out for milk and bread, even if we hadn't needed it, and the ticker across the bottom of the six o'clock news told us that most Wednesday night prayer meetings had been canceled. Wake County schools would be on two-hour delay the following morning, just to be on the safe side. But our snow would be gone by ten a.m., leaving only white triangles on roofs slanted away from the sun and a faint memory that, yes, sometimes it does snow here in the south.

It was cold, so cold I shivered and saw my breath condensing in the middle-of-the-night air. The snow had stopped, and at that hour of the night, the white lawns were still foot-printless. The roads, however, were clear, too warm for the snow to accumulate. I climbed into my car, knowing I would be safe from skids, started the engine, and revved up the heater.

As I sat, waiting for the car to warm, I fiddled with the radio until I found the Beach Music-24 station out of Greenville, North Carolina. I had introduced Mark to beach music when we'd met. He took right to it—loved the sultry beat, the simple melodies, the perfect harmonies. Beach Music-24 had been his favorite station. He'd turn it on softly after our love making and let it lull us.

The sleep-inducing DJ crooned, "And now from the 50's, The Platters with *I'm Sorry*."[5]

"*I'm sorry for the things I've done; I know that I'm the foolish one...*" I sang along as I backed out of the driveway. I knew the song well, had watched Mama and Daddy slow dance to it many times.

The houses were dark; the streets were deserted. The clock on the dashboard read 2:17.

"*I should have known from the start I'd break your heart, I'm sorry. Please be kind and I know you'll find it's so easy to forget...*"

The hell it is easy to forget! The tears sprang to my eyes, and I punched the off button to kill The Platters.

I turned left and headed for town. Just nine miles to comfort.

I drove the familiar streets, past Patty's house with Mr. Pelletier's bird houses still hanging in their enormous front-yard magnolia trees. Patty and I used to help her dad paint his bird houses. He paid us in movie tickets to the Rialto Theatre. His bird houses were looking a little weathered. Perhaps he needed my help.

Broughton High School, on the left, where I had been salutatorian, inched out of the valedictory spot by a Korean kid who had been in the country only two years and barely spoke English. I've never forgiven that little twit for moving to America. Last I heard little Woo-jin Kim was nuclear physicist Dr. Woo-jin Kim, working on some secret government project in the desert of New Mexico.

I still didn't forgive him.

I cut over to Hillsborough Street, to the NC State campus. From a distance I could see the Bell Tower glowing red in the night. I guessed we'd beaten somebody in some sport—the only reason the Bell Tower would be illuminated red. Football? Probably not. It was February. I figured we had won a basketball game. I hadn't paid attention. I'd been too preoccupied with my victimhood.

Almost there.

As I got closer, my mouth began salivating. When I turned the last corner, I saw the bright red neon sign:

HOT!

It's what every Krispy Kreme lover wants to see at 2:30 in the morning. That sign means that the donuts are hot off the conveyor belt, just the way God intended for them to be eaten.

Krispy Kreme has been a constant, a staple of my life. I can't remember not knowing Krispy Kreme. Every summer Mama and Daddy would go out of their way to this same Krispy Kreme on Person Street in downtown Raleigh to buy the two dozen glazed that we'd take to Emerald Isle. My brothers and I would have them eaten before we reached the bridge that connected the mainland to the island.

And Daddy used to pile all us kids in the station wagon on Christmas eve and take us to Krispy Kreme.

Mama would say, "Daddy," (She called our father Daddy.) "you're just gonna get those children all sugared up. We'll never get 'em to sleep."

But Daddy sugared us up anyway and then drove us all over town. We'd sing Christmas carols loudly and off key and look at the decorated houses. One year we passed a mobile home, its side adorned with aluminum pie plates. There was a string of Christmas lights tacked to the side of the home, a different colored bulb protruding through the bottom of each pie plate. My little brother Sam thought it was the most beautifully-decorated house he had ever seen. We all decided that everyone's idea of beauty was different and that Sam's favorite house really was beautiful, in its own way. The following year Sam asked Daddy to take us to see his pie-plate house. Daddy obliged. The lot was empty, except for an abandoned, harvest-gold oven.

Still, year after year, Sam would say, "Remember the pie-plate house? I loved that house."

And he'd look off, wistfully, remembering his favorite Christmas decorations.

Eventually, all us kids would get drowsy, and Daddy would take us back home so Mama could bed us down.

Every year there's a race from the NC State Bell Tower to Krispy Kreme, two miles away. Once the runners reach the donut shop, they have to eat a dozen glazed before turning around and running the two miles back, without losing their donuts. What started out long ago as a silly campus dare has turned into quite an ordeal. It's now a huge fundraiser that attracts national attention. There's a plastic donut on a stand for the winner—the one who can complete the course first without barfing his or her donuts. But, mostly, there are the bragging rights for all who can accomplish the mission. I've never participated, but I've seen lots of runners lose their Krispy Kremes along the way.

Mark's and my first date ended at Krispy Kreme. Lots of dates end at Krispy Kreme. We had gone to the midnight showing of *The Rocky Horror Picture Show* at the Rialto. All Raleigh residents have to experience *Rocky* at midnight, so it had been my suggestion. Mark came out of the theatre wired and excited, anxious to return to throw toast at the screen and dance the Time Warp in the aisle. Since there wouldn't be midnight *Rocky* showing for another week, I made an alternate suggestion to placate him: Krispy Kreme.

When we arrived, we found the HOT! sign glowing, much to my delight. Three firsts for Mark in one night: *Rocky*, Krispy Kreme, and HOT! The usual late-nighters greeted us: theatre goers in tuxedos and furs, bikers in torn jeans and leather vests, and the homeless with their shopping carts.

It's no wonder I turn to Krispy Kreme for comfort.

As I pulled into the small parking lot, I found that mine was the only car. But I wasn't the only customer. I could see other sleepless folks, who had apparently walked there, lining the counter, scattered at small tables, hunched wearily over their donuts topped with sprinkles, filled with jelly, iced with chocolate.

I killed the engine and sat for a moment, eyeing the bedraggled-looking man lurking by the front door, shoulders hunched around his ears, his hands crammed deep into his pockets. He appeared to be wearing layer upon layer of tattered clothes, possibly everything he owned. Homeless, I assumed. I pulled two crisp dollar bills from my wallet and got out of the car. I approached the man, but he didn't look my way. I held out the bills to him but couldn't find anything to say. Neither could he. He finally peered into my face with exhausted-looking, bloodshot eyes, took the bills from my hand and turned to leave. He shuffled out of the parking lot and down the sidewalk, disappearing into a thicket of overgrown Red Tip bushes. I'd thought he wanted donuts. Guess donuts weren't strong enough to dull his pain or provide the comfort he needed.

I tugged at the heavy glass door, and the heavenly scents of deep fried dough and sugary glaze assaulted me. I closed my eyes and let the memories the place conjured envelope me. I approached the glass case laden with lemon filled, glazed with sprinkles, jelly filled, custard filled, chocolate glazed, vanilla iced, crullers, cake with cinnamon, with powdered sugar, plain. But why tamper with perfection? To me the only true Krispy Kreme donut is a simple glazed, preferably hot off the conveyor belt.

And the sign had told me the donuts were HOT!

A very weary looking black woman shuffled her ample frame to the counter and said, "Hep you, ma'am?"

"Yes, please, I'd like two glazed, hot off the belt."

"Be right back," was all she said.

With that, she disappeared through the swinging doors behind the counter and within seconds was back, cradling two hot donuts on a waxed paper. She took them to the cash register to ring me up, saying, "Some'pm to drink?"

"A large decaf, please."

Once we'd settled up, I took my treasures to an empty table at the back of the shop where I could watch the donuts being born. The wall was glass, and through it I could see all the workings of donut magic. In the back of the room were the vats where the donuts were deep fried. Once they left their vats, they traveled down conveyor belts, prodded along by little metal wheels. I watched as dozens toddled along, wending their way toward the glaze waterfall. A constant sheet of delicious, teeth-aching icing cascaded toward the belt as the donuts passed through. Once they were glazed, workers wielding a chop stick in each hand scooped them up and deposited them into cardboard boxes of a dozen each. Watching the process is like watching a favorite movie that never ends.

Although there's a tendency to scarf Krispy Kremes while they're hot, I had learned to nibble instead, to savor every bite. After about an hour of nibbling and watching my favorite movie, I contemplated another pair. Thinking better, I opted for a little more coffee instead.

I shuffled my bedroom slippers over to the counter and said, "Refill, please."

The clerk groaned and kneaded the small of her back as she hoisted herself from her stool and, reaching for my cup, said, "That was regular, right?"

I started to correct her but said instead, "Sure, why not?"

I figured I'd already given up on sleep for the night.

As I headed back to my table, I looked around for the first time since I'd arrived and found that everyone else had left. While I sipped my coffee, I returned my gaze to the donuts rocking down the conveyor belt toward the icing waterfall. As mesmerizing and entertaining as it was, at some point I figured I'd better get on home. Why, I don't know. It just seemed like something I should be doing.

I stood and tightened my coat around me, re-wrapped my scarf around my neck, dropped my half-empty cup in the trash, and said to the woman behind the counter, "Thanks."

Without looking my way and still clutching her back, she grunted, "Hrmmmm."

Back in the car I tried Beach Music-24 again. It must have been all Platters, all night long because *"Only youuuuuuu could make the darkness bright,"* [6] wailed from the speakers.

Click! I couldn't abide their plaintive cry.

I drove in silence through the sleeping streets until I was back home. In nine miles I had not passed a single car. My hometown had never felt so silent, so lonely. I pulled into my driveway and killed the engine. I didn't have the energy or desire to leave the car, so I sat until the chill crept in and I began to shiver. Only then did I hop out and race to my porch as fast as my flapping slippers would take me. When I opened the front door, who should be awaiting my return? Why, Nick Nack, of course. It never fails. But how does she know?

And she was looking at me as if to say, "And just where have you been at this hour of the night, young lady?"

I brushed past her and said over my shoulder, "Oh, shut up. Your judgment is the last thing I need tonight."

I trudged up the stairs, Nick Nack hot on my heels. We entered our bedroom, and she was asleep on her rug before I could drop my coat and scarf on the floor and kick off my slippers. Apparently, she really didn't need an explanation for my whereabouts, just as long as she was confident I was home safe.

I fell across the bed and lay staring into the darkness. I was still alone. And my heart still hurt.

Krispy Kreme hadn't been much comfort.

Nine

I couldn't seem to escape that destructive, self-pitying rut on alternate weekends: send Alex off to be with Mark and Tawni; cry from loneliness; take my anger out on Nick Nack, eat whatever crap I could find in the fridge (or at Krispy Kreme); put on a phony smile just as I heard Alex returning.

So when she came shrieking in the front door, thundering down the hall toward the kitchen, I was all smiles and full of phony glee. She was so excited that she didn't even bother to close the front door but just let it bang against the hall tree that stood in the corner. I heard it topple and crash to the floor, but, still, she kept running toward me, screaming.

"Mama, you're not going to believe this!" she yelled, hopping up and down, shaking her hands.

I took a very deep breath, willed my self-pity away, composed myself, and stretched my lips over my teeth into a grin.

"Calm down, Alex. What are you screaming about?"

"I have the best news, Mama! Tawni is pregnant! And we're not just having a baby! We're having *two* babies! That's right, Tawni is going to have *twins*! I'm going to be the big sister to two little babies! Isn't that fantastic? I mean, have you ever heard such great news?"

The room was doing flip flops. I knew that it was going to just turn upside down, slamming me on my face. So I sat down to catch my breath and to keep from doing a face plant on the kitchen floor.

Pregnant. Tawni was pregnant. With twins. Mark had been gone only five months, and already he and his girlfriend were expecting twins. How far along must Tawni have been? Two months? Isn't that about the time she'd learn? Hell if I knew; I'd never had twins, but that sounded about right. Guess those condoms hadn't done much good.

So that's why Mark had gone to Las Vegas to get a quickie divorce. He'd said that he and Tawni were going on vacation, and he figured while he was there, he'd just go ahead and get it over with, do us all a favor. I should have smelled a rat.

As if the news weren't painful enough, Alex's delight was a kick right to the gut. How could she think I'd believe this was good news? Had I gone overboard with my phony acceptance of the situation? Had my false eagerness over the arrangement made her think that I was okay, really okay, with her father and Tawni's relationship and with the part she played in it. She was just a child and I couldn't expect her to reason as if she were an adult, but her lack of empathy wounded me deeply.

And as I felt the pain seep from my heart to my other organs and ooze into my extremities, she continued to chant, hop up and down, and chatter about what good news this was, waiting for me to join in her excitement.

But what could I say? "Hell, no, this isn't good news, and you're an insensitive brat. And if you were paying any attention, you'd be able to see the seeping, oozing pain."

Didn't think so.

So I tried to act happy for her, though she was so wrapped up in her excitement over being a big sister, that she'd have ignored any response to her good news. I could have put my head on the kitchen table and wept, and she wouldn't have noticed.

After running out of breath, Alex, still shaking her hands furiously in the air, said, "I'm just so excited I can't stand still. I'm going to go call Chelsea and Sara Beth. I can't wait to tell them my good news."

And as she thundered up the stairs to her room to call her friends, I put my head on the kitchen table and wept.

❧❦❧

Just as Mark had rushed to Las Vegas to get a quickie divorce, he and Tawni rushed to book a place for their wedding. June, two months away, was the earliest they could find a venue. As the plans progressed and Alex, who would be Tawni's flower girl, got swept up in all the excitement, the wedding-flurry fallout made its way to my house.

"No, Alex, I am not going to Daddy and Tawni's wedding."

"But, why not, Mama? They said you could come."

"Alex, they were only being polite. They never would have mentioned it had you not brought it up. So, once again, and for the last time, I will not be attending Daddy and Tawni's wedding. Let's drop it."

"But…"

"Alexandra Rowdy," I said, in that tone that means I mean business.

"Oh, all right," said Alex, and flounced up the stairs to her room and slammed the door.

She didn't understand why we couldn't all be just one big happy family. Why, we—yes *we*—were having twins, weren't we? Apparently, my child just wasn't old enough to understand what had truly happened to her father and me. She didn't know about broken hearts. She only knew that three adults loved her. Why, then, couldn't all those adults love one another? Sure, she understood that I was lonely sometimes and that I missed her daddy, but I just couldn't explain to her the pain that Mark and Tawni had caused me without also causing her pain. And I would go to any lengths to protect my child from pain.

Weekend after play weekend Alex came home, shivering with excitement over the upcoming nuptials. Tawni had taken her shopping at an expensive children's boutique for her flower girl dress. I wasn't aware such an establishment existed, considering that my clothes shopping was limited to Target. It was a calf-length pink tulle number with red velvet sash and red velvet rosebuds around the hem. With it she would wear white patent Mary Janes and lace-trimmed socks. I never thought that pink was a good color for redheads, but my little red-headed girl looked beautiful in her pink flower-girl dress.

One weekend she returned home carrying a small white wicker basket with red ribbon streamers. She tiptoed up and down our long hall in her Mary Janes, practicing tossing imaginary pink rose petals. Tears stung the backs of my eyes as I watched the joy my child was experiencing handing over her father to another woman.

"Oh, Mama, Tawni's dress is so beautiful. It's white and has little thin straps."

Of course, it was white because isn't white the color for pregnant-with-twins brides?

"The skirt is real full because it has to fit over her tummy. She's already getting big in the tummy, so she's bound to get bigger before the wedding because she's having twins, you know."

Yes, god damn it, I know!

"Why, yes, Alex, I remember your telling me that Tawni and your daddy were expecting twins."

Ten

It's amazing how finding a lump in your breast can derail your plans.

As the date of Mark and Tawni's wedding drew nearer and Alex got giddier by the day over the part she would play in their union, I became more and more despondent.

I had just seen Alex off to school to begin her last week of classes before summer vacation and The Event. I had two hours before I needed to report to the library, a job that I no longer found satisfying or rewarding but simply filled my empty, pointless mornings. I trudged upstairs to make the beds and take a shower.

After giving the beds a quick, half-assed smoothing, I shuffled to the bathroom. That's when I caught sight of myself in the mirror. How long had it been since I'd seen my image? *Really* seen it. I was taken aback.

But how is a woman supposed to look five days before her former spouse is to marry a woman half his age and pregnant with his twins, and her daughter is in a glee over the whole screwed-up mess? Just about like I looked, I guess: like shit. The break-up, Mark's move-out, the new woman, the twins, and my daughter's delight had sucked the life right out of me. I'd stopped watching my diet (as evidenced by my middle-of-the-night excursion to Krispy Kreme) and exercise regimen and was beginning to strain the buttons on my once-roomy pajamas. My complexion was suffering from lack of care, and my once-beautiful red hair, my crowning glory, was unkempt and greasy.

How had I allowed Mark and my victimhood the upper hand? I

was in control of me, if nothing else, and I had become completely out of control. My appearance, the physical evidence of that lack of control, repulsed me and really pissed me off.

"Damn it," I thought to myself, "I'm mad as hell, but moping and crying isn't going to make Mark come back. He's gone. He's always going to be gone, and I've got to get a grip."

With a rush of adrenalin and a feeling of power I hadn't experienced since Mark took a hike seven months before, I grabbed my loofah, my exfoliating cream, my razor, my peppermint-shea butter shampoo, and my honey face mask. I stepped out of my slippers and sloughed my pajamas, leaving them in a puddle on the tiled floor. I turned on the shower, waited for it to warm, then stepped in. I began soaping my body, and as I ran my hands across my newly-doughy midriff, once sleek and firm from hours of swimming laps, I made a mental note to call the gym to reinstate my membership.

I had exfoliated months of dead skin, shaved every shaveable surface, loofahed till my skin was raw, and shampooed and rinsed twice. I was showering off the last of my cucumber bath gel...

I went hot all over. I felt my knees turn to jelly, and I had to grab the towel bar to keep from falling. I slid down the wall until I was sitting on the cold, hard tile shower floor.

My thoughts ricocheted around my brain like staccato notes:
"No, it can't be."
"Oh, but it is."
"It's just fibrous tissue."
"Oh, no, it's not!"
Round.
Like a ball.
The size of a marble.
Hard.
Not painful.

Where had it been hiding? Why hadn't I felt it? Would a mammogram have detected it? But I was only thirty-five, too young for regular mammograms. Or so the experts say.

I kept pressing and prodding, hoping I could make it be something else. Then I became terrified that the pressing and prodding had made the marble explode and had released cancerous poison that was, at that moment, surging through my body.

I wrapped my arms around my head as I sat on the cold tile, the shower raining down on me. The water was warm, yet I was shivering. I felt like crying but was too scared to cry. I was so terrified that I probably couldn't have remembered how to cry. What do I do? How could this have happened to me? How in the hell could Life slap me with a lump in my breast when I'm dealing with so much other shit?

Then I got angry. Ordinarily, I'd have screamed for Mark, he'd have come to my side, and he'd have supported me as we figured out how to handle this. But where was Mark? Getting ready to marry his pregnant-with-twins girlfriend.

I sat there long after the water turned cold. Finally, shaking, I managed to get to my knees and paw my way up the shower wall until I was once again steadying myself with the towel bar. I turned off the shower and grabbed my towel, but my rubber legs wouldn't support me. I made my way to the toilet and sat on the seat to dry and calm myself. The drying I accomplished; the calming I did not.

What was I supposed to do? This was all so foreign to me. And I was young. Thirty-five year olds were not supposed to have lumps in their breasts. Were they?

Still trembling, I wrapped my towel around me and headed downstairs, my hair wet and dripping down my back.

In the kitchen I rummaged through the junk drawer until I found my address book. I made a mental note to transfer all the phone numbers to my cell, though at that moment transferring phone numbers didn't seem pressing. Flipping to the M's, I ran my finger down the page and stopped at Dr. Moore's number. My hand shook as I punched the key pad. While the phone rang, I reached under my towel. I was pressing the lump when Dr. Moore's answering service picked up.

"Doctors Moore, Hathaway and Clevenger. May I help you?" the operator sort of sang-spoke.

"I need to talk with Dr. Moore right away," I said, near panic.

"This is the answering service. The doctors' office isn't open yet," she said, still in that melodic voice.

My doctor's practice was one of the few remaining that hadn't gone to an automated phone answering machine. Dr. Moore and his partners still believed in the personal touch and felt their patients wanted to hear a human voice when they called the office, regardless of the time of day or night.

So I said to the human voice at the other end of the line, "I know the doctors' office isn't open yet and I know I'm speaking to the answering service and I know that Dr. Moore isn't in his office. But I need to talk with him, wherever he is."

My abrupt and rude response astounded me, but I just couldn't seem to stop myself. This personal service wasn't doing me any more good than an automated answering machine would.

"Ma'am, I can take a message and pass it on to him, but if this is an emergency, please hang up and dial 9-1-1."

"*Ma'am*," I replied, still with sarcasm dripping from my voice, "this *is* an emergency, but not a 9-1-1 emergency. It is a *gynecological* emergency, and I need to speak to my *gynecologist* right away. Now, where is he?"

"Ma'am," she said again, her sing-speaking voice having completely disappeared, "Dr. Moore is on rounds at Rex Hospital this morning. I'll leave him a message and let him know that this is an emergency and that you need to talk with him right away."

Then I softened.

"I'm sorry, but I'm just so scared." I said. "I've found a lump, and I'm alone."

By this time I was crying, and even though I knew I was talking to someone who just took messages and had no medical training whatsoever, I really needed to hear a comforting voice.

"I'm so sorry. I know how terrified you must be," said the faceless voice at the other end of the line, and I cried harder at her kindness. "Take your time, and when you're ready, I'll jot down your name and the number where Dr. Moore can reach you."

Sniffling and trying to stem the flow of tears, I blubbered, "Rowdy Murphy, my name is Rowdy Murphy, and Dr. Moore can reach me at 919-828-9979. I'll be waiting by the phone."

"Okay, Ms. Murphy. I'll reach him as soon as I can," said the compassionate operator, the song returning to her voice.

"Thank you," I whispered.

And the line went dead.

As I waited to hear from Dr. Moore, I remembered that I'd be expected at the library soon. I punched in the number I knew by heart and waited for an answer. Checking the clock on the kitchen wall, I realized that the library, too, would not yet be open. My call went straight to voicemail.

"Hi, this is Rowdy Murphy. It's Monday morning," I said to the machine.

I didn't know what to say. I wasn't on life-crisis-sharing terms with the library staff, so I wasn't familiar with I-can't-come-to-the-library-today-because-I-have-a-lump-in-my-breast protocol.

So I said, "I'm so sorry to call at the last minute, but something has come up and I won't be able to come in this morning."

I paused, not knowing what else to say. Finally, I just blurted, "Bye," and hung up the phone to wait for Dr. Moore's call.

I crossed the kitchen and grabbed a paper towel to wipe my eyes. I was staring out the kitchen window, blowing my nose, when the phone rang.

"Hello?"

"Rowdy girl, what's going on over there?"

"Dr. Moore?"

"That's right. What's happening?"

Then I *really* started crying.

My kind doctor waited patiently until I slowed enough to say, "A lump, I found a lump in my breast."

"Well, let's not panic. About eighty percent of breast lumps are benign. But, of course, we'll want to take a look just to be sure. How about coming to the office first thing tomorrow morning?"

Then I started crying again.

"Oh, please, Dr. Moore, I can't wait till then. I'm all by myself, and I'm a wreck. Can't you see me today?"

Without hesitation, he said, "Sure, Rowdy, I understand. The office will be open at nine. I'll head over there when I finish rounds. Come in as soon as you can, and we'll work you in."

I slowed to a sniffle and said, "Oh, thank you so much, Dr. Moore."

My doctor was such a dear. He'd been my OB-GYN since my pre-wedding physical. He had seen me through my pregnancy and had delivered Alex. If I had to have a lump in my breast—and apparently I did—I wanted Dr. Moore taking care of me.

I hung up the phone, and when I turned to head upstairs to dress, I nearly tripped over Nick Nack.

"Damn it, Nick Nack, get out of my way!"

She wouldn't budge but just stared up at me with a confused look on her face. I'd lived with her long enough—rather, *she'd* lived with *me* long enough—for me to gauge her reactions. She was clearly confused. And concerned. She stepped closer, looked up at me, and laid her head against my arm.

"Go away, Nick Nack. I don't have time to deal with you this morning."

Still she stood her ground. So I stepped around her and headed upstairs to get dressed. She stayed hot on my heels, following me up the stairs and into our bedroom, hovering while I stepped into the jeans that I'd dropped on the floor the night before. I slipped my sweatshirt over my head, but not before prodding the lump once more, and stepped into my flip flops. I shook my head; my hair was still damp, but I'd just let it dry naturally. I ran my fingers through it and let it fall where it wanted.

I ran down the stairs and grabbed my purse and keys from the hall table, Nick Nack still my shadow. When I tried to leave, she stood between me and the door, whining. Ordinarily her intrusion would have infuriated me, but as I trembled with fear, I found her devotion touching.

So as I gently pushed her aside and eased open the door, I said, "It's okay, Nick Nack. I'm okay."

I let myself out and headed for my car. As I got in and began to back out of the driveway, I noticed that Nick Nack had made her way to the living room and was watching me from the front window, something she had never done before. She continued to stare as I backed into the street and pulled away.

Morning traffic was light until I got to Crabtree Valley Mall, where the shoppers' cars were bumper to bumper. There must have been something special going on, maybe a big sale. But so early in the morning? And on a Monday? I used to keep up with such things, but I couldn't remember the last time I'd been to the Mall. In the big scheme of things, shopping just didn't seem too significant. I clutched the steering wheel, willing the traffic to part like the Red Sea. Perspiration broke out on my forehead and trickled down my spine as I inched along with all those people who had no idea that I had a lump in my breast and was chauffeuring my terror to my doctor's office. Had they known, they'd have surely pulled over or, perhaps, ordered me a police escort. But these clueless drivers just bobbed their heads to music, checked their lipstick in the rearview mirror, and talked or texted on their cell phones as I shook with fear. After about fifteen minutes that felt like an hour, I broke free and was sailing up Edwards Mill Road and into the care of Dr. Moore.

Eleven

The receptionist behind the front desk slid the frosted glass window aside and said, "Morning, may I help you?"

"Yes, I'm Rowdy Murphy."

And before I could finish, she said, "Oh, sure, Ms. Murphy, Dr. Moore is expecting you."

She stood and handed me a clipboard and pen and said, "Please fill out these forms, and we'll get you back to see the doctor soon."

"Thanks," I said and took the clipboard to the nearest chair.

As I sat and dropped my purse on the floor beside me, I glanced at the clipboard and realized they held the same damn forms with the same damn questions I had filled out every time I had been in any doctor's office. Why did I have to fill them out again?

Yes, I know that I am protected by HIPPA laws and that I can sue the shit out of you if you share any of my medical information with anyone. And, no, I still don't take any medications, either prescription or over-the-counter, unless you count that Midol I took for menstrual cramps four months ago. I am one year older than I was when I came to see you a year ago. My name hasn't changed; my address hasn't changed; my insurance carrier and coverage haven't changed; my telephone number hasn't changed; my social security number hasn't changed; my medical history hasn't changed.

Only my medical present has changed. I have a lump in my breast. All you need to know is that I have a lump in my breast. All the rest is old news. All the rest is irrelevant.

All that matters right now is that I have a lump in my breast and I am so terrified I think I am slipping away, my head is getting light, and I'm falling down a black hole. And if someone doesn't hurry and rescue me, the hole is going to close over me. And then it really won't matter if someone comes to rescue me.

"Ms. Murphy, Ms. Murphy, are you okay?"

I was crouching on the floor, there was a wad of paper in my hand, and the voice crying, "Ms. Murphy, Ms. Murphy," sounded muffled, as if the person talking were speaking through a wad of cotton balls.

Then I was sitting on a sofa in Dr. Moore's office. I have no idea how I got there, but Dr. Moore was beside me, holding a cup of water to my lips, saying, "It's okay, Rowdy. Breathe deep, and take a sip."

A nurse was hovering nearly, waiting for the doctor's instructions.

"Okay now?" Dr. Moore asked, as I tried to push the cup away.

"I have a lump in my breast," was all I said.

"I know, Rowdy, and I know you're scared," he said, still coaxing me to take a sip.

"I have a lump in my breast. I have a lump in my breast and Mark has left me and he is getting married Saturday. Mark is marrying a woman who is pregnant with his twins. And I have a lump in my breast."

I was babbling. I knew I was babbling, but I couldn't stop myself. It all came tumbling out. It was more than I could grasp. I just kept saying it over and over. Maybe I thought that if I said it enough, I could just spit it out and make it all disappear into thin air. But no matter how much I chattered, my screwed-up life was still my screwed-up life.

So Dr. Moore patted my back, still holding the cup to my lips, and said, "I'm so sorry, Rowdy, but let's not get ahead of ourselves." And ignoring my marital catastrophe, he continued, "Like I told you on the phone, most breast lumps are benign. We'll take a look and see where we need to go from here. Okay?"

He kept asking if I were okay. I was not okay. I was terrified and alone. Being swallowed by a black hole was looking more appealing by the minute.

When I didn't respond, he took my hand, still offering me water. I let him hold my hand, but I refused his water.

"Rowdy, are you in any pain?"

Did he mean heart pain because, if so, the answer was a screaming, "Yes!" I assumed, though, since I was here about the breast lump and not my broken heart, he was referring to breast pain.

"No, no pain."

"How about discharge? Have you noticed any discharge from your nipple?"

"No discharge. Just the lump."

"When did you discover the lump, Rowdy?"

"This morning. In the shower. I found it this morning."

"Okay, then," Dr. Moore said and released by hand, "let's take a look," and to his nurse he said, "Martha, please put Ms. Murphy in two, and I'll be right in."

He gave my shoulder a pat as Martha turned and led me to examining room two.

"Undress from the waist up," she said, "and slip into this gown, open in front. Dr. Moore and I will be in when you're ready." And before turning to leave, she said sweetly, "I know you're scared and that's normal, but you're in good hands."

I smiled weakly and watched her walk out and close the door behind her. I was alone, alone in a cold, institutional-green cubicle. I didn't want to be alone—ever again.

Before I began to panic and slip back into my black hole (I had decided that I really didn't want to be consumed by the black hole.), I quickly shed my sweatshirt and slipped into the yellow hospital gown—but not before prodding the lump once again.

I climbed up on the examining table and was perched on the end, my legs fidgeting nervously, when Dr. Moore knocked lightly, cracked the door a bit, and said, "Ready?"

"Yes," was all I could manage.

He came into the room, Martha right behind. She pulled out the leg rest and told me to lie down as Dr. Moore turned his back and washed his hands in the mini sink in the corner of the examining room. Once I was settled, he turned and, drying his hands on a paper towel, joined his nurse at my side.

Martha lifted my left arm and parted the gown as Dr. Moore tossed his paper towel and pushed his glasses up his nose. He bent over me and began gently prodding my breast.

There was no pain, only terror. He examined in silence, with no comforting positive affirmations. I tried to read his mood, his facial expression, but he wouldn't give me a clue. When he finished his exam, he took his glasses off, stuck them in his lab-coat pocket, and managed a semi-smile.

"Get dressed, Rowdy, and come on back to my office so we can talk."

My panic mounting with each minute, I wanted to scream, "What is it? Why do we need to talk? I don't want to talk! I want you to tell me to go home because I'm fine!"

But he didn't do that. He left the examining room to return to his office, to wait for me to join him so that we could talk.

I took my time shedding my gown and dressing and then sat on a low, metal stool with wheels, catching my breath, careful not to roll into the black hole. When I thought I'd dawdled as long as I should, I gathered my purse and tried to gather my courage and headed for Dr. Moore's office.

"Come on in, Rowdy, and have a seat," Dr. Moore said when he saw me cowering in the doorway. He motioned to the chair in front of his desk.

"Rowdy, I'm just not sure what we're dealing with here, so I'm going to order some tests."

"Tests? What kind of tests?"

"I want you to go to Raleigh Imaging for a diagnostic mammogram."

"What's a diagnostic mammogram?"

"It's similar to the routine screening mammogram, only the diagnostic mammogram is more meticulous."

Comparing a diagnostic mammogram to a screening mammogram was like comparing flying a jet to flying a helicopter. I'd done neither. This was a brand new experience for me. But, given a choice, at that moment I felt as though I'd rather have been handed the keys to a jet.

But still insisting that I succumb to a diagnostic mammogram, rather than fly a jet, he continued, "The technician will take more images, examining the lump and surrounding breast tissue more thoroughly. And we won't make you wait a week for the test results, as is customary with a screening mammogram. The technician will send the films directly to the radiologist, and she'll request that he review them right away."

Martha stuck her head in the door.

"Excuse me, Dr. Moore," she said, and smiled faintly in my direction. "Raleigh Imaging doesn't have an opening today; it really doesn't matter, though, 'cause Dr. Sherron won't be in till tomorrow."

I took a deep, ragged breath and dug my fingers into the chair arms.

"But they'll work Ms. Murphy in at ten tomorrow morning, and Dr. Sherron will be there to read the x-rays then.

"Great news," Dr. Moore said and reached across his desk for my hand. I didn't turn it over to him but just kept clutching the chair arms. He didn't withdraw the offer in case I changed my mind. Talking and smiling, hand still outstretched, he continued, "Dr. Sherron, great diagnostician. He'll take a look and report his findings right away. Martha will print out my orders for your mammogram and quick reading, as well as a map showing you how to get to Raleigh Imaging."

"Now, Rowdy, I want you to relax for the rest of the day, take it easy, and try not to worry. I know that's easier said than done, but regardless of what we're dealing with, we're in this together. You and me. And one more thing, Rowdy: I want you to eat something. You may not be hungry, but you need to eat. You got mighty light-headed out there in the waiting room, a sign that you need something on your stomach. Okay?"

I wasn't hungry and I really didn't want to eat, but I promised him that I would.

He smiled, stood, and came around to my side of the desk. I was still clutching the arms of the chair. He gently patted my back, causing my fingers to unclaw, my body to relax. Dr. Moore had always had that effect on me.

As I stood to leave, he followed me to the door saying, "Stop by the check-out desk. Martha will have all your paperwork waiting for you."

By the time I left Dr. Moore's office, it was near noon. Time for lunch, and I'd promised my doctor that I would eat something. I was just blocks from Char-Grill, the home of the ultimate comfort food. A 50's-themed hamburger joint with no eat-in dining but only outdoor picnic tables, Char-Grill is known and well loved by all Raleigh residents. My parents dated at Char-Grill when Daddy was a student at State and Mama a coed at Meredith College. And when my brothers and I were little, Daddy would take us for Char-Burgers on Saturdays so that Mama could have a little peace and quiet, a break from her five children. Maybe a Char-Burger was just what I needed. So I pulled out of the parking lot beside the medical building and headed for Char-Grill.

The place was teeming with folks; most of them looked like workers on their lunch breaks. I parked the car, crossed the lot, and got in the long line. After a lengthy wait, I reached the window. I wrote my order—Char-Burger all the way, fries, medium diet—on the order pad, scrawled my name at the top, ripped off the sheet, and slipped it through the slot in the window.

Office workers in suits and laborers in paint-splattered pants and muddied boots stood in twos, fours, sixes, waiting for their food. I stood off to the side, by myself, trying to think of happy times at Char-Grill, trying not to think of the unknown that lay ahead for me.

"Rowdy, order for Rowdy. Char-Burger all the way, fries, medium diet. Rowdy, order for Rowdy."

I stepped to the window, paid the cashier, took my food, and turned to look for a picnic table. They were all occupied.

Just as I was resigned to eating in my car, balancing my lunch on my knees, a young man turned, smiled, and said, "Ma'am, we're just leaving. You can have our table."

Ma'am. Southern gentlemen are so polite. I could have been twenty-five, and he'd have still called me Ma'am. The guy and his friends stood and turned to leave. They looked as if they were right out of college, all fresh-faced and delighted with their low-paying, entry-level jobs. The boys wore cheap suits and loafers, the girls demure black pumps and short dark skirts. They looked optimistic, enthusiastic, and happy to have enough money for Char-Burgers after making their monthly student loan payments.

I thought, "Don't get too comfortable, kids. Just when you think you have life by the balls, it'll laugh in your face and kick you in the ass."

As they relinquished their table and strolled innocently and cluelessly to their compact car that would return them to their identical cubicles, I sat and peered into my paper sack of comfort.

I was spreading a napkin on the table when two painters I had seen at the window approached and said, "Ma'am, mind if we share your table?"

"No, help yourselves," I said, unenthusiastically, and motioned to the empty spaces.

"Joe," said the larger of the two, extending his beefy hand.

Concerned about germs, I realized I hadn't packed hand sanitizer. "Oh, what the hell," I thought and reached to shake Joe's hand. "Hi, Joe, I'm Rowdy."

"Rowdy, this is Anthony," he said, motioning toward his buddy across the table.

Too far apart to shake, Anthony and I just semi-smiled, bobbed our heads in greeting, and said, "Hey."

Once they'd sat and unwrapped their hamburgers and fries, they fell silent and ate quickly. I'm guessing they were on the clock and needed to get back to their painting.

I, on the other hand, had time to kill. I laid out my Char-Burger and too-hot-to-eat-yet fries (real honest-to-god fries, not those skinny, hard, shoestring things), and prepared to be comforted. The comfort never came. And though Dr. Moore said I needed to eat, I just couldn't. My throat tightened, my stomach knotted, and I couldn't have eaten under threat. I sat and stared, tears welling, the fear escalating. I tried a fry, still so delicious, but not what I needed. I wrapped my uneaten lunch in the place mat I had fashioned from the paper napkin and put it back in the bag.

I stood to leave, and four laughing, chatting newcomers claimed the table before I could clear it. I passed a trash container and shed my almost-untouched meal. I had planned to take my drink along with me to nurse throughout the afternoon but, at the last moment, decided that I didn't want it either. I dropped it in the trash can and headed for my car and home.

I didn't remember the twenty-minute ride. I just appeared in my driveway. The thought of being on auto pilot all the way frightened me.

I remembered Gramma, Daddy's mother, bragging that she'd never had a wreck, and Grampa saying, "True, Maude, you've never *had* a wreck, but God knows how many you've *caused*."

I prayed I hadn't caused any wrecks as my car, somehow, got me home with no help or recollection from me. As I sat there in the driveway, gaining my composure, I looked up to see Nick Nack staring at me from the living room window. Had she been there since I'd left for the doctor's office before nine o'clock that morning? Was she really so concerned that she had kept vigil for over four hours? My instincts told me she had.

I got out of the car and headed for the house. When I opened the door, Nick Nack was there to greet me. She seemed overly attentive, hovering more than usual. I dropped my purse and keys on the front hall table and headed for the kitchen. Though I hadn't been able to eat my lunch, I was suddenly parched. As my devoted shadow trotted along beside me, I opened the fridge, grabbed a bottle of water, uncapped it, and downed most of it in one gulp.

Nick Nack stood and stared. Was she picking up on my terror vibe? Was I carrying a fear aura? Her extra attention and her sense of concern were freaking me out. Did she know something I didn't know, intuit something that I couldn't?

"You okay, Nick Nack?"

Still she hovered and stared.

I reached into the cupboard and grabbed one of her favorite doggie treats, hoping to divert her attention.

"Want a biscuit, Nick Nack?"

She ignored it, her full attention trained on me.

Exhausted from the morning, I flicked her treat on the kitchen floor and headed upstairs to rest a while before Alex's return from school. Nick Nack left her snack right where I'd tossed it and followed me down the hall and up the stairs to *our* bedroom.

I lay across the bed, and Nick Nack rested her head on the edge of the bed, still studying me.

"All right, Nick Nack, this is creeping me out."

Still she watched, attentively.

Finally I said, "Lie down, Nick Nack," and motioned to her rug by the bed.

She lay down obediently but did not rest. She craned her neck, still on guard.

As I drifted off, she was standing watch.

Twelve

"Mama?"

I woke with a jolt.

"Oh, hey, Sweetie. Caught me napping," I said groggily.

Alex rarely found me napping when she got home from school, and there was a look of surprise on her face—as if she had caught me smoking pot or having sex.

"What's wrong?"

I couldn't say, "Nothing," because something was certainly wrong. But I didn't want to mention the lump in my breast until I knew what it was, what I had to do about it, and what impact it was going to have on our lives. And, who knew, maybe I was worrying for naught. Perhaps the lump was benign, I wouldn't have to do a thing, and Alex would be none the wiser.

So I chirped, "Just droopy, I guess. I ran errands today, and I must have overdone it. But I'm fine. Now run put your backpack in your room, wash your hands, and come tell me about your day."

She backed out of my room, still eyeing me suspiciously. By the time she had deposited her backpack on her bedroom floor and washed and dried her hands, I was revived, my best mommy smile plastered in place.

I went through the motions of preparing Alex's supper, but I was so accustomed to fixing macaroni and cheese and applesauce that I could have done it in my sleep. To make it simple, I ate mac and cheese and applesauce, as well. While we had our bland, textureless meal, I asked Alex about her day and feigned interest.

Normally after supper Alex would begin her homework at the kitchen table while I washed the dishes and tidied the kitchen. Then I'd join her, helping her with her lessons, drilling her on her spelling words, working on science projects. But we were just days from summer vacation; there was no more homework, no spelling words, no science projects.

So I made a bowl of popcorn, and we settled in our pj's on the sofa to watch TV. I had no idea what was on, so I let Alex choose a show. She picked The Bachelor. God help us! I couldn't concentrate on the inane chatter among the plastic girls and the preening Adonis, but it seemed to hold Alex's attention.

She prattled, "I hope he picks Kelly. She's pretty, and I like her pink dress and her sandals. I don't like Hilary, though. She's mean, and she says mean things about the other girls. She even says mean things about Kelly. And Kelly's so nice. She shouldn't say mean things about her. And, you know, Mama, they live in a really big house. I like that house. It's so pretty. I hope I have a house like that when I grow up. And I want a pool like that, too. I can go swimming any time I want. And you won't have to take me to the club. I can just walk outside my back door and jump right in. And I can swim all by myself. There won't be lots of stupid boys playing Marco Polo and doing cannon balls and splashing all over the place. And, Mama, you could come swim with me any time you wanted."

"That sounds like fun, Alex," I said, when what I really wanted to say was, "Oh, please, stop talking."

But, instead, I sat with my arm around my precious child, my smile in place, while she chatted animatedly about her new favorite TV show. I was so relieved when the hour show that seemed to last several days finally ended.

"Well, Darlin', that was fun, but it's time to hit the sack. Tomorrow is your field day, and you have to be well rested so you can run the sack race and play corn hole."

"Oh, I know, Mama. I just can't wait," she trilled excitedly and clapped her hands, as she sailed upstairs to brush her teeth and get ready for bed.

I turned off the TV—the silence was golden—straightened the throw pillows on the sofa, and headed upstairs to tuck Alex in. She was already under the covers when I got there. I sat on the edge of the bed and leaned over to kiss her good night.

She wrapped her arms around my neck and breathed her little minty breath in my face as she kissed me on the cheek and said, "I love you so much, Mama. Heather's mama would never watch The Bachelor with her. You're so cool."

Blessings come when you least expect them and need them the most. I was at my lowest, but my daughter thought I was cool.

I kissed her on the forehead and said, "And I love you, Alex."

I stood, crossed the room, and turned out the light. I left her door ajar out of habit; I wanted to hear her should she call out in the night. She hadn't called out in the night for years, but just in case... I padded across the hall to my bedroom, where I found Nick Nack already curled by the bed, waiting for me to turn in.

She looked up as I approached, and I said, "Nick Nack, did you know I was cool? Neat, huh?"

She just smiled and slapped her tail with a muffled thud on her rug before settling into her pile of fur.

I climbed into bed, though I didn't expect to sleep. And I didn't. I watched the green numbers on the clock advance until, at 6:30, the obnoxious sound of the alarm made me pound the OFF button.

Nick Nack did not roll onto her back, yawn loudly, and stretch to her full length before standing on wobbly, sleepy legs. She just lifted her head and looked at me with her loving brown eyes. I could tell she hadn't slept either. She stood and rested her head on the edge of the bed and let out a plaintive sigh.

"Guess it's time to start our day, Nick Nack," I said, and slid out of bed and climbed over her.

I stepped into my slippers and crossed to Alex's room.

Sticking my head in the door, I sang, "It's field-day day. Time to rise and shine."

She rolled over, stretched, and smiled a sleepy smile at me.

"Hi, Mama."

"Hi, Sweetie. What do you want for breakfast?"

"Hmmm, Pop Tarts."

Not too healthy, but at least it wasn't mac and cheese.

"Sounds good to me. Now go wash your face and get dressed and come on down to the kitchen. Your Pop Tarts and I will be waiting for you."

I shuffled down the stairs in my slippers, hair frazzled, face unwashed, Nick Nack clicking down the steps beside me. Once I'd released Nick Nack to the outdoors and filled her bowls, I pulled Alex's strawberry Pop Tarts with sprinkles, her favorites, from the pantry and dropped two into the toaster. I started the coffee and poured a glass of milk for Alex. She sailed into the kitchen just as her Pop Tarts jumped out of the toaster, dressed, but hair as frazzled as mine. She handed me her brush and an elastic band.

"I need a pony tail, Mama. I can't do field day with my hair all hanging down."

She turned her back to me so that I could brush her long red hair and pull it back in a thick, fluffy pony tail. Then she faced me, all smiles and dimples, sweet baby curls framing her beaming, freckled face. She didn't know her mama's fear. Her only thought was on three-legged races, relays, and corn hole. I wanted it that way.

She gobbled her Pop Tarts and gulped her milk, wiping her mouth on the back of her hand.

"Run brush your teeth and get your back pack."

"Okay, Mama," she called over her shoulder, bounding up the stairs.

By the time I ushered her out of the house and to the bus stop, my mommy smile was beginning to hurt my face. I didn't feel like smiling, and the effort had been a strain. But I knew I had to hold it together for my child.

I called the library again, this time leaving a message that I had a family issue to deal with and that I'd let them know when I'd resolved it. I trudged upstairs, halfway made the beds, showered, and climbed back into my jeans and sweatshirt.

Nick Nack didn't leave my side.

Once again, she tried to prevent my leaving the house, and, that failing, she raced to the living room window and nervously watched my departure. I was certain she'd be there at her post in the window when I returned.

I followed Dr. Moore's map and, without a hitch, pulled into the Raleigh Imaging lot in twenty-five minutes. There was a space right at the front door. Good omen? I was hoping.

"Good morning, I'm Rowdy Murphy. Dr. Moore has scheduled an appointment for me," I told the woman at the reception counter.

She scanned her schedule and said, "All right then, diagnostic mammogram at ten," and she put a check by my name. "You can sit right over there and fill out these forms," she said, as she handed me a clipboard and a pen.

I clenched my teeth as I took the forms from her and promised myself that I would try not to have another meltdown over the medical profession's morbid curiosity about my personal life.

I was still working on the no-I-don't-take-any-drugs-except-Midol section of the questionnaire when I heard, "Ms. Murphy, Rowdy Murphy."

I halted the inquisition and looked up to see a young woman in green scrubs and white Crocs standing in an open doorway, scanning the room—I was guessing for Ms. Murphy, Rowdy Murphy.

"Right here," I said. "I'm Rowdy Murphy."

I stood, crossed the room, and handed my almost-finished forms to the woman and followed her to a miniscule dressing cubicle where she said, "Clothes off from the waist up. Put your personal belongings in that plastic bag and bring it with you. Slip on this gown, open in front, and then go sit in the waiting room at the end of this hall till the technician calls you."

And then she disappeared.

Didn't she know that I was scared and that she was supposed to pat my back, offer me water, hold my hand, and smile at me? Most importantly, she was supposed to say, "It'll be okay 'cause you're in good hands."

I figured she must have been new. She didn't know yet that she was supposed to be easing my terror and singing the praises of the great hands that were working at Raleigh Imaging.

Alone in my cubicle, I noticed that my gown was pink. Doesn't pink mean breast cancer? I did not like that one bit. It felt like bad karma. But I put on the pink gown for the lack of any other available color, open in front, just as the young woman had ordered me to do, stowed my sweatshirt and personal belongings in the plastic bag, and headed for the holding room to await my turn.

I grabbed a magazine but was only three paragraphs into "Are Brad and Angie Caput?" when I heard someone call my name. I followed the voice to a pleasant-looking plump woman with a long, blonde ponytail and three graduated silver loop earrings in one ear, none in the other. As I approached, she smiled an eye-disappearing smile. I once told Mama that if people's eyes disappear when they smile, they are smiling sincerely. This young woman who was escorting me to the machine that would predict my future was

smiling at me sincerely. Sincere smiles usually make me feel good.
Hers did not.

"Hey, my name's Alicia," she said, as she led me to a room with a big, white machine that I guessed was going to be used for my diagnostic mammogram. "Okay, Sugar," she drawled, "you just put your things on that chair over there and step right here. Now, I'm so sorry my hands are cold this morning," she said, rubbing them together briskly, "and this dang machine is *always* cold. Just can't be helped."

I stepped forward and let Alicia man-handle my breast with her cold hands and her cold machine.

As she was tugging and spreading and flattening and squeezing my breast, she chattered cheerily, "Now, I guess Dr. Moore told you that we're doing a *diagnostic* mammogram this morning. We'll be taking more pictures of your breast than we would with a screening mammogram, more angles so that Dr. Sherron can get a real good look."

She stepped on a pedal that made the clear, Lucite trays that were holding my breast press together, further flattening it, making it look like an anemic, veiny pancake. Just when I thought I couldn't stand the pain another second, she said, "Hold your breath, Honey," and raced behind a Plexiglas shield and pushed the button to take a picture.

Eight times Alicia squeezed at varying angles, said, "Hold your breath, Honey," raced behind the shield, and took a picture. By the end of the session, I was bathed in perspiration, and tears were welling in my eyes.

"Here, Darlin', let's sit right over there for a minute," she said, as she gently covered my breast with the pink gown and guided me to a straight-back chair.

I held tight to her and hobbled with wobbly knees.

"You all right, Hon?" she asked, rubbing my back.

I couldn't answer but just shook my head up and down weakly.

"You sit right there while I run these films to be developed. Then I'll get you a ging' ale. Would you like a ging' ale?"

"Yes, thank you, ginger ale would be nice," I said.

Fifteen minutes passed before Alicia returned with my ginger ale. By that time the pain had subsided and I had calmed, no longer perspiring, tearing, shaking.

"Sorry that took so long. Here's some ging' ale, and I got you some graham crackers, too. Sometimes these exams can make you right queasy; the graham crackers will help settle your stomach. Now, once the films are developed, Dr. Sherron is going to take a look at them. We want you to stay here, just in case he needs another picture. He'll also want to discuss his findings with you. So let's take your stuff back out to the waiting room, and you can read a magazine and have your ging' ale and crackers till he's ready for you. You okay, now?"

"Sure," I squeaked, "I'm fine. I'm just scared."

"Course you are, Honey. That's natural."

She didn't promise that I was going to be all right or that I had nothing to worry about or that the hands that were taking care of me were good ones. She just validated my feelings of fear and gently led me back to the waiting room where I could finally find out if Brad and Angie were really caput.

Turns out it was a ruse, a come-on just to drag me inside their magazine. Brad and Angelina really weren't caput, and, furthermore, Jennifer Aniston had done absolutely nothing to cause a rift in their relationship. The bright red, angry headlines on the cover had indicated otherwise. I also discovered that Lindsey Lohan was in trouble, yet again. And that's newsworthy? I learned that JLo wore the dress better than Jessica Alba—by a whopping 74% to 26%—and that Matthew McConaughey was still sexy as all get out. I didn't need a magazine article to convince me of that.

Ordinarily I wouldn't have given a shit about Brangelina or JLo and Jessica or Lindsey or Matthew McConaughey (well, maybe Matthew McConaughey), but as I sat in the waiting room, gowned in breast-cancer pink, trying to keep my terror at bay, I'd have read an article about NASCAR or snake handling to divert my attention from the elephant in the room.

I was well into dog-eared magazine number three, shivering from fear, not cold, when a very tall, beautiful woman the color of strong coffee came into the waiting room and said in a soft, soothing voice, "Ms. Murphy, I'm Tracey, Dr. Sherron's nurse. He has reviewed your x-rays and will see you now. Come with me. I'll take you to his office."

Thirteen

I followed her down the hall where a fiftyish-looking man in the same green scrubs and white Crocs as everyone else, graying at the temples, bushy eyebrows, glasses at the end of his nose, sat behind a desk, working at his computer.

"Ms. Murphy," he said, turning his computer screen from my view, removing his glasses, standing, and motioning to the chair in front of his desk. "I'm Dr. Sherron. Please sit down."

I didn't speak, just clutched my plastic bag of belongings and sat in the chair he offered.

"I've had a chance to study your x-rays. They show a suspicious-looking area, so I'd like to take a closer look, just to get a better idea of what we're dealing with."

He paused to let me talk, should I feel the need. I did not.

So he continued, "I want to perform what is called a needle biopsy. It's a simple, relatively painless procedure to remove a piece of the tumor and cells from adjacent lymph nodes to examine for abnormal cells. We'd do it right here at the clinic. We'll use a local anesthesia to numb the area, so you'll be fine to drive home afterward."

He said it in such a matter-of-fact manner, as if he did this every day. Well, he *did* do it every day, but I *didn't*. I could feel the blood drain from my face and my hands begin to shake. To ward off another meltdown, I closed my eyes and took slow, deep breaths. I had wanted him to tell me that all was fine and that I was free to go home to live a happy, healthy, carefree life. But he refused to do that.

"Ms. Murphy, do you have any questions?"

I sat and stared silently at my hands resting in my lap.

Finally I looked up and asked, "Do I have cancer?"

He didn't seem surprised. That's probably the first question every terrified woman with suspicious-looking areas asks.

"We just can't be sure until we examine a section of the tumor. Only then will we know for certain what it is."

"When do you plan to do this test?"

"Well, since you're already here, I'd like to go ahead with the procedure."

"Now? You mean right now?"

"The sooner we proceed, the sooner we'll know what kind of tumor it is. Wouldn't you rather have some answers right away, instead of being in the dark and playing the guessing game?"

"I guess so," I said meekly, but I wasn't sure. Isn't ignorance bliss?

"Great. We'll take care of it now, and then you and I can meet back here on Thursday. I'll have the test results by then, and you and I can talk about what we do next."

"Do next?"

"Yes, if it is a malignancy, we'll talk about treatment options. If it's benign, I'll send you on home with instructions about what to be on the lookout for in the future. Okay?"

"Okay," I said weakly, my head spinning, my heart racing.

But I was not okay.

"Tracey," Dr. Sherron said to his nurse, "please prep Ms. Murphy, and I'll be with you shortly."

Tracey took my arm, helped me from the chair, and guided me down the hall to the procedure room. The only sounds were Tracey's Crocs squeaking on the green tiled floor and my heart pounding in my ears. As she prepped me for the needle biopsy, she chatted animatedly, but her voice was just a bunch of garbled sounds because of the thrumming in my ears.

Dr. Sherron had been right: once he numbed the area of the tumor, the biopsy was relatively painless. The doctor had an assistant, freeing his nurse, Tracey, to stand by me, rubbing my arm comfortingly and holding my hand. When Dr. Sherron finished his work and, I'm assuming, gotten the specimen he needed, he covered the area with a small bandage and sent me on my way, saying he'd see me at one o'clock Thursday to discuss his findings.

I was getting damn tired of these regular visits, and I was becoming more and more concerned and frightened by the day. But it was mid-afternoon and Alex would be home from school soon. So I had to head on home, as well, and get myself together and act as if all were right with the world...and me.

This time I drove cautiously, making sure I paid attention, was aware of my surroundings, didn't cause any accidents, and arrived home safely. Just as I suspected, Nick Nack was still staring out the living room window when I pulled into the driveway. She disappeared when she saw my car and was waiting by the door when I stepped inside.

"It's okay, Nick Nack. You don't have to stand vigil. Now, move it and give me some room. I don't think I can abide your devotion today."

But there was still no ditching her. I dropped my purse and headed for the kitchen, Nick Nack beside me. I grabbed the pitcher of tea from the fridge, poured myself a glass, and filled Nick Nack's water dish at the kitchen faucet. I coaxed her out the back door, but she flew out, did her business, and was back in an instant. She was still hovering when Alex got home from school.

Flushed pink, her hair stuck to her face in wet ringlets, she was animated and excited about field day.

"Mama, me and Bethany" (Her poor grammar didn't seem at all important.) "came in third in the sack race. And guess what! I was the grand-prize winner of corn hole!" she crowed and spun around and flashed her blue ribbon at me.

I wasn't surprised at all that she had won the grand prize ribbon in corn hole, that wonderfully-southern redneck game. She and Mark had been playing it at the beach and at football tailgate parties since she was a toddler. Her dad would be so proud.

I went through the mama motions, fixing her mac and cheese, overseeing bath time, getting school clothes ready for the following day. As the numbing wore off and my breast began to throb, I took some Tylenol but, mostly, grinned through the pain and the fear and the uncertainty. Again Alex and I put on our pajamas and watched a little TV; this time, thank heavens, it wasn't The Bachelor. I really don't recall what we watched. My focus on the lump prevented my concentrating. By the time Alex wound down and I tucked her into bed, I was exhausted and relieved. It was all I could do to brush my teeth and topple into bed.

I slept through the night, I'm guessing from sheer exhaustion from prior nights' sleeplessness and the trauma of my medical visits and procedures.

The following morning after I got Alex off to school and showered, I was staring at an empty day of fear and uncertainty. I decided to head to the library to shelve some books and fill book-club orders. I needed to stay busy, to keep my mind focused somewhere other than on my breast.

I thought that the library staff would be surprised to see me after I'd left the message not to expect me back until further notice. Instead, they all offered a lackluster "Hey" and appeared not to have gotten my messages or noticed my absences.

Volunteers came and went, and we tended not to bond, with the paid staff or with each other. Once I'd tried to engage a newbie in conversation while we sorted and shelved, only to have a *real* librarian *shhhhhhh* at us very loudly. The young woman was so mortified for having been chastised as if she were a child. Her cheeks flamed, she ducked her head, and, after a single day of volunteering, never returned to the library. As a result, I worked in silence and didn't try to buddy up. So I spent the morning and a good part of the afternoon catching up on my stocking and order filling in solitary silence. No one seemed to care, notice, or even appreciate that I was working overtime.

Or that I had a lump in my breast and was terrified.

I tried to concentrate on book stocking until it was time to head on home. There I shifted my focus to Alex, to the television, to house tidying, to mac and cheese preparation; but my fear was just too huge to be displaced by mindless activities, or even the care of my child.

I was just eager for Thursday to arrive so that I would *know*. Know what? I had no idea what to expect. So unable to avoid it any longer, I began playing the what-if game. What if it is cancer? Will I lose my breast? Both of my breasts? Will I lose more than my breasts? If it is cancer, has it spread to other parts of my body? Who will take care of Alex while I'm sick? Who will take care of *me* while I'm sick? How long will I be sick? Will the treatments make me nauseated? Will the treatments makes me lose my hair?

I grabbed handfuls of my heavy, thick red hair. Then I shook my head and let it cascade over my cheeks and past my shoulders. I just couldn't lose my hair, my beautiful red, wavy hair. Mark fell in love with me because he noticed my beautiful red hair. As I ran my fingers through my healthy, full, shiny, long, red hair and realized I might lose it, tears spilled from my eyes and down my cheeks. Then the question I'd been running from slapped me in the face.

Will I die?

⊰⊱

When I got to Raleigh Imaging the following afternoon, the same woman with the green scrubs and white Crocs escorted me to Dr. Sherron's office.

"Come in, Ms. Murphy. Sit down, please."

I could tell by the sympathetic look on the doctor's face that the news was not good. He was smiling sweetly but not optimistically. And not sincerely.

I sat in the chair opposite him, took an extra-deep breath, sank my fingernails into the chairs arms, and braced myself for what the doctor had to say.

"Rowdy—may I call you Rowdy?—our biopsy concluded that the lump in your breast is malignant."

My bracing hadn't done any good. My face flushed hot and I began shaking, so I clenched the chair arms even tighter and held on so that I wouldn't fall into the black hole. I could feel the blood drain from my face as the room began to spin. Dr. Sherron stood from his desk and came to me. He crouched by my chair and took my hand.

"It's all right, Rowdy. I know this is frightening," he said, still holding my hand, his other hand gentle on my shoulder.

I waited until the spinning room slowed and the black hole disappeared before I said, "What happens next?"

"Well, Rowdy, we'll begin treatment right away. The sooner we tackle this, the sooner you'll be on the road to recovery."

"What treatment? What are you going to do?"

"We've assembled a treatment team, a group of specialists we feel best suited to take care of you. I've asked them all to join us today." And looking at his watch, he said, "They should be here any time now."

It was just more than I could absorb. Even though I'd played the brutal what-if game, I came to Dr. Sherron's office hoping for the best: the lump was benign, and I'd just go on home and keep an eye

88

out for future lumps and have regular check-ups. But that wasn't going to happen. Instead, I was facing cancer with a team of specialists.

Patting my shoulder, Dr. Sherron said, "Are you up to meeting your team?"

Did I have a choice? I didn't see any other options, so I squeaked, "Okay."

We waited quietly, and Dr. Sherron didn't leave my side until we heard a tap at the door and saw a woman pop her head in.

"Ready for us, doctor?" she asked.

"Sure, Celeste, come right on in, " Dr. Sherron said, standing to greet her.

Celeste, a petite woman with a sharp little face and short, gray hair bustled in, followed by two men and two women.

Dr. Sherron greeted them all by name, and, once they were seated, said, "Rowdy, this is your treatment team. They will be with you every step of the way, from today until the day we pronounce you cancer free."

They all smiled warmly and nodded in my direction.

First Dr. Sherron motioned to a tall, handsome man with blond hair and said, "This is Dr. Travers, the surgeon I recommend to remove the lump from your breast."

Surgeon? He looked like a surfer dude. A very *young* surfer dude. How would he know how to perform surgery? But I was in no position to question or argue. I didn't know any surgeon replacement whom I could recommend to carve on me. I'd just have to trust Dr. Sherron's judgment that hunky Dr. Travers was the dude for the job.

Then he turned to two of the women and said, "This is Dr. Rahn, our diagnostic radiologist, and her radiology therapist, Kathleen Kerrigan. They'll administer radiology, if that should become part of your treatment."

It was just more than I could wrap my head around, but we still had two people to go.

"Rowdy, meet Dr. Easterling, your medical oncologist. He will be responsible for your chemotherapy treatments, should we decide that chemotherapy is the way to go."

At the mention of chemotherapy, I reached up and touched my long, thick hair. It made me sad.

"And this," Dr. Sherron said, as he pointed to the woman who had lead the group into his office, "is Celeste Raymond. Celeste is your nurse coordinator. She will see that your surgery, treatments, and appointments are scheduled and move like clockwork. She'll arrange everything for you. All you'll have to do is show up."

He paused for me to talk, just as he had during our last visit. Still I said nothing.

He picked it up: "I know this is a lot to process, Rowdy. Let's just take a deep breath, and you tell me if you have any questions."

They all waited silently and patiently.

Finally, I squeaked, "When?"

"When? Do you mean when will we perform the surgery?"

"Yes."

"Well, we felt it would be good to schedule it as soon as we could. Dr. Travers has freed his calendar and will be able to take care of it Monday morning at nine-thirty. Celeste has already pre-admitted you to Rex Hospital and has set up an operating room. She has also made arrangements for you to go from here today over to Rex and have your preliminary blood work done."

"Monday?" I croaked.

"Yes, Rowdy, don't you want to get this taken care of right away?"

"But I can't. I can't have surgery. I have a daughter. I don't have anyone to take care of my daughter. And my ex-husband is getting married this weekend."

"Rowdy, your health is more important than your ex-husband's wedding. Surely, he'll understand."

"But he's going on his honeymoon…."

Then, through my tears, I burst into laughter. All of a sudden, my disrupting Mark and Tawni's honeymoon with a lump in my breast seemed hysterical. I could almost hear Mark accusing me of planning it just so I could sabotage his wedding.

My team stared, expressionless, as I laughed uncontrollably. Dr. Sherron just held onto my hand.

My life was resembling a redneck opera, with all the angst and melodrama of Verdi and all the tackiness of The Dukes of Hazzard. There was infidelity, the pregnant-with-twins Daisy Duke, and the mangy mutt. There was even a garage apartment, a hide-a-bed, and a water park, for god's sake. And in the midst of all the tackiness was the long-suffering, put-upon, abandoned wife ready to go under the knife. The absurdity and unbelievability of it all made me laugh and cry and laugh some more.

When my hysteria slowed to a snuffle, Dr. Sherron handed me the box of tissues from his desk. I grabbed a handful and mopped my sopping face.

"Okay?"

Well, I wasn't okay, but I shook my head *yes*.

"I'll talk with Mark," was all I could manage.

"Rowdy," Dr. Sherron continued, "as I said, Celeste has taken care of everything with the hospital. You'll need to show up at Admitting over at Rex Hospital Monday morning at seven o'clock where they'll have your orders waiting for you. Dr. Travers will be there to perform the surgery at nine-thirty. We'll keep you in recovery till you come out of the anesthesia, and then we'll transfer you to a private room. If all goes well, and we have every reason to believe that it will, you'll have to stay in the hospital just overnight for observation. Celeste has the paperwork for this afternoon's blood work and your instructions to follow on the night before surgery."

Still I stared, stunned into silence.

"Just one more thing, Rowdy: you'll need to have someone drive you to the hospital, take you home at the end of your stay, and be with you for about ten days following your release."

Someone to stay with me?

But who?

Fourteen

There were the friends in Mark's custody and the non-buddies at the library. Not a single Florence Nightingale in the bunch.

My high school girlfriends would have rallied. As much as we'd grown apart, we did have history. Surely they would have come, but it would have been problematic for them to drop jobs, kids, and husbands and rush to my side from California or even the mountains of North Carolina.

How about my neighbors? We had been cordial but not chummy. We'd attended neighborhood gatherings in one another's back yards, where we'd stood around balancing a beer in one hand and a paper plate of carb-and-mayonnaise-laden food in the other, pretending to be interested in Heather's harp lessons or Preston's honorable mention in the Leesville Road Elementary School Science Fair. Then a month later we'd show up in another back yard, eat the same artery-clogging food, and feign shock and awe over the achievements of the same precocious neighborhood youngins. Alex's claim to fame was that she had been potty trained in one day and that Mark had taught her to recite the alphabet backward and burp it forward. Though I was impressed with my little genius's talents, I kept them to myself and hoped she would as well.

Most of the neighbor wives worked and didn't have time for bridge, girlfriend lunches at Panera Bread, or sugar borrowing. Those back-yard thingies were their only attempts at adult socializing. On weekends those over-achieving moms would wave and smile as they rushed off to soccer games and ballet lessons, making sure their children's lives were perfectly coordinated, because we all know that little geniuses don't know squat about how to play without instructions. And while the moms structured their children's lives, the grumbling dads stayed behind to tend the lawns they thought they couldn't live without when they had moved to the burbs five years earlier.

When Mark left, one by one the power moms appeared on my doorstep, brow furrowed, head tilted in pity, arms open for a semi-comforting hug. But once they made the initial I'm-so-sorry visit, complete with condolence bought-bakery-goods baskets, they retreated, as if divorce were contagious.

I was certain they'd all rush over with Whole Foods pound cake and deli chicken salad when they learned of my illness, but I didn't think I could depend on any one of them for the long haul. I felt it would be pretty presumptuous of me to request that they drop those husbands and kids and houses and jobs to spend ten days with me, tending my wound, preparing my meals, keeping my house, and caring for my dog. That level of imposition just didn't seem at all neighborly.

Then I thought of Eugenia. Genie. She'd have come to me. She'd have wrapped me in her ample arms and rocked me and sung to me and nursed me till she was sure I was able to care for myself.

Eugenia had helped raise Mama and her brother, Emmett, and when Mama had five babies in five years, Grandmama said, "Aurelia needs you more than I do, Genie. I can take care of myself. Now, get on over there and rescue my daughter."

So Genie came to be our second mama, doling out treats and hugs, as well as switchings.

Sometimes I'd get whiney, so she'd yank me up by my arm and give me a pop on my hiney. I'd dance around and scream as if she were killing me, when, in fact, my feelings were hurt lots worse than my behind. I hated disappointing my Genie.

She'd gather me in her broad lap in the big old rocker in the corner of the kitchen and press my head against her fluffy bosom. She always smelled like Woolworth talc and raw onions. And as I snubbed and squeezed out as many tears as I possibly could, she'd rock and hum me some tuneless tune, something I think she'd made up on the spur of the moment. When I'd finally decided that I had acted pitiful enough, I'd sit up straight and look Genie in the eye to let her know I was done and had finally forgiven her for hurting my hiney and my feelings.

She'd lift the corner of her apron with her huge hand, the back as black as pitch, the palm as pink as a plastic baby doll, and as she mopped my wet face, she'd say, "You know yo' mama's my baby, and I can't have you whining at my baby.

"Yes, ma'am."

"Miss Aurelia got her hands full with five youngins."

"Yes, ma'am."

"I know sometimes you feel pushed aside 'cause of all them little boys needing yo' mama's attention."

"Yes, ma'am," I'd say, trying to swallow that truth with the lump growing in my throat before it could make me cry again.

"You a good girl, Rowdy, and Eugenia loves you to pieces," she'd say and smile broadly, showing me her big white teeth for the first time.

That's when I'd know she'd forgiven me—when she'd show me her big white teeth.

"Now you go get two cookies from the jar and run on out back till I call you to help me set the table for supper."

I'd slide off Genie's lap, and she'd give me a send-off tap on my behind, a tap that healed the pop she had given me earlier.

I'd give anything to climb onto Genie's lap and rest my head and my frightened body against her pillowy bosom. I was certain she could calm my fears with tuneless humming and soothing words and homemade ginger cookies like no ordinary friend could. But we'd lost Genie, lost her to cancer of her lady parts, so she said.

My family went to her funeral at the First AME Zion Church. There was standing room only for a single, childless woman who had held many a child, black and white, in her broad lap and hummed tuneless tunes to soothe them. My family wept as copiously as Eugenia's kin. My staid, elegant grandmother, who loathed public displays of emotion, cried shamelessly, mopping her wet cheeks with her lacy linen hanky.

At that moment I wanted and needed my Genie worse than I'd ever needed her, worse than I had needed her when my mama had four little boys and I needed a soft lap to climb onto.

The tears slid down my cheeks as I whispered, "Oh, Genie, I'm so scared. I need you so bad."

I had not realized, until that moment, how alone and lonely I'd become. I really had planned to find those post-divorce friends. Honest. But I was still licking my wounds and feeling sorry for myself. I thought I had plenty of time to get back on the friend circuit. Cancer just sneaked up on me, unaware. Really shitty timing on my part.

Then I thought of Sandy, my brother Greg's wife. Since she was a school teacher, she would be off for the summer. She had a home and a husband, but she didn't have kids to care for. Granted, I hadn't seen her in years and we'd never been real tight, but we'd gotten along just fine. And just fine was about the best I could do under the circumstances. And she was family, so to speak. I remembered how she had taken charge during that last beach trip with Mama and Daddy: cooking, cleaning, coordinating family games, caring for Alex. She could do it all. She was just the kind of person I needed taking care of me.

But would she come? I'd have to take my chances. I'd give her a call as soon as I got home. But first: blood work.

My team gave me comforting reassurances, and Celeste handed me a packet of instructions to carry me through till Monday.

The lab already had my paperwork, and I breezed through the blood work and was back home in an hour. I figured that would be the last breeze I'd face for a very long time.

Of course, when I got home, Nick Nack was waiting in the living room window and was at the front door by the time I parked the car. She followed me as I reached for my cell phone and dropped my purse on the hall table.

I thought I'd put Greg and Sandy's phone number in my cell, but I couldn't find it. And I didn't know it by heart. My own brother. I didn't remember my own brother's telephone number, hadn't considered it important enough to record among my special cell phone numbers. The thought made me so sad. Sadder, still, was I when I considered that Greg most certainly didn't remember my number either. I swallowed my pain and called the operator.

The phone rang eight times before Sandy answered. She sounded out of breath.

"Hello?" she huffed. "Whew! Sorry about that. I was in the garden. I'm a little out of breath from running."

"Sandy, I'm sorry to call, but I need your help badly."

After a long silence, she said, "I'm sorry, who's speaking?"

"It's Rowdy."

No response.

"Your sister-in-law. Greg's sister."

"Oh, sure, I didn't recognize your voice. It's been so long. You say you need my help? What's up?"

Then the tears came again. I'd begun to realize that tears were one of the fallouts of breast lumps.

"Sandy, I found a lump in my breast. I've already had a mammogram and biopsy. It's cancer. I'm having surgery Monday morning. I need to be at the hospital by seven o'clock. My doctor says I'll need someone to stay with me after surgery, and you were the first person I thought of."

I rattled it off bam, bam, bam. I didn't want to pause to give her time to ponder, for fear she'd say, "No," before I could make clear my level of desperation.

When I paused to take a breath, she said quietly, "I was the first person you thought of?"

"Oh, Sandy, I'm so sorry. I wouldn't ask this of you," I said between tears, "but I just didn't know who else to call. All of my friends were Mark's friends..."

Sandy interrupted, "Of course, Rowdy, I understand. I'm glad you thought of me. You know I'll help any way I can. I'll be there as quickly as I can. Just let me rearrange a few things with Greg."

"Really, Sandy, I wouldn't ask..."

"I know, Rowdy, it's okay. It'll be fine. We'll... I'll... Let me..."

"Sandy..."

"Rowdy, you just hold on, and I'll call you right back."

In about forty-five minutes the phone rang.

"Rowdy, we're all set. I have a benefit Sunday night that I can't wiggle out of, but I'll be there bright and early Monday morning, say six o'clock. Okay?"

"Sure, Sandy, that's fine. And, Sandy, thank you so much. You know I wouldn't..."

"Rowdy, it's fine. I'm glad I can help. You just hang on, and I'll be there Monday morning. Now, is there anything I can't do for you before then?"

"No, I don't think so."

"Well, then, I'll see you Monday. But before you hang up, Greg would like to speak with you. Bye, now. See you Monday."

"Hey, Rowdy."

"Hi, Greg. It's good to hear your voice."

"Sandy tells me you're sick. I'm so sorry. Is there anything I can do?"

I thought for a minute before saying, "I can't think of anything."

I was hoping he'd be moved to jump into his car and run to his big sister's side. But I could see that that wasn't going to happen.

"Well," he said, "you let me know if you can think of anything."

So I just said, "Thanks, Greg. I'll let you know if something comes up. And, Greg, I really appreciate Sandy's agreeing to help."

"Sure, sure. And, Rowdy, I've called Will and Kevin and Sam to let them know. They send their love and said to let them know if they can do anything to help. Now, you take care, okay?"

They send their love? I needed, wanted more from my brothers, but I didn't have the time or the strength to dwell on that. Or beg for it.

"Yeah, thanks, Greg. Bye, bye."

The line had just gone dead when the front door banged open and I heard, "Mama, I'm home!"

Alex was home from school. I'd lost track of time. She came sailing in the door, breathless.

"Just one more day of school," she panted, doubled over, clutching her side. "Yea! Then the next day is the wedding! I gotta go upstairs and practice."

"Would you like a snack first?"

"Oh, no ma'am, I'm not hungry. Noah's mom brought cupcakes to school today. And I *really* need to practice."

Still breathing hard, off she ran, up the stairs.

In minutes I heard her clacking up and down the hall in her Mary Janes, practicing to be Tawni's flower girl.

I needed to make another phone call. While Alex was out of ear shot, I dialed Mark's number.

"Mark, can you come by. I need to talk to you."

"Rowdy, I'm really kind of busy. Can it wait till Tawni and I get back from our honeymoon?"

"No, Mark, this can't wait."

"Well, what is it, Rowdy? Is this about Alex?"

"No, Mark, Alex is just fine, but I need to talk with you, and it's not something I can discuss over the phone."

"I have an appointment with a student this afternoon, and Tawni's folks are coming to town tonight. It'll have to be tomorrow. You want me to come by tomorrow?" he asked, his voice dripping with exasperation.

"Yeah, Mark, that'll be fine. How about eleven in the morning?"

"Sure, Rowdy. I'll be there."

"Thanks, Mark. Bye."

"Why didn't you tell me? Why did you wait until the day before my wedding?"

That was so like Mark to make this about him. I started to lash out, to tell him what a selfish ass he was, but I needed his help, needed for him to take care of Alex. This was no time for anger or harsh words, no time to mention his selfishness.

"I just found the lump Monday. I've spent the past four days going through a battery of tests and procedures. After my initial visit with Dr. Moore, I had a diagnostic mammogram and a needle biopsy. I didn't know until yesterday afternoon that the lump was malignant. As soon as I found out, my cancer team sent me for preliminary blood work for the surgery on Monday. Mark, I called you just as soon as I could." Changing my tone, I said, "It must be pretty urgent, though. Otherwise, my team would allow me to wait for the surgery until after your and Tawni's honeymoon."

Mark grasped the sting in my voice and backed down. "I know it's urgent, Rowdy. I'm so sorry. Of course our honeymoon can wait. I'll keep Alex for you."

He sounded as though he felt he were doing me a favor—keeping *my* child.

I wanted to scream, "She's yours! You're not doing me a favor! You're being a parent!"

But I couldn't. I was at his mercy. I needed his help, regardless of how I could get it.

"And there's Nick Nack, too," I said. "You remember Nick Nack, don't you? That dog I didn't want but you couldn't live without?"

He opened his mouth, to protest, I'm certain. Instead, he said, "Sure, Nick Nack. I'll make sure she's fed and walked."

"Thanks, Mark."

"When do you want me to take Alex? This afternoon?" he asked.

"No," I said, "I promised her I'd get her dressed for your wedding, and I want to do that. And I'll make sure she gets to the church, too."

"Are you sure?"

"Yes, Mark. I need this. I'll need to hold onto her as long as I can. And I'll need the diversion. This coming week is going to be a tough one, for a lot of reasons."

I stopped myself before the tears came, again.

Mark leaned across the kitchen table and reached for my hand, to comfort me, I assumed. My first inclination was to pull away, but I was far too vulnerable and needy to distance myself from him.

"Take care, Rowdy. See you tomorrow," he said, and patted my hand gently, as if I were a pet or an elderly aunt.

It was so final. I wasn't expecting hugs and kisses and promises to return to nurse me back to health. But *take care* and a pat on the hand? I don't think I've ever felt more lost and alone than I did as I watched Mark stand and walk out the door.

Fifteen

Alex's giddiness had reached new heights when she came bounding through the front door. School was officially over for the summer, and she was just one day away from her first-ever job as a flower girl.

To divert her attention from *everything* that was making her twirl and skip and hop and squeal and make me want to run screaming from the house, I said, "How'd you like to go to Pizza Hut for a cheese pizza? And then we can come home and have toenail night."

"Oh, Mama," she trilled, with no sign of winding down from her euphoria, "that would be just *awesome!*"

And she twirled in celebration.

"Run wash your hands," I said, as I grabbed my keys and purse and headed for the door.

Back in a flash, wiping her wet hands on her shorts, she skipped out the front door and down the sidewalk to the car.

Nick Nack, now constantly by my side, looked up at me in confusion over Alex's sudden hysteria.

"I know, Nick Nack, it's driving me crazy, too. But I'll get her out of your hair for a while. We'll be back later," and I inched out the door, leaving her to race to the living room window.

Alex ate three slices of cheese pizza, a record. She chattered around bites and swung her legs back and forth furiously while we ate.

Exhausted from her animation, I rubbed my stomach after only one piece of pizza and said, "Well, I'm full. I'm ready to head on home for toenail night. How about you?"

Wiping her mouth with her napkin, instead of the back of her hand, she said, "Sure," and hopped off her chair.

All the way home she talked about the last day of school and her excitement over the upcoming wedding. My mind was elsewhere, but I kept my smile in place and nodded and um-hmmmed from time to time.

I knew that I had to tell her that she'd be staying with her dad and Tawni for a while. And I needed to tell her why. But how much should I tell her? Surely, she'd find out about the lump in my breast. She'd have to know it was cancer. She needed to know that I was having surgery.

But that's what toenail night is all about: girl talk. I'd know what to say when the time came because toenail night makes talking easier.

Once we'd stripped down to our panties and donned our pink terry cloth robes, Alex crawled under the bathroom vanity and pulled out the wicker basket full of polishes and polish remover and file and buffer and cotton balls.

As we settled on the bathmat, I looked up to find Nick Nack standing in the doorway, one paw raised over the threshold. Her hovering had reached new heights. When I was at home, she hated leaving my side, even if Alex offered treats and a promise to play. It's hard to admit that I was finding her devotion touching.

"It's okay, Nick Nack," I smiled and said, "you can come in."

With that she joined us in the bathroom and eased herself to the floor, just inches from my side. There she sat quietly, monitoring my every move.

I had finished painting Alex's nails a pale shell pink and she was painstakingly working on mine, her tongue sticking out in concentration, when I said, "Alex, do you know what cancer is?"

She kept painting as she said dismissively, "I've heard about it, but I don't know what it is. I think it makes people sick, though."

"That's right, Alex, it does make people sick. Cancer happens when someone finds a tumor or a lump in her body." I paused, took a deep breath, and continued, "I have a lump in my body."

Alex stopped painting and looked up at me, fear in her eyes. I made sure to remain calm, though, to keep the smile firmly in place to allay her concerns.

"But I have lots of doctors and nurses looking out for me. One of them is going to take the lump out Monday so that I can get all better."

"Where is the lump, Mama?"

"It's in my breast."

"Can I see it?"

Though I wasn't expecting her to ask to see the lump, without hesitation I pulled her close, opened my robe, and reached for her hand. I had removed the small bandage from the biopsy site that afternoon, and, once again, the lump was exposed.

"Here, hold your fingers like this," I said, and took her small hand and guided it to my breast.

As Alex gently touched the site, Nick Nack cautiously rose and sniffed at the area where Alex's fingers rested. Then looking up at me, she sighed heavily and settled back by my side, this time resting her head on my knee.

"Can you feel that?" I said to Alex, swirling her outstretched fingers lightly over the area.

"Yes, Ma'am," she said faintly, no longer trilling with enthusiasm. "Does it hurt?"

Although the area was still somewhat tender from the biopsy, I said, "No, not at all," and shrugged casually. "I just happened to feel it one morning while I was taking a shower."

"Is it making you sick?"

"Not now, but I'll have to get sick before I get all well."

"Mama, I don't want you to get sick."

"I know, Sweetie, I don't want to get sick either. But sometimes we don't have a choice. You remember when you had strep throat, how bad you felt? You didn't have a choice about having strep throat. It just happened. But you got over it. And, even though I'm going to get sick, I'll get over it."

I couldn't tell her that I was going to get sicker than strep sick and that my illness was going to last a lot longer than strep, but it was the best I could do, because I honestly didn't know how sick I was going to be, how long it was going to last. I didn't even know if I would ever get better.

Alex was silent as she finished painting my toenails. After she dabbed the last dot on my pinkie toe, she quietly returned all of our nail paraphernalia to the basket and shoved it back in the cabinet under the vanity.

I took her face in my hands and smiled as I said to her, "Alex, I don't want you to worry at all. I'm going to be fine. I just wanted to let you know that you'll be staying with your dad and Tawni while the doctors are taking care of me. Okay?"

"Okay, Mama," she said, as she wrapped her arms around my neck. Then she added, "Can I sleep with you tonight?"

"Sure thing," I said, "but, first, let's watch a little TV."

I felt we needed to decompress after our chat, to have a few laughs before we went to bed. I didn't want cancer to be the last thing on her mind before she dozed off.

As I rose, so did Nick Nack, still staring at me with furrowed brow. Sensing her concern, I stroked her head and said, "It's going to be okay, Nick Nack." For the first time in days, she gave me a doggy smile and happily wagged her tail.

Alex and I padded down the stairs in our robes, cotton balls wedged between our toes. Nick Nack trotted along beside us, one of the girls, and joined us in front of the TV. As soon as I sat, Alex curled up beside me and rested her head in my lap. Nick Nack lay on the floor in front of us, and Alex reached out and scratched her on the head as she settled into her fluffy, relieved puddle. We found an episode of America's Funniest Videos, and Alex and I laughed hysterically at the silly antics until we both had tears streaming down our faces. Who wouldn't laugh at a dog playing the piano and a cat diving into a fish tank? By the time the show ended and we were ready to turn in for the night, we were all smiles and cancer had taken a back seat.

For one of us.

Alex hadn't asked to sleep with me in ages. "Too baby," she'd said. But tonight was different, and we both welcomed the closeness. As Nick Nack settled on her rug by the bed, Alex crawled in beside me and snuggled up to my side. In moments she was asleep. I lay awake as I listened to her purr, wanting to cherish every moment with her until she left me for Mark and I left for that frightening unknown.

I dozed but was aroused by Alex's thrashing. I cracked my eyes and peeped at the bedside clock.

"Alex, please go back to sleep. It's only six-thirty in the morning. The wedding isn't for," and stopping to calculate in my early-morning haze, said, "seven and a half more hours."

"I know, Mama, but I'm just too excited to sleep. And I have so much to do!" she exclaimed as she leaped from the bed.

Right, the duties of a flower girl are extensive.

"Okay, Alex, but please just do it quietly, and I'll get up in a little while and fix your breakfast."

"Oh, I'll just get Pop Tarts," she trilled, unable to contain her excitement.

"Okay, and please feed Nick Nack."

"Yes, ma'am," she said and went thundering down the stairs, screaming, "Come on, Nick Nack!"

Nick Nack stretched, yawned loudly, and teetered on her sleepy legs. Smacking her lips, she peered over the edge of the bed to make sure I was still there.

I shooed her and mumbled into my pillow, "Yeah, I'm still here. Now, go on with Alex and eat your breakfast."

I was in no mood to deal with Nick Nack this early in the morning on Mark's wedding day and just two days before I was scheduled for cancer surgery.

Nick Nack slowly turned and walked reluctantly to the door, looking back just to make sure I meant for her to leave.

"Yeah, Nick Nack, I meant it. Now go on with Alex."

Still she stood motionless in the doorway, staring at me.

"Nick Nack, go!"

Finally, she sighed heavily, hung her head, turned, and unenthusiastically followed Alex, her toenails clicking down the stairs to the kitchen.

I knew I wouldn't get back to sleep—and I didn't yet trust Alex alone in the kitchen—so I dragged myself out of bed and padded down the stairs, barefoot and disheveled.

I found Alex eating cold Pop Tarts and drinking milk, her legs flinging wildly.

"Can I fix you something else to eat? Eggs? Oatmeal?" I asked, as I stretched and dug my fists into my eyes, not yet ready to face the day.

"No, ma'am, this is fine," she said, waving a Pop Tart at me.

I put a filter in the coffee maker, measured the coffee and poured in the water, and pulled a mug from the cupboard. Then I sat at the kitchen table, smiling at Alex as she prattled.

"Keep it normal," I told myself.

When the coffee stopped dripping, I poured a mug and rejoined Alex as she ate. I kept my smile in place and feigned interest in all of her prattling.

When she'd finished half a Pop Tart, she said, "I'm full. May I be excused?"

"You sure that's all you want?"

"Yes, ma'am. I need to go take a bath. Will you help me?"

"Sure, I'll be glad to help," I said, and gave her a hug of delight because my little girl still needed and wanted my help.

I piled Alex's hair on her head with a big plastic clip and drew a bath for her. Normally, she is in and out of the tub in a flash, but on her special day she asked for a bubble bath. She soaped and scrubbed every inch of her body until she was pink and glowing, and since she had hours to kill, I let her stay till the water turned cold and her fingers were pruny. When she finally stepped from the tub and I wrapped a big, fluffy towel around her, I inhaled her precious little-girl smell. I dusted her with my Chanel bath powder and let her sprits a little #5 behind her ears. Then she headed for her bedroom to dress. As she tiptoed, naked, down the hall, I noticed that my baby was no longer a baby. Her little tubby tummy was flattening and her waist was beginning to take shape. Though she was only nine, her breasts were beginning to bud, and her legs were showing signs of stretching long and lean, just like mine.

She assembled all of her wedding finery on her bed, ready to transform herself. She stepped into her new panties with the pink rosebuds and bows and climbed onto her bed to put on her lace socks and white patent leather shoes. My heart broke as I watched her dress herself for this important occasion, with no help from me. We were experiencing so many firsts that day, one I continued to will myself to ignore. When she finished struggling with her shoe buckles, she hopped off the bed, her Mary Janes clacking on the hardwood.

"I'm going to have to remember to tiptoe so my shoes don't make clackety noises when I walk down the aisle," she said, as she made a practice tiptoe around her bedroom.

I held my tears as she finished parading and lifted her dress from the bed. She slipped it over her head, pushed her arms through, and patted it into place.

"Help, please, Mama," she said, as she backed up to me, holding her long, red curls out of the way so I could button her dress and tie her sash.

She did still need me.

I fell to my knees and let the tears stream silently down my cheeks as I took my time buttoning and tying my little girl so she could commence with the most exciting day of her life.

I raked my sleeve across my face, sniffed loudly, and said, "Let's get that hair brushed and that pretty little hair band in place."

Sensing my mood, Alex stood quietly as I gently brushed her red hair into cascading curls. I pushed it back from her face with her pink-rosette hair band. A few baby-hair curls sprang free, as they always did, and framed her freckled face.

I kissed her on her nose and said, "All ready to tiptoe down that aisle?"

"Yes ma'am," she said sweetly.

"Then grab your basket, and we'll be on our way. Go on down to the living room and sit still while I throw on some clothes."

I heard her practice tiptoeing down the stairs as I made my way to my bedroom.

What does one wear to deliver one's daughter to her daddy's wedding? I picked up the same jeans I'd worn all week and stepped in. Pretty soon they'd be able to stand on their own. I pulled a red NC State sweatshirt from my dresser drawer and slipped it over my head. I slid my feet into white tennis shoes. Dressing to impress didn't seem important. I went to the bathroom, where I brushed my teeth, splashed some cool water in my face, and tamed my fly-away hair with my damp hands. Drying my face and hands, I headed downstairs where I found Alex perched daintily on the living room sofa, her lacy ankles crossed, her flower-girl basket dangling from her arm. She looked up and smiled sweetly when she heard me coming.

"Alex, you look so pretty. Your daddy is going to be so proud of you." It was hard to say, but it had to be said.

"Thank you, Mommy," she said.

Alex hadn't called me *Mommy* in so long. It was just too baby. I'd become *Mama*. At least she hadn't yet graduated to the I'm-just-so-cool-and-mature *Mom*. But I guess she needed a *Mommy* on her daddy's wedding day; perhaps she sensed I needed a *Mommy* too.

Kids can be pretty perceptive, after all.

"Okay, Miss Priss, let's get a move on."

She hopped off the sofa and headed for the front door. Once in the car, Alex was relatively quiet on the ride to the church, probably still sensing this wasn't an easy day for me.

The church yard was teeming with people dressed in their wedding finery, and cars circled round and round, trying to find a place to park. I had not realized that the wedding of a pregnant bride and a divorced, middle-aged groom would attract such a huge following. I pulled around to the back of the church, where I found Mark standing with his hands in the pockets of his tux pants, waiting for me to deliver our daughter to him. When Alex saw her dad, she flung open the door and was out as soon as the car came to a complete stop.

As an afterthought, she hopped back in, hugged me, and said, "Thanks, Mama. I love you. Are you going to be okay?"

"Yes, Alex, I'm going to be okay. Now run on with your daddy. You have a job to do," I told her, as I smiled and kissed her on her forehead.

She got out of the car, and with a slam of the door, she skipped to her daddy's arms. He swooped her up and held her to him. She wrapped her arms around his neck and gave him a kiss on his cheek.

"How are you doing, Rowdy?" Mark asked.

I said, "Hangin' in there."

He furrowed his brow and cocked his head toward Alex.

"She knows, Mark. I talked with her about it last night. I told her that I'm going to go to the hospital and that she'll be staying with you and Tawni. I'm assuming Tawni is okay with that."

"Sure, Rowdy, she's fine. We can go out of town any time."

Out of town. I knew that Mark and Tawni had planned to go to Paris on their honeymoon. That was a little more than out of town. It was kind of Mark to downplay the loss for my sake. Kindness was not his strong suit. But his caring touched me.

"Thanks, Mark, and please tell Tawni I appreciate her help."

It felt good to say that.

"She knows you appreciate it, Rowdy, but I'll be sure and tell her you said so."

Before I pulled away from the church, I handed Mark a key to my house. "So you can feed Nick Nack while I'm in the hospital."

"Right. I'll take care of it," he said, reaching for the key and slipping it into his pocket.

As I drove away, I watched Alex in the rear view mirror, skipping down the sidewalk, holding her daddy's hand, on the way to *her* wedding.

Sixteen

Staring ahead at two empty, fear-filled days, I decided to head to the library. I was certain the staff wouldn't be expecting me because I was still convinced they hadn't even missed me. I could sort and shelve my books unnoticed. That's just what I needed to occupy my mind, to fill the empty hours. I drove straight from the church to the library wearing my non-regulation sweatshirt and not wearing my regulation volunteer lanyard around my neck. Who cared? Would anyone notice?

I parked my car at the far end of the parking lot, as the head librarian had instructed all volunteers to do because the spaces closer to the entrance were to be saved for *real* readers. As I strolled to the front door, I passed a mother dragging a toddler having a screaming meltdown because she wanted more *"Boots! Boots! Boots!"* The child had made a limp lump out of herself, and the mother looked harried and in need of a stiff drink. There was a time I'd have sympathized. Today an out-of-control child didn't seem like such a big deal.

A teenage couple sat face-to-face on the bench by the front door, her legs draped over his, and they were making out. He wore a wife beater over his chiseled abs, displaying colorful tattoo sleeves on both arms, a tattoo of black barbed wire circling his neck. She had blue spiky hair, a stud in her nose, and two rings in one eyebrow. Her black, pleather jeans were painted on and rode low in the back, displaying a tramp stamp of fluffy, white angel wings fanning out above her in-full-view butt crack.

I wondered if upon first meeting her he'd said, "You have

beautiful hair," and when she turned to face him, he'd added, "and I love your face jewelry."

I could have found a better place to make out than the entrance to the public library, but then I recalled all the times Mark and I had been caught in the throes of passion and hadn't cared where we were or who watched us pawing each other.

Instead of thinking they should get a room, I wanted to say, "Always keep that flame burning. Don't ever let your passion get stale."

Instead, I said nothing.

I bypassed the front desk to avoid the lackluster greetings or no greetings at all and headed straight to the holding room of returned books. There I began to sort and stack books on my cart in preparation for re-shelving. For hours, until the library closed its doors, I worked silently, pushing my cart on wheels through the stacks, filling up the empty spaces on the shelves and the empty spaces of my day.

When the loud speaker announced, "Last call, library closing," I considered hiding in the women's restroom until the place was vacated. When the library was empty, I'd emerge and have the whole building to myself. I'd find my favorite books, those that comforted me, those that had, at one time, made me laugh, and I'd take them to the children's room. I'd line up all the little beanbag chairs, making a mushy, yellow vinyl bed out of them. Then I'd settle down on my yellow bed, surrounded by my books, and I'd read the night away, the words illuminated only by the small flashlight on my cell phone, so as not to attract attention from the outside world. But I figured there was an alarm somewhere, and I'd probably set it off, wandering around alone in the library after hours.

And then there was Nick Nack, Nick Nack waiting at home in the living room window, frantic for my return and probably frantic to be let outside after the long day.

So I returned my three-quarters-empty cart to the holding room and shuffled out the front door, where a library employee impatiently held the door for the last stragglers to leave so she could lock up and, I assumed, set the alarm.

I sat in my car in the parking lot until the last real reader and the last employee and the last volunteer pulled away. I told myself I didn't want to get in the tangle of traffic. In truth, I was still trying to wish the minutes away. When the lot emptied, I started the car and turned on the radio. I punched buttons, trying to find something to soothe me on my ride home. I settled on the classical station. Before putting my car in reverse, though, I changed my mind and settled on silence. I turned off the radio and eased out of the parking lot, headed for home.

I was not surprised to find Nick Nack in the living room window, dancing excitedly when she caught sight of my car. By the time I parked and got to the front door, she was there to greet me, as usual.

"Hey, Girl," I said, as I breezed past her and dropped my keys on the hall table. "Let's get you outside."

I strolled to the kitchen and opened the back door, just in time for Nick Nack to streak past me and fly to her favorite tree. I felt guilty for having made her wait so long, but hadn't I said I wouldn't be responsible for a dog, in any way? But she was a helpless creature and she was devoted and oh, shut up! I had other things on my mind. I didn't need to be getting soft on a dog.

Though I wasn't hungry, I knew I needed to eat something. I hadn't had a thing since that cup of coffee at breakfast. I opened the fridge and peered inside: fixings for a tossed salad, apples and oranges, a shriveled kiwi, lasagna that was so old it was probably growing hair and needed to be tossed, chicken breasts, half pound of bacon, three eggs, leftover green beans, Neapolitan ice cream covered with freezer crystals. Nothing appealed to me. Then I spotted the cheese, my parmigiano reggiano cheese.

I buy my clothes at Target, my toiletries by the twelve-pack at Costco. But my parmigiano reggiano, my one decadent, extravagant indulgence, I buy at my local wine and cheese merchant. I don't know what gives my wine and cheese merchant the right to charge me twelve dollars a pound for cheese, but his calling himself a wine and cheese merchant somehow makes me feel that he is a bona fide something or other. And I freely hand over twelve dollars to my expert cheese man.

And if you were to taste his parmigiano reggiano, you would cry just as I do: "Here, please, take my twelve dollars and give me that!"

I allow myself snippets—not tastes, not bites. I shave a paper-thin wafer occasionally, on self-designated special occasions, and let it languish on my tongue as I close my eyes and savor the flavor that lingers for hours. It's a religious experience, an orgasmic experience, one of my few pleasures that remained after Mark's departure.

I chuckled to myself as I recalled the last time I'd bought parmigiano reggiano. But I certainly hadn't chuckled then.

I had just returned from Target and my wine and cheese merchant. I'd dropped my purse and my pricey parmigiano reggiano on the kitchen counter and taken up to my bedroom my $9.99 Target stretch pants I'd purchased to accommodate my expanding midriff, the result of my late-night forays to Krispy Kreme.

When I returned to the kitchen, there I found Nick Nack stretched out on the floor, legs splayed in sheer ecstasy, dining on my golden treat, as if she had been invited. My blood-curdling scream made her abandon her snack and sent her leaping to her pallet, where she cowered with a what-have-I-done-this-time look in her eyes.

I grabbed the remaining $11.90 worth of an almost-brand-new brick of parmigiano reggiano, stomped on the pedal of the trash can, and hurled it in. As I released the metal lid, it thwanged shut loudly, reverberating like a tuning fork, making Nick Nack get real flat and try to become invisible.

But still able to see her clearly, I screamed, "Why are you doing this to me? Why are you still here? I hate you and don't want you! What did I do to deserve you?"

Anger brings out the drama in me.

Amused by the memory but no longer enraged by the incident, I pulled my new brick of expensive cheese from the refrigerator and took it to the counter. I rummaged for a sharp knife in my jumbled cutlery drawer and, locating one, I carefully shaved two thin slices. I placed them on a paper towel and carried them to the table. I sat and picked up a sliver of my delicious parmigiano reggiano.

"Come here, Girl. You want some?"

Nick Nack stood from her pallet, cocked her head at me, and inched slowly forward, her toenails clicking lightly on the kitchen floor. Stopping at a distance, she craned her neck and sniffed the air.

"Here, Nick Nack, you can have it," I said, and she stretched forward and gently took the sliver of cheese from my hand.

She lay down beside my chair, and together we enjoyed our parmigiano reggiano treat. She smiled and smacked her lips as she happily slapped her fluffy tail on the kitchen floor, so delighted that she was finally invited to the party.

"I think we deserve another, don't you, Nick Nack?" I said, as I stood and sliced us both a generous piece, not knowing and not caring if dogs were supposed to eat cheese and not giving a damn that parmigiano reggiano cost twelve dollars a pound.

Nick Nack finished her treat, stood up, and crossed to her water bowl, where she lapped noisily.

"Good idea," I said, as I went to the refrigerator and got myself a bottle of water.

I was standing at the kitchen window, sipping, when the phone rang.

"Hey, Rowdy, how you doing?"

It was Mark. He'd just gotten married, and he was calling to check on me. Perhaps I'd underestimated him. Maybe he did have a kind streak, after all.

"Still hangin', Mark. How's Alex?"

I, on the other hand, wasn't kind enough to inquire about his wedding.

"She's fine, Rowdy. She was the star of the show. Everyone fawned over her and told her how pretty she looked. She's worried about you, though. But Tawni's keeping her busy, and we're assuring her that you're going to be all right."

"May I speak with her?"

"Sure, hold on."

Shortly I heard her sweet little voice: "Hi, Mama."

"Hi, Precious. How was the wedding?"

"It was pretty, Mama. I wish you could have been there to see me."

"I know you did great, Sweetie."

"Mama, are you okay?"

"Sure, Alex. But I'm going to the hospital Monday. Aunt Sandy will stay with me, and I'll make sure she calls Daddy. Okay?"

"Okay, Mama, I love you."

Mark took the phone and said, "Please have Sandy call us."

"I will, Mark."

His calling to check on me should have helped. It only made me more aware of my loneliness.

I hung up the phone, stepped out of my week-worn jeans, and dropped them in the washer. I poured in some detergent, a little extra because I felt my grungy jeans deserved it, closed the lid, and set the machine to heavy wash. I took my water bottle upstairs, Nick Nack close behind, and headed for my bathroom. I needed a bath.

I ran the water in the tub and poured in a little lavender bubble bath because I'd been told that lavender had relaxing qualities. I shed my panties and sweatshirt and stepped over Nick Nack into the tub. She lay by the tub and watched attentively as I submerged in my bubbles, leaned back, and closed my eyes. Only when the water reached my chin and the bubbles were tickling my nose did I turn off the faucet.

But I didn't relax. The terrors returned. Once my mind wasn't occupied with books or wedding or Alex or cheese, there was nothing to keep the fear at bay. I reached up and prodded the lump which, over the course of five days, had gone from lump to tumor to cancer. My breast was still a little tender from the biopsy, so I touched it gingerly, ever so lightly. But I could still feel it. It had not miraculously disappeared as I'd so hoped it would.

Nick Nack did not nap, as she was accustomed to doing, but sat at attention as I soaked.

Only when the water cooled did I soap my body, rinse, and pull the plug. I stepped out, dried, prodded once more, and slipped my nightgown from the hook on the bathroom door. I pulled it over my head, and Nick Nack followed me downstairs to take my jeans from the washer and toss them in the dryer. As I left the kitchen, I could hear them dancing merrily, so happy to be clean after a week of hard living.

My shadow and I climbed the stairs together. I fell into bed, and she resumed her watch beside me on her rug. It was still daylight.

I reached for a book in the stack on my bedside table and settled on my mother's copy of A Tree Grows in Brooklyn. Even one of my favorites couldn't corral my terrors and keep them at bay. I stared at the words, but they couldn't get past my eyes. My brain was too full of my fear to let anything else in.

When I was still wide awake at five in the morning, I gave up and got up. Nick Nack jumped to her feet without her usual stretching-and-yawning ritual and followed me to the bathroom and then down the stairs to start our day. I opened the kitchen door for her to go out back and decided to leave it open so she could come and go as she pleased. I went to the front porch and collected the newspaper.

The News and Observer had been a constant in my life, but I hadn't gotten much out of it lately. But I had another day of empty hours ahead of me, so I decided to give it a try.

I stuck a filter in the coffee maker and dumped in some coffee. I retrieved the mug I'd rinsed the day before and left to dry in the dish drainer. I stuck two pieces of bread in the toaster and pulled the butter from the fridge. While I waited for my toast and coffee, I filled Nick Nack's food dish and gave her fresh water. When she heard her dish rattling, she stopped playing in the back yard and joined me in the kitchen. She ate while I buttered my toast, poured my coffee, and doctored it with a half pack of Sweet 'n Low. Then I sat at the table to try to find something of interest in the morning paper.

The provincial assembly of Sindh, Pakistan observes a minute of silence in honor of Michael Jackson at the anniversary of the pop singer's death. You've got to be kidding! *North Korea promises to unleash destruction of biblical proportion on its enemies.* And that's new news? *Political crisis erupts in Syria.* Once again, news? *Who are the Ten most successful Mouseketeers?* I slammed the paper shut and rested my forehead on the kitchen table in exasperation.

I finally gave up on news and nibbled my toast and sipped my coffee in silence. Nick Nack, already full from her breakfast, was relaxing on her pallet. I rinsed my plate and mug and, once again, left them to dry in the drain. With over twenty-four hours left before I needed to head for the hospital, I decided to get out of the house to clear my mind and, once again, use up some time. I reached in the dryer and pulled out my oh, so happy clean jeans and stepped into them.

"Nick Nack, let's go to Shelley Lake."

At the mention of Shelley Lake, she leapt to her feet and yelped. It was one of her favorite places: a beautiful lake bordered by a paved walking trail that meandered through woods and meadows for Nick Nack to romp and chase geese and other dogs' Frisbees. What dog wouldn't cry tears of joy for such a place?

When Mark, Alex, and I were a family, we'd spent Sunday afternoons at the lake, picnicking and strolling the path. Nick Nack loved going along with us to romp and play until she collapsed from exhaustion. But I hadn't taken Alex or Nick Nack there since Mark's departure.

We arrived at the lake shortly after seven o'clock, long before the hikers and bikers and sun worshippers arrived. Nick Nack and I had the place to ourselves. I'd been told that it isn't safe for a woman to go to the lake alone when it is deserted, but on that morning the thought of being harmed by someone lurking nearby didn't frighten me at all. I was carrying my harm in my own body. Nothing could have been more threatening.

Nick Nack and I strolled the path. The silence was eerie. Nick Nack couldn't find a single dog with a Frisbee to steal. (I made a mental note to buy Nick Nack a Frisbee of her own. But perhaps stealing a friend's Frisbee was part of the fun.) She didn't seem to mind, though. She was content to trot by my side at my pace. When, after forty-five minutes, we'd completed the loop around the lake, we got back in our car and headed for home.

Now with only twenty-two hours left to kill, I decided to do something I'd avoided since I'd learned that I had cancer. I went to my desk in the living room and punched the button that would boot up my computer. I was going to research what I was facing.

Breast Cancer, I typed. The more I read, the more frightened I became. I had feared the surgery, but that was going to be a piece of cake compared to the aftermath. I'd recover from the operation in a heartbeat, but the treatments, whatever My Team chose, were going to be brutal: weeks and months of blistered skin, nausea, fatigue, hair loss, loss of appetite. I might not recover. I might die. The more I read, the more terrified I became. Why had I done this to myself? I should have adopted the ignorance-is-bliss ideology. But, no, I had to find out. I put my head on my desk and trembled with fear.

Nick Nack, who, as usual, was by my side, stood and whimpered and laid her head on my knee. When had I gotten over my fear of dogs and my anger at having had dog ownership forced upon me. I couldn't remember, but I was glad I had. I needed Nick Nack's gentle comfort when I was so frightened.

"Thank you, Nick Nack," I whispered, as I wiped my perspiring face on my sleeve and patted her on her head. "I think we've done enough research."

I punched the off button.

I spent the remainder of the day in a house-keeping frenzy. I felt it would take just the minimal amount of concentration to divert my attention from the next day, the next week, the next month, the next...

Nick Nack and I headed upstairs, where I pulled a set of clean sheets from the linen closet. I took them to the guest room that

Sandy would call home for ten days and ripped the soiled sheets from the bed. I flung them into a pile and began pulling the fresh contour sheet over the mattress.

"Nick Nack, could you get that corner over there?"

I half chuckled at my lame attempt at humor and was relieved to find that my mindless diversion was already working.

After making the bed, I ran the soiled sheets down to the washer and started a load. I grabbed the Pledge and a dust cloth from beneath the kitchen sink and headed back to Sandy's room, where I gave all the furniture a good polishing. Then I pulled out the vacuum and cleaned the floor, along with the upholstered chair and valance above the curtains. But I didn't stop there. I vacuumed the other two bedrooms, the stairs, and the entire downstairs. I was dripping with perspiration, but I was on a roll. I returned the Pledge and grabbed the Comet and a sponge and headed to the guest bath. Once I'd scrubbed months of neglect and had the place sparkling, I proceeded to my bath. By mid-afternoon I was panting from exhaustion, and my stomach was growling, my having ignored lunch.

I pulled my wash cloth from the rod, wet it with cold water, and mopped my steaming face and neck. I washed my hands and headed to the kitchen to peruse the same fridge whose contents hadn't interested me at all the day before.

It still didn't interest me.

But I grabbed lettuce and tomatoes and cucumbers and chopped myself a salad, adding some creamy cucumber dressing. I poured myself a glass of iced tea and took my lunch to the swing on the back porch. I dreaded slowing down, for fear the terrors would return.

Nick Nack refused to let that happen. While I ate, she put on a show of epic proportion out in the back yard. She found an old, dirty tennis ball in the bushes, and while I ate my salad, she ran and spun and tossed the ball in the air. She'd catch it before it hit the ground and then fling it in the bushes. She'd disappear for a minute and then come charging out, head high in triumph, the ball clenched in her teeth. Then she'd start the act all over again.

When I'd finished my lunch and Nick Nack had ended her stage show, we were both exhausted. I rinsed my dishes, folded the clean sheets and put them away, and headed upstairs to the shower.

Though it was still light outside when I toweled dry, brushed my teeth, and slipped into my nightgown, I was ready to turn in for the night. So was Nick Nack.

❦

I awoke with a start. Had I missed my surgery? I looked at the green numbers glowing in the dark. It was four-thirty. Sandy would be here in an hour and a half. Since I couldn't have breakfast, not even coffee, before surgery, and I'd taken my shower before going to bed, I had nothing to do but wash my face, brush my teeth, and step into my Target stretch pants. That wouldn't take an hour and a half. I lay in bed till the clock read five.

Nick Nack stood and looked over the edge of the bed, her snout just inches from my face.

"Yeah, I know I gotta get up."

She huffed and headed for the door, looking back to see if I'd follow. I dragged myself from bed, my muscles aching from the previous day's flurry of activity. I massaged my back and groaned as I padded down the stairs in my nightgown and bare feet. I shuffled to the kitchen where Nick Nack was waiting to go outside. I opened the door, once again leaving it open so she could return when she pleased. I filled her food dish and gave her clean water.

Back upstairs, I yanked up the covers on my bed, washed my face, brushed my teeth, and pulled on my stretch pants and a tee shirt and slipped my feet into my flip flops. I picked up my canvas bag that I'd packed with toiletries and clean underwear to take to the hospital.

It was five-thirty.

I went downstairs to find that Nick Nack was eating her breakfast. I closed the back door and headed to the living room, where I sat and waited for Sandy.

Seventeen

As soon as I saw her, I realized that it had been a long time since we'd been together. When Greg had married Sandy, she'd been a wispy little thing with expressive blue eyes and long, lustrous dark hair held back with a preppy little head band. She wore the most fashionable clothes, always perfectly matched, always size four. She had put on a few pounds, she wore wire-rimmed glasses, and her once-dark-brown hair was now shot through with gray. Instead of trendy size-four clothing, she wore gym pants, a tee shirt, and tennis shoes. Guess she'd figured out the dress-for-comfort thing, just as I had.

She was alone. For some reason, I'd thought that maybe, just maybe, Greg would surprise me by coming along. His oldest sibling, his only sister, was having major surgery just an hour and a half from his home, yet he didn't show. But the years and the pain had kept us, all of us siblings, apart. I'd tried, but had I tried enough? My correspondence had become one of obligation, not one of love.

I sent all of my brothers Christmas cards, but they were the same cards I sent Alex's teacher, my dentist, my newspaper delivery boy. Delivery girl? I had no idea. And that newspaper delivery boy or girl even got a crisp ten dollar bill in his or her card. And the card was always some generic holiday greeting card, rather than an honest-to-god Christmas card that might offend one of Mark's liberal, non-Christian colleagues. And it was signed by a machine: *Season's Greetings from the Murphys.* One Christmas the card company printed *from the Murphy's,* and Mark sent the cards out anyway, showing how little

119

thought he had put into it and how unimportant the ritual was. Small wonder my brother felt no compulsion to be at his sister's side when she didn't even care enough to remove an errant apostrophe, slip in a ten dollar bill, or, better yet, write a personal note. The tears caught in my throat, and I made a mental note to do better, if, I prayed, I'd get a chance to do better.

Sandy and I stood and stared at each other for an uncomfortable moment, and then she smiled. The beauty I'd remembered was back. She beamed, and the tenseness between us melted.

"Hey, Rowdy," she said and embraced me with her free arm, her other full of purse and overnight bag.

"Thanks for coming, Sandy. Come on in."

She stepped inside and deposited her purse and bag on the hall floor. She pulled a pad and pencil from her purse and headed for the living room to sit on the sofa.

"Okay, then, let me know what you need for me to do?"

Now, that was the Sandy I remembered: efficient, thorough, always in control.

But I didn't know what I wanted her to do. I didn't know what needed to be done. I just knew that I had to be at the hospital in an hour to have the malignant lump removed from my breast. Beyond that I was clueless. And my cluelessness made me sad and lonely and terrified.

So I just put my face in my hands and cried, "I don't know, Sandy, I just don't know."

She reached up, took my arm, and pulled me down on the sofa beside her. She wrapped her arm around my shoulders and said, "I know, Honey. You've had a rough time, a really rough time. I'm so sorry. But we'll figure out what needs to be done. Okay?"

"Um hum," was all I could manage while she rummaged in her pocket for a handful of tissues to mop my leaky eyes and nose.

"A teacher always has a pocket full of tissues," she said, smiling and pressing the tissues into my hand.

"Thanks," I said and wiped my face obediently.

"How about food? Laundry? I'm sure you haven't had time to shop or do laundry with all you've had on you."

"Well, I washed my jeans," I said and immediately realized how silly that sounded, an indication of my scattered frame of mind.

"That's a start. How about I just check and see what needs to be done. I can figure it out. Are you all right with that?"

"Yes, I'm fine with that."

I showed her the house, let her put her bag in her room and use the powder room. I took her to the kitchen and introduced her to Nick Nack, who had been dozing on her pallet. She hopped up immediately, to prove she hadn't been snoozing on the job, and greeted our guest graciously, wagging her tail and nuzzling Sandy's hand. The formalities out of the way, Sandy opened the refrigerator, and I could see her making a mental note that she had her work cut out for her.

"Okay, Rowdy, why don't you just give me a key to the house, and then I think it'll be time to get you to the hospital."

❦

"Rowdy Murphy," I told the front-desk attendant, a gray-haired lady wearing a pink flowered smock over white slacks. "I'm scheduled for surgery this morning."

She smiled sweetly, showing red lipstick smudges on her startlingly-white, perfectly-aligned false teeth.

"Hi, Ms. Murphy, I'm Evelyn," she said, as she got up from the desk, walked around, and placed a gentle hand at the small of my back. She was a tiny lady, probably no more than four-ten.

She looked up at me, still smiling with the lipstick stain on the her new teeth and said, "Right this way, Honey. They'll have your records just down the hall here at Intake."

She guided Sandy and me to the Intake desk where she said, "Elma, this is Ms. Murphy. She's here for surgery." And, turning back to me, she said, "Good luck, Honey. It was nice to meet you." Still smiling, lipstick still in place on her teeth, she headed back to her station to calm more terrified patients on their way to surgery.

"Paperwork, please, Hon," said Elma, a short, squat woman with a tight perm in her jet-black hair and fingernails gnawed to the quick. She wore a mechanical pencil on a chain around her neck. I hadn't seen a mechanical pencil on a chain since my grandma Maude wore one to make lists and notes to herself when her memory started to slip. I smiled at the recollection of my precious grandmother. I wondered who had gotten her pencil on the chain when she died.

I handed my packet to Elma, and she opened it, examining its contents.

"Everything looks in order, hon," and to Sandy she said, "and you'll be staying with Ms. Murphy?"

"Yes, I'm Sandy Alexander, Ms. Murphy's sister-in-law. I'll be with her throughout her stay here at the hospital."

I looked over at Sandy and smiled; she returned it with a wink. Then she reached for my hand. As terrified as I was, a feeling of calm and relief washed over me as she squeezed my hand and said, "Yes, I'm staying as long as she needs me."

"Good, that's nice to hear, Ms. Alexander," Elma said, though I'm sure the length of Sandy's stay was none of Elma's business and none of her concern.

Elma ran through some computer screens, typing furiously with her pale, pudgy fingers, and several sheets of paper shot out of the printer by her side. She yanked them from the tray, clipped them to my packet, and returned it all to me.

She stood, leaned forward, and pointed to the right, saying, "Now, Hon, you and Ms. Alexander take that hall right yonder down to the door that says Insurance. Miss Genevieve will be waiting down there to get your insurance information."

Sandy and I followed Elma's directions and passed through large swinging doors to the insurance office, where we found Miss Genevieve.

"I'm Rowdy Murphy, and this is my sister-in-law, Sandy Alexander."

"Hey, Girls," said, Miss Genevieve, a large bleached-blonde woman with lots of rings and lots of exposed cleavage, who smelled like vanilla. "Just sit right there, Sweetie," she said to me, "and give me your insurance card. This'll only take a minute."

I handed Miss Genevieve my card, and, sure enough, she flew through all the computer screens, her long, red fingernails clicking on the keyboard, and returned my card to me in a flash. Then a small slip of paper with my name, social security number, insurance information, and lots of hospital code I couldn't decipher shot out of a little black box beside her computer. Miss Genevieve grabbed it between two long, red nails, slipped it into a yellow plastic band, and clamped it around my wrist.

"See there, that wudn't so bad, now was it?" she said, smiling and winking.

She picked up the phone on her desk, punched a button, and said, "Wayne, Sweetie, come on over here and get Miss Rowdy, will ya?"

Then turning to me, she patted my hand and said, "Hold tight, Honey, Wayne'll be right here to take care of you."

I couldn't remember ever having been treated with such kindness. Perhaps they were trained to smell terror. All of a sudden I wanted to sell my house and move in with these sweet-talking people. I'd wander the halls all day, while people called me *Sugar, Honey, Sweetie, Darlin'*. Just as I was staging my home to put on the market, Wayne, a large young man dressed in blue scrubs and yellow rubber Crocs, his hair red and spiky and his glasses red and square—framed, came sashaying through the door.

"Hey, Precious."

Another sweet name caller.

"Let's get a move on. You need a wheel chair, or can you keep up with me?"

I tried to muster a smile and said, "I don't think I can keep up with you, Wayne, but I don't believe I'll need a wheel chair."

Wayne threw his head back and let out a belly laugh. It wasn't that funny, but I was still wallowing in the kindness.

As we shuffled down the hall, Wayne's yellow Crocs making squishing noises on the tiles, he said, "You're a hoot! Now, let's get you back to pre-op and fix you up with a pretty little peignoir."

He pushed through double swinging doors and greeted all the nurses with, "Hey, Doll. Whatcha doin', Gir'friend? Hi, Cutie." And to me he said, "Step right this way to the bridal suite, Miss Rowdy," as he unfurled the curtain of a four-by-six cubicle. "See, there's the pretty little peignoir I promised," he said, lifting a limp, worn, blue dotted hospital gown from the gurney. "Just strip to your birthday suit and slip into this sexy little number and hop up on your throne there. One of the nurses will be right outside if you need anything."

Then he reached for my hand and cupped it between his two soft, gigantic palms and patted gently. When I looked into his face, his eyes softened, and he said, "Take care, Sweetie."

Then he slipped out, closed my curtain, and left me to strip to my birthday suit.

"Would you like for me to step outside, Rowdy?" Sandy asked.

I smiled wanly and said, "Not necessary, Sandy. You'd better get used to my naked body. I'm guessing you're going to be seeing a lot of it."

"You're probably right," she laughed. "Now strip down to your birthday suit, and give me those clothes."

I did as she instructed and slipped into my peignoir. Sandy put my clothes in a plastic bag labeled PERSONAL BELONGINGS and sat in the chair by the gurney, cradling my clothes, her purse, and a half-dozen magazines. I climbed onto my throne and waited for what was to come.

A young Asian woman with shiny black hair pulled back in a long ponytail and a name tag that said Erin Sun, RN stepped through the curtains to my cubicle and took my wrist, looking at my arm band.

"Birth date?"

"November 26."

"Full name?"

"Rowdy Alexander Murphy."

"Great! Just making sure we have the right person. Don't want to take the wrong patient to surgery."

"That wouldn't be good," I smiled weakly, "though I'd gladly give up my spot."

"I know you would, Ms. Murphy," she said and squeezed my hand.

"Now I'm going to start your IV," she said, moving the stand closer, unraveling the tubing that would connect it to the back of my hand. She lifted my right hand, thumped my vein, and inserted the needle. "These fluids will keep you hydrated during surgery, and the anesthesiologist will administer your anesthesia through this same port."

Once she was sure she had my IV secured, she turned to Sandy and asked, "And you'll be staying with Ms. Murphy?"

"Yes, I'm Sandy Alexander, Ms. Murphy's sister-in-law."

"Well, Ms. Alexander, we'll be taking Ms. Murphy to surgery soon. You're free to go on down to the surgical waiting room. Just follow the signs outside those swinging doors. Dr. Travers, Ms. Murphy's surgeon, will come get you when she's out of surgery and in recovery."

Sandy stood and said, "Would it be okay if I go to surgery with her. I'd rather stay with her as long as I can, if I may."

Erin smiled and said, "Sure, Ms. Alexander, that'll be fine. You can go as far as the surgical suite with Ms. Murphy."

"Thanks," Sandy said, taking my hand, "I'd like that."

Then two orderlies dressed in scrubs, caps on their heads, booties covering their shoes, pulled my curtain back and announced that they were there to wheel me away. While Erin stepped back to make room, they put a cap identical to theirs on my head and began maneuvering my gurney from the small space. Sandy gathered her magazines, her purse, and my personal belongings with one arm and grabbed my hand with the other.

She ran alongside me, holding on all the way, until the orderlies said, "Well, we're here. You can wait for your friend right down the hall in the waiting room."

Sandy leaned over the gurney rail, kissed me on the forehead, and said, "I'll be right here, Rowdy."

They were the sweetest words I'd heard in a long time.

Then she disappeared from view as the orderlies wheeled me through swinging double doors.

Operating rooms are intimidating places. I hadn't been in one since I'd had a tonsillectomy at seven. I'd forgotten how loud everyone sounds, how stainless steel everything looks. There was nothing warm and inviting about the place. There was efficient bustling, paper rustling, and masked people scurrying about. No one was calling me *Sugar* or patting my head lovingly. I didn't like this faceless, sterile, industrial place. And I was still terrified.

Several of the masked, faceless people gathered around me, and one said, "On three—one, two, three," as they scooted me from the gurney to the operating table.

Then Dr. Travers, still looking every bit the surfer dude, was by my side, his blond hair peeking out of his surgical cap, his tan and blindingly-white teeth glowing beneath the surgical lights.

"Hey, Ms. Murphy. We're going to be in here a couple of hours, I'm thinking. From here we'll move you to recovery for a few more hours. You just relax, and Dr. Winters is going to begin administering your anesthesia."

With that Dr. Winters stepped forward and said, "Good morning, Ms. Murphy. I'll take care of your anesthesia this morning throughout your surgery. You'll be in a deep sleep and won't feel a thing. Do you have any questions?"

"Don't think so," I told him.

"Good. Then I want you to begin counting backwards from one hundred."

"One hundred, ninety-nine, ninety-eight, ni..."

Eighteen

I opened my eyes. Had I finished counting? What was I supposed to do now? I looked around and realized I was not in the stainless steel room? But where was I? Then I noticed Sandy sitting in a chair a short distance away, reading a magazine, her legs crossed, her foot swinging back and forth. When I stirred, she dropped her magazine, hopped up, and stepped to the side of my bed.

She took my hand, smiled broadly, and said, "Hey, Rowdy, you did great. Dr. Travers said everything went just as planned. You were in recovery for a few hours, but I don't believe you remember his coming in to talk with you. You were pretty woozy. You're in your own room now," she said, sweeping the room with her hand, as if she were offering me a door on Let's Make a Deal. "He said to let him know when you were awake. Here, let me call the nurse for you. Right here, this red button, you can call for help any time you want," she said, pointing to the button on the bed railing.

Within moments a nurse appeared, bustling, talking way too loudly, being more efficient than I could handle in my foggy state, looking at my arm band, thumping my IV. She pulled at my gown to examine the bandage at the surgery site and straightened my covers. I was beginning to regret opening my eyes.

"How are you feeling, Ms. Murphy?" she yelled.

Had I been able, I'd have said, "The surgery didn't make me deaf."

But my mouth felt as if it were full of glue.

Prying my tongue from the roof of my mouth, I managed, "Water, please."

"Sure," she said and poured some water from a Pepto-Bismol-pink plastic pitcher into a Pepto-Bismol-pink plastic cup.

She stuck in a straw, and Sandy said, "May I?" reaching for the cup.

"Sure," said my nurse and handed it to her.

As Sandy bent the straw and guided it to my lips, the nurse, whose name tag read Myra Oberlin, RN, said, "Dr. Travers asked that we page him as soon as you were awake. He's right down the hall with another patient. He'll be in to see you when he's free. Now, can I get you anything else?"

"No thanks, I think Sandy has it covered," I said, as I attempted a feeble smile and took another sip of water.

When Nurse Myra left, Sandy continued to hold the straw to my lips and stroke my arm gently. We didn't chat.

Dr. Travers rushed in, all smiles. "Well, you did great, Rowdy." The last time he and I had spoken, he'd called me Ms. Murphy. I guess handling my breast for hours made him feel he had the right to call me by my first name. "How are you feeling?"

"I'm still a little foggy, Dr. Travers, so why don't you tell me how I am."

"Well, everything went as planned. We were able to avoid a radical mastectomy and perform only a lumpectomy, with minimal damage to the surrounding breast tissue."

I assumed that was good news because he smiled broadly and waited for me to say something.

When I didn't, he continued, "Your cancer is what we classify as Stage IIIA, meaning that the tumor was greater than five centimeters and that we found abnormal cells in six ipsilateral ancillary nodes. The really good news, though, is that we are confident the cancer was confined to your left breast because we got clean margins."

In my fogginess, all I could do was let him talk. What he was saying sounded so foreign, as if he were talking about someone else. Stage IIIA, ipsilateral ancillary nodes, clean margins. Those things just couldn't apply to me. How could I have, in just one week, gone from divorced mother who shelves library books to cancer patient with affected ipsilateral ancillary nodes and clean margins?

"I've already talked with the rest of the team about your adjuvant treatment, that is the follow-up treatment to your surgery. Though the decision will ultimately rest with you, we feel that the best course would be six weeks of radiation therapy, five days a week, followed by eight months of chemotherapy, one day a week. You'll have a recovery period, about two weeks, before you'll need to begin the radiology. I'd like for Mrs. Alexander or another friend to stay with you for about ten days," he said, looking at Sandy for affirmation. When she smiled and shook her head *yes,* he continued, "After that time you'll be free to drive and resume your normal activity. You'll want to continue to rest, of course, take it easy, no heavy lifting, but you'll be able to care for yourself just fine."

I wanted to go shelve library books.

"Rowdy, I know this is a lot to throw at you, but we'll be with you all the way. I do want to keep you here for observation until tomorrow. You can just rest for now, and I'll be back this afternoon to check on you, see how you're progressing. By then I'm sure you'll have questions."

With that he patted my hand and left Sandy in charge.

Sandy chattered nervously, not ready to discuss what lay ahead. We'd have plenty of time for that. Around five o'clock in the afternoon, a tall, voluptuous woman the color of cinnamon strolled in, pushing a meal cart. She smiled a beautiful smile, revealing the most perfect white, very natural teeth I'd ever seen.

"Hey, Precious. How you doin'?"

The sweet name callers were back. Somehow they didn't seem so special anymore.

"Looky what I got," she said, as she plopped my meal on the bedside tray with a clang and whisked the dome off my plate with a flourish. "Mmmm, mmm, don't that look yummy? We got chicken broth and lime Jell-O and tea." Then she chuckled and said, "Sorry I can't do better than this for you, but doctor's orders, you know. But you'll be eatin' fried chicken and 'nana puddin' 'fore you know it."

But I had no appetite for anything, not even green Jell-O.

"Thanks, this looks fine."

She pushed the tray around so that it would be close enough for me to reach, spread my paper napkin, and laid it across my chest.

"By the way, I'm Jacqui. That's Jacqui with an I. What's your name?"

"Rowdy. My name's Rowdy."

With that she pulled a small piece of paper and a stub of pencil from her pocket. Posing the pencil to write, she said, "Spell that for me, will you, please?"

"R-O-W-D-Y," I said, wondering why she needed to know.

Sticking her tongue out and concentrating on writing my name, she said, "Now you're on my prayer list. I hope you don't mind me praying for you."

Touched by her offer, I stammered, "Why, no, thank you. That's very thoughtful of you."

"Well, I believe the doctors are wonderful, but they can just do so much."

Then she said, "I'll be thinking 'bout you," and left me to ponder her remark about the doctors being able to do just so much.

After Jacqui whooshed out the door, Sandy stepped to the side of the bed, picked up my spoon from the tray, and began feeding me the first of many meals.

One by one, my cancer team came in to see me and share their suggested treatment plans. Sandy took copious notes. I was so grateful since there was just so much to absorb. I couldn't have done it alone.

By the time I was ready for discharge the following morning, I had decided to trust my team and go with the treatment they felt best— six weeks of radiation followed by eight months of chemotherapy— since they were the experts and I had no past cancer experience.

Sandy loaded me into her car, tender parts padded with pillows, and drove me home. When we pulled into my driveway, we saw Nick Nack standing at the living room window. How long had she been waiting? Had she been there since Monday morning when I left for the hospital? If not, how did she know when she was supposed to begin her vigil? By the time Sandy helped me to the front door, Nick Nack was waiting for me. She ignored Sandy, focusing all of her attention on me, showing me how glad (Relieved? Concerned?) she was that I was home.

Only when I said, "Nick Nack, say 'Hi' to Sandy," and motioned toward her did Nick Nack break away from me and greet her. Once she'd welcomed her, though, she returned her full attention to me.

Sandy bedded me down and immediately began to care for me as well as any professional could have done. There was a drain from my incision which had to remain in place for a week, and the tube leading from the drain had to be milked every few hours and the fluid measured, charted, and the results reported to my doctors. She took on the task with grace. She also changed my bed, prepared my meals, administered my medications, and gave me sponge baths.

And as she cared for me, Nick Nack watched her every move and did not leave my side.

I'm certain Sandy found Nick Nack's constant hovering a nuisance, but she didn't let on if she did. She cared for my dog, just as she did me, feeding her, walking her, and scooping her poop. And she took care of us both with poise and dignity and without one sign of squeamishness or disgust. I marveled at her fortitude and felt so fortunate that I'd thought to call her. But, mostly, I felt so blessed that she'd agreed to help.

We didn't warm to each other immediately; it had been so long since we'd been together. But it's hard to remain distant when the relationship takes on the intimacy of cancer patient and caregiver. I was forced to be completely vulnerable in her hands, and she didn't shy away from the most intrusive and personal responsibilities.

The first night she bedded me down, dragging in pillows from the linen closet and Alex's room to cradle my arm, protect my incision. She fed me more broth and Jell-O, helped me to the bathroom, sponged my hot body with a tepid cloth.

She was sitting in my bedside chair, reading her magazine, Nick Nack vigilant on her rug, when my pain meds kicked in and I finally dozed off. But I awoke throbbing in the middle of the night to find her still there, asleep, her glasses down her nose, her magazine on the floor. The moment I stirred, she was wide awake and at my side.

"Why aren't you in your bed?" I asked groggily.

"I didn't want to go far, in case you needed me. And it looks like you do. What can I do, Rowdy? Are you in pain?"

"Yeah, it hurts, Sandy."

"Dr. Travers said you should expect some pain for the first few days," she said, smoothing my hair away from my face. "It'll soon subside, but until then, you can take your pain medication. Here," she said, pouring a glass of water for me, dropping a pill in my hand, and gently helping me to sit. "You'll feel better soon. Can I get you anything else?"

"Just move that pillow a little. Yeah, just like that. Thanks, Sandy."

"While you're awake, let me milk your line and measure it. Your doctors need for us to keep track."

And she set to work in the middle of the night, milking, measuring, charting, like the professional I knew she would be.

Nick Nack had awakened when we stirred, and she watched protectively as Sandy cared for me. When Sandy finished and had me settled, she turned to Nick Nack, patted her head gently, and said, "She's fine now, Nick Nack. You can go back to sleep."

Each day she made a pallet for me on the sofa, my pillows plumped just so, while she washed my bed sheets. She insisted upon putting fresh linens on my bed each day; she said it would make me feel so much better to sleep on crisp, clean sheets. Once she had me situated on the sofa with Nick Nack by my side and the sheets washing in the machine, she'd clean the house, make lists, fill the fridge with food I didn't want, and fill my phone with contacts I also didn't want.

She was amazing.

By the third day, house clean, fridge stocked, phone numbers in place, I was feeling somewhat better, and we were chatting like school chums. She'd climb into bed with me and rub my back while we talked and I, in time, would drift into sleep. I cried from her tenderness, tenderness I hadn't felt in so long and had missed so much. She understood and didn't hold back.

Toward the middle of her stay, my pain somewhat diminished, I was propped up in bed, Sandy painting my fingernails.

I said, "Sandy, I don't want to heap any more responsibility on you, but I need to be with Alex. I thought I didn't want her to see me like this, but I miss her so much. I want her to come home. I know Mark said he'd take care of her, but I really have to see her."

Sandy looked up at me, beaming, and said, "Oh, Rowdy, I was so hoping you'd say that, hoping I'd get to spend some time with her. It's been so long, and I know she is still the darling little girl I remember from our last visit at your mom and dad's beach cottage. She was such a cunning little child. I can still see all those red curls, those beautiful dimples."

"Well, she still has those red curls and dimples, but she's a big girl now. She's my heartstrings, Sandy. I'm glad you want to see her 'cause I can't wait to get her home."

"You know, Rowdy, I've always wanted to be a mom. People think we're childless by choice, but that's not the case at all. We've tried. In fact, I've been pregnant five times, but I can't seem to carry

131

beyond three months. I've had every test known to the medical establishment, but my doctors say there's nothing physically wrong with me. So we keep trying. It's just not happening."

"Oh, Sandy, I didn't know. I'm so sorry."

"We haven't told anyone but my mom and dad. But I wanted you to know," she said, a sad smile trying to tamp down the tears welling in her eyes.

To take the focus off her sadness, she said, "I sort of expected you to have a house full of kids, just like your mom."

Then it was my turn to tamp down the tears.

"I did want a brood. Then Mama and Daddy died, and all my brothers went away. Losing Greg, Will, and the twins has been heartbreaking. I knew I couldn't prevent Alex from losing her parents, but I had it in my power to keep her from losing siblings. If she didn't have them, they couldn't desert her."

Before she could respond, I said, "Sandy, I know I'm just as much at fault as they are, but that's how I've felt: deserted. I tried, really I tried. Maybe I just didn't try hard enough. But since I'm the oldest, it was probably my responsibility to keep us together, and I just failed." By now I was sobbing, "Oh, Sandy, I love my little brothers, and I miss them so much."

Grabbing a handful of tissues from the box on the bedside table, Sandy dabbed at my face and said, "Oh, no, Honey, you can't be responsible for four other adults. You can only be responsible for yourself. You did all you could do. They just didn't reciprocate. I can't speak for the others, Rowdy, but please don't give up on Greg," she said, still mopping my leaking eyes. "He tries to reconnect, and then he goes to pieces. It's so sad. He's in so much pain."

"Sandy, I know. He was Daddy's favorite. We all knew it, and Daddy didn't try to hide his favoritism. They were just alike, and Greg was Daddy's little shadow. I know how hard Daddy's death must have been on him."

"Yes, Greg told me he was your dad's favorite. He loved him so much, Rowdy. He still cries in his sleep. It's so sad to hear a grown man cry in his sleep over his daddy."

Now she was sobbing, too, tears sliding down our cheeks before the tissues could catch them. I still ached for my parents, but the thought of my little brother harboring so much pain just broke my heart.

"He loves you, Rowdy, but the memories hurt so much that he just can't seem to make that move. But please, please keep your door and heart open for him. He's a wonderful man, Rowdy. I love him so much. And please know that he loves you and Will and Kevin and Sam, even if he can't show it right now."

Now I wrapped my free arm around her as we comforted each other. I promised that my heart would forever be open to Greg, to all my little brothers.

When our sobbing slowed, Sandy went to the bathroom, mopped her face with a cool cloth, and brought one for me to do the same.

Then she handed my phone to me and said, "Please call Mark now and tell him to bring Alex home."

I punched in the number and waited for Mark to answer. Only Mark didn't answer the phone. Tawni did. As soon as I heard her voice, I realized that it was the first time I'd heard it. I'd seen her in the car when Mark came to pick up Alex, but I'd never had a conversation with the woman I'd entrusted with my child's safety and well-being. All of our messages had gone through Mark.

"Tawni, this is Rowdy."

"Oh, Rowdy, I'm so glad you called. How are you feeling?"

"Well, I'm doing much better, thank you. In fact, I'm doing so well that I'm ready for Alex to come home. Can Mark drive her over?"

"That's great news!"

I thought she was intimating that it was great news that she was finally getting rid of my child. I realized, though, that she meant it was good news that I was doing much better.

"Mark isn't here right now. He had to run to campus to meet with a student. But I'll be glad to drive Alex home. Right now, though, she is helping me ice cupcakes. We'll be through in about fifteen minutes. Will that be okay?"

"Sure, sure," I said, "that will be fine."

"Great. That way she'll be able to bring some cupcakes to you."

"Thanks, Tawni, I'd like that."

"And, Rowdy, thanks so much for trusting me with Alex. She's so wonderful. I really love her."

Damn, Tawni was making it hard to hate her. And I *really, really* wanted to hate her.

"Okay, Alex and I will see you in about thirty minutes."

In thirty minutes flat Alex came bursting through the front door, bearing cupcakes and yelling, "Oh, Mama, I'm so glad to see you. Here, I made these for you," and she handed me a plate with a half dozen pink-iced cupcakes, each bearing sprinkles and a message of love and get well wishes in her little-girl hand writing.

She kissed me on the cheek but didn't grab me in her usual hug. I assumed Mark and Tawni had explained the nature of my surgery and cautioned her against hurting me.

When she saw Nick Nack standing aside, waiting patiently to be greeted, she fell to the floor on her knees and wrapped her arms around her dog.

"Oh, Nick Nack, I missed you so much! Did you take good care of Mama while I was gone?"

In response Nick Nack smiled proudly, thumped her tail on the floor, and licked Alex on her cheek.

Then Alex returned to my side, to weave her arm gently around my waist, careful not to jostle me. She laid her head on my arm and looked up at me, smiling sweetly, her dimples glowing.

"I'm so glad you're feeling better, Rowdy."

I looked up to see Tawni framed by the doorway, carrying Alex's bag and backpack. She was more beautiful than I'd expected, with her flowing blonde hair, her large doe eyes, legs that went on forever, and her very pregnant glow.

"Thanks so much, Tawni," I said, wrapping my well arm around Alex protectively and, I hate to admit, possessively. "I can't thank you enough. Your help has been a life saver."

"Well, I love her, and it's been my pleasure," she said, but did not approach Alex to counter my possessiveness with a squeeze of her own.

A pleasure? She'd given up a trip to Paris to care for someone else's child? She could have been making love in the most beautiful, most romantic city in the world; instead, she'd been making cupcakes in her toy kitchen for her husband's ex-wife. A pleasure? Hard. Really hard hating this woman. Damn it!

"Tawni, this is my sister-in-law, Sandy Alexander," I said, turning to Sandy who had been standing by silently.

Tawni deposited Alex's bags beside the hall table, and the two women stepped forward to shake hands and exchange pleasantries.

And to me Tawni said, "Call me if you need anything. If you can't reach me at home, Alex has my cell number. And honest, Rowdy, I'm cool with Alex staying with us whenever you need. Bye, now," she said and floated out the front door, down the stairs, and out to her car.

"Run your things upstairs, Sweetie. Then you and Aunt Sandy and I can have a snack, maybe one of your cupcakes. They look delicious."

"Okay, Mama," Alex said and, grabbing her bag, clattered up the stairs, screaming, "Come on, Nick Nack."

Nick Nack looked at me for permission to join Alex, and I said, "You can go play, Nick Nack."

Without hesitation, she bounded up the stairs to join her little buddy.

When Tawni had disappeared and Alex was out of earshot, Sandy turned to me and said, "Hard to hate that, isn't it?"

"Damn it!" was all I said.

We both laughed.

When Alex came skipping back down the stairs, Nick Nack close behind, we headed for the kitchen, where we ate cupcakes and Alex told us all about *her* wedding.

It was wonderful to have by child back home. Having her with me brightened my outlook and, I believe, lessened the pain. She and Sandy had so much fun getting reacquainted, and the school teacher came out in Sandy when they were together. She knew the coolest games, said the funniest kid stuff, and just knew how to interact with Alex on a level that I'd never know.

Ten days flew by, and it was time for Sandy to return to Greensboro. The house was spotless, my appointment calendar was up-to-date, and Nick Nack was well cared for and sweet smelling and glossy from the bath that Sandy had given her—and she had given Sandy.

The neighbors spun into action after Sandy saw super-mom Bernadette Collins at the mailbox and reported to her that I was ill. Bernie coordinated the effort, and, within two days, the kitchen was full of fresh bakery breads, roast chicken, potato and pasta salads, Edible Arrangements, and enough desserts to render me diabetic.

"I'll be glad to stay for as long as you need me, Rowdy."

"Thank you, Sandy, but it's time you got back to Greg. He needs you. And I am okay to take care of myself. My larder is full, thanks to you and Bernie, and I can drive and shop for myself just fine. And if I need you, I know where to find you."

"Yes, you do. And you know you can call me any time."

The following morning, after washing my sheets and making my bed for the last time, Sandy tossed her bag in her car, prepared to leave.

"Sandy, I just can't find words…" I said, and truly meant it. There were just no words to express my gratitude for her selflessness.

"Rowdy, when you called, I was taken aback. But I wouldn't take anything for this time we've had together. Thanks for trusting me to help you."

She hugged Alex and me and scratched Nick Nack on the head; then we watched her climb into her car to head back to Greensboro. She backed out of the driveway and coasted slowly down the street, and as she turned the corner, she stuck her hand out the window and gave us a big thumbs-up.

How would I ever repay her? First of all, I'd keep in touch. In addition to regular calls and letters, I would still send Christmas cards. I pledged, though, to delete all misplaced apostrophes and to include a personal note. Maybe I'd tuck in a gift card. Once when Sandy was rubbing my back, she confided that she and Greg enjoyed going for pancakes at IHOP on Sunday mornings. Maybe an IHOP gift certificate would be a good gift. But what denomination? There wasn't a denomination large enough to repay her for her kindness. Perhaps I should buy her an IHOP franchise.

Nineteen

As soon as Sandy left, I had to start thinking about caring for myself. I had gotten comfortable with her tender, loving care, but I no longer had someone making my decisions, making my bed, and making me feel safe and protected. I was on my own.

After ten days the pain from the surgery had pretty much subsided, but I still had to be cautious, handle myself with care, so to speak. I couldn't do any heavy lifting, which ruled out house work—what a pity—but I was cleared to stay alone and to drive.

Nick Nack continued to hover out of love for me, and I'd gotten accustomed to her adoration. Alex, however, hovered out of fear. I tried to act as normal as possible under the circumstances, so as not to alarm her. I believe I did a pretty good job, as there were times when Alex seemed to forget that her mom was even sick. I cherished those times, those ordinary, normal times. I found that I even enjoyed the ordinariness of fixing her mac and cheese and applesauce, watching The Bachelor, and toenail night. Especially toenail night.

Shortly after Sandy left, Celeste Raymond, my nurse coordinator, called to check on me and to fill me in on the progress of her scheduling.

"I've set up your radiation treatments to begin Monday. You'll report to Raleigh Imaging at ten in the morning. Dr. Rahn's therapist, you recall Kathleen Kerrigan, is expecting you."

"Sure," I said, "I remember," though the get-together with My Team seemed so long ago that it had become one big blur. Hard to

137

believe that it had been only a few weeks. So much had happened since then.

"Now, you'll be reporting to Kathleen five days a week for six weeks, for a total of thirty treatments. You have the brochure about radiation therapy in your packet. You might want to review that before you go, just so you'll know what to expect. Now, remember, Rowdy, if you need anything at all or have any questions, you just give me a call. That's what I'm here for."

"Thanks, Celeste, that's comforting to hear."

"Okay, Rowdy, you take care, and I'll check in on you Monday after your first treatment."

Before she could hang up, I said, "Just one thing, Celeste, my daughter is out of school for the summer. Will I be able to take her along to my radiation treatments?"

"How old is she?"

"She's nine."

"Oh, sure, she'll be fine. There's a waiting area right outside the therapy room, and your treatments will take just a matter of minutes. That shouldn't be a problem at all."

∾☙

Monday morning Alex hopped into the car with me, and we pulled away as Nick Nack watched us from the living room window.

"Is it going to hurt, Mama?"

"I don't believe so, Honey?"

"Are you scared?"

"Ummm, maybe a little, but I have lots of good people looking out for me, taking care of me."

"How many people?"

"Oh, about six, I think."

"That's a lot. Are they nice?"

"Yes, Alex, they are all very nice."

Her little-girl chatter revealed her concern. I tried my best to put her at ease but was so glad when we reached Raleigh Imaging and I could stop pretending that I wasn't terrified and acting as though I knew what was going on, when, clearly, I was just about as clueless as Alex.

Kathleen, a petite, perky brunette, was waiting for me in her green scrubs when we arrived at ten on the dot.

"Hey, Rowdy, good to see you again. And this must be Alex," she

LESSONS I LEARNED FROM NICK NACK

said, smiling and reaching out to pat Alex's shoulder.

I was so grateful she was there to greet us, to make Alex feel welcomed and put her at ease.

"Whatcha got there?" she asked Alex.

"It's a video player."

"Oh, cool. May I see it?"

"Sure," Alex said, as she turned on her small hand-held machine.

They put their heads together, and Alex said, "See, you just turn it on here and scroll down with this button to find the video you want to watch."

"Wow, that's awesome! I wish they'd had this when I was a kid."

She took it from Alex's hand and, scrolling up and down, said, "Whatcha watchin'?"

"Harry Potter," Alex told her.

"No way! Which one?"

"*Sorcerer's Stone.*"

"Awesome! That's my favorite." Kathleen said, and handed Alex's video player back to her. "Come on with me, and I'll show you where you can watch your movie while I'm with your mom," she said, as she guided her down a narrow hallway to the waiting room.

Once she had Alex settled and smiling, she said, "Your mom and I will be back real soon. Okay?"

Alex nodded, said, "Sure," and returned to Harry.

Kathleen was just as gentle and comforting with me as she had been with Alex.

She guided me to the radiation room, chatting all the way, and said, "Just put your bag over there, Rowdy. Then slip off your top and put this gown on, open in front."

While I undressed and put on the gown, Kathleen busied herself, readying her equipment.

"Just hop up here on the table; this will only take a few minutes."

Once she had me arranged on the table the way she wanted, she pulled a marker out of her scrubs pocket and peered closely at my breast. She uncapped the marker, made an X, and said, "We mark your breast so that we know exactly where to aim our radiation. With that she lined up the overhead machine, focused on her mark. "Now, hold still while I go into the next room and administer the radiation. You'll be able to see me right through that window. This won't take long at all. You okay? Comfortable?" she said as she stroked my arm.

She was right. It didn't take long, and within ten minutes I was dressed and back with Alex in the waiting room.

"That was quick, Mama," she said and hopped down, took my hand, and walked beside me to the car. Looking up at me she asked, "Did she hurt you?"

"No, Sweetie, it didn't hurt at all," I was happy to report and squeezed her hand.

We had macaroni and cheese and applesauce for lunch, as usual, and Alex finished watching her movie in the afternoon. I was glad that she was occupied with Harry because immediately the side effects kicked in. After just one treatment my breast felt as if it had been badly sunburned, and the feelings of fatigue were evident right away. Day after day the burn and fatigue increased. By week two the skin on my breast became hard and drawn. Though I was somewhat uncomfortable and very, very tired, it was nothing I couldn't handle to assure my best shot at conquering the cancer.

About halfway through my radiation, I began anticipating the chemotherapy treatments that would begin in about three weeks. Though the radiation was quite manageable, the chemotherapy, I'd been told, would be another story.

I was scheduled for a treatment each Wednesday for eight months. Each session would last from two to six hours, and though Alex could entertain herself through radiation treatments, I felt that chemo was something I just couldn't subject her to. I was terrified by the mere anticipation; I felt it would frighten her, as well. But I would be out for hours on Wednesday, I'd be sick with nausea all day Thursday, and I'd be recovering on Friday.

It was August, and Alex was out of school on summer break for another month. I had to make a plan for her care on those days when I wouldn't be able to mother her, and I'd already decided that the plan did not include Mark and Tawni. I told myself that I'd imposed enough, but there was more to it than that: as much as I appreciated their help, our agreement still called for Alex to stay with them only on alternate weekends. And that's all I wanted.

Then one afternoon my neighbor Bernadette Collins dropped by to see if the fridge needed restocking.

"How's everything going" she asked.

"Pretty well, I think."

"Enough food, or do we need to restock?" Bernie asked in her get-it-done, matter-of-fact way.

"Thanks, Bernie, I think y'all have it covered."

"How's Alex doing?"

"I believe she's pretty scared, but she seems to be holding up okay."

"Hey, do you think she'd like to go to the summer program at the Y with Conner and Everette? I take the girls in the morning on my way to the office, and Roger picks them up in the afternoon. We'd love to have Alex go with us."

I'd never considered the Y summer program, or any program, for that matter. Alex had spent summer mornings with me in the library, and I'd spent summer afternoons with her at the club pool. And when Mark had breaks from school, we'd head for the beach. But this was a new ball game. We needed a new plan. And the Y summer program seemed like a plan to consider.

"My girls love it, Rowdy. They have a great pool, and they do all kinds of crafts. They learn all sorts of dances, and they even put on plays. And they go on fantastic field trips to the science and art museums. They hike in Umstead Park, and the counselors even take the kids down to Fort Fisher, below Wilmington, for a day trip."

Already it was sounding like something she'd enjoy and something that would solve my child-care problem.

"Would she have to go every day?" I asked, because I really didn't want to send Alex away on those days when I'd be well. Not knowing what the future held, I wanted to spend as much time with my child as I could.

"Oh, no, she can go whenever you'd like. You just have to work out your schedule with the Y. Just go on line and check out the program. If you're interested, you can download an application and fill it out."

"You know, Bernie, I believe Alex would love camp, especially if Conner and Everette are going. And it sure would help me out while I'm taking my treatments. I'll check it out and get right back to you."

"Sounds great. Well, I'll be on my way; sorry I've kept you so long, Rowdy," Bernie said, standing to leave. "I'm sure my girls really would like for Alex to go with them. They think she's so cool." We both laughed as she said, "Did we even know *cool* at their age?"

"Thanks so much for thinking of us, Bernie. This just may be the life saver I've been looking for," I said.

Then Bernie added, "Rowdy, I'm so sorry I didn't know sooner that you were sick. I'm just glad I ran into your sister-in-law at the mailbox. I swear, I feel so out of the loop. If I'm not at the office, I have some kid activity. And if we don't have our children in dance lessons and piano lessons and soccer lessons and any other lessons the lesson fairies can think up, people treat us like slackers. Believe me, I want to be a good mom, but when are we going to have a minute for ourselves or each other? When the kids go to college?"

All of a sudden, Bernie looked exhausted. All along I'd thought she *enjoyed* coordinating everyone's lives. Seems she just felt an obligation, not a desire. Already she was looking forward to her nine- and ten-year-olds going to college so she could catch her breath and probably take a nap.

"But you have my number," she chirped, reverting to take-charge mom. "Please let me know what you decide about camp, and call me if there is anything you need. I can skip a soccer practice, I think," she said, and gave a nervous, guilty laugh.

"Thanks so much, Bernie. I don't think I'll need for you to skip practice, but the offer to take Alex to camp is so generous. I'm going to call the Y this afternoon, and I'll get back to you as soon as I figure out a plan."

I explained my situation to Shirley Austin, the coordinator of the YMCA summer program, and she was most accommodating.

"Oh, sure, Ms. Murphy, we'd be glad to have Alex three days a week. Mrs. Collins has already contacted us and told us you might be calling. She and her girls are real anxious for your daughter to join us, and we look forward to seeing her. Just download the on-line application and fill it out. Get us a copy of your daughter's inoculation record, and we'll get her registered."

Alex was in a glee over the prospect of going to day camp with Conner and Everette. The fact that Conner was a year older and thought she was cool delighted her.

That first Wednesday Alex had just finished packing her backpack with her towel, swimsuit, hat, sunscreen, a granola bar, and water bottle when Bernie wheeled her huge, silver Mercedes SUV into my driveway. I walked Alex to the car while she hopped excitedly beside me.

"Hey, Ms. Murphy," sang Conner and Everette in unison. "Hey, Alex, love your shirt. That's so cool!"

I leaned on Bernie's window and said, "I can't thank you enough for this. You're a life saver."

"My pleasure, Rowdy. The kids will have fun. Roger will have them home by 5:30." She reached over and took my hand and said, "I hope your treatment goes well today. I'll be thinking about you."

"Cool," I said, and we both laughed.

I squeezed her hand and waved them away. As I saw Bernie drive down the street, a sense of sadness came over me. It had taken cancer for me to become friends with my neighbor.

Twenty

C hemo was a bitch.
I don't care how you look at it, there's just nothing good you can say about it. As pleasant as everyone tried to make it for me, it beat me up and left me a weak, whimpering husk. And a raving bitch.

I swore I wouldn't be pigeonholed by my illness, but I was the classic cancer patient. I was ticking off the characteristics of each stage of the sickness as if I'd written the book. When I arrived at chemo for the first time, I'd already passed through the shock, disbelief, denial, and fear stages and had arrived, full blown, at the really pissed-off stage, more commonly and delicately known as the anger stage. And, by the way, these stages don't necessarily occur in this order, and there's no telling how long each will last. And here's the real kicker: once you've passed through a stage, there's no guarantee that it'll never come back. You might experience shock, disbelief, denial, and fear all in one day, only to be pretty chill for a few days. Then, blam, out of nowhere, disbelief and denial can blindside you all over again. It's an emotional roller coaster, the emotions being side effects of the illness, just as loss of appetite, fatigue, nausea, and hair loss.

Ah, the hair loss. To this day I can hardly say those words without tearing up. Cancer can be so cruel. It kicks you in the ass, and then it rips the hair right out of your head. How mean can it get?

For some cancer patients losing their hair is a badge of honor. They wear their baldness as if it were a beacon of bravery, a spit in the eye of cancer, an I'll show you, god damn it! Many cancer patients even shave their heads just as soon as they see their hair begin to fall. I guess it's one of the few things they feel they can control. They call the shots before chemo calls them for them. I admire their bravery, their bravado, and so wish I'd had their balls.

But for some patients the hair loss is devastating. I was of the devastated-variety cancer patient. To me losing my hair was the physical manifestation of the ravages taking place inside my body. It terrified me. But it also robbed me of a huge part of my identity—my beautiful, lush, copper-red, attention-grabbing hair.

It was my calling card. It was what attracted my only love to me. What would Mark think if he could see my lovely hair falling into large ringlets on the floor, in the shower, on my pillow, in my lap? Would he be repelled? Or would he comfort me and tell me that I'm not defined by my hair? I'll never know.

It starts in the hairbrush: a few more strands than normal, then a handful, then a clump. Sobbing is also a side effect of cancer, so when I saw my beautiful copper-red hair waving like a flag from my brush, I dissolved. I knew what was coming, and I knew I was helpless to prevent it. But I tried, nonetheless. I felt if I didn't wash my hair so briskly or brush it so vigorously, I could be the one, the only chemo patient who didn't lose her hair.

When it became apparent that cancer was stronger than I and that I wouldn't be that person who hung onto her hair, I looked on my list of *things you might need* that Sandy had compiled for me. I ran my finger down the page until I found Angel Wigs. I called and made an appointment.

I wrapped a huge scarf around my head, tied it tightly under my chin, and pulled it low on my forehead. I looked like a Ukrainian potato farmer's wife, but that didn't bother me. At least I didn't look like a breast cancer patient who was losing her hair.

Charmaine was waiting for me. Tall, thin, beautiful, with snow-white hair—her own, I believe—she looked to be in her early sixties. She had a soft peaches-and-cream complexion, and sparkling blue eyes. She wore pastel blue linen slacks and a matching sweater. I'd never seen a lovelier woman.

"Hi, Rowdy, please come in," she said in a soft, throaty voice. She took my arm gently and ushered me into her shop, closing and locking the door behind us, saying, "Angel Wigs is all yours, my dear, for as long as you need. We'll take our time."

The place was very comforting and warm. Soft classical music drifted from speakers, and there were pastel chintz slipper chairs and a love seat in an inviting grouping toward the back of the store.

"Just put your purse right over there, Rowdy, and let me get you something to drink. How about some juice or a soda. Maybe a glass of wine. I even have champagne, if you'd like."

"Champagne at ten in the morning?"

She placed her hand gently on my back, smiled coyly, and said sweetly, "Dear, you have earned champagne at any hour of the day or night you please."

"Okay, then," I said, "champagne it is."

When she floated through sheer curtains to pour champagne, I dropped my purse on the plushly-carpeted floor and, for the first time, noticed the shelves of wigs—wigs of every color, every cut, every length.

Charmaine returned with two flutes of champagne, handed one to me, and sat on the love seat. She patted the space beside her and said, "Come, join me."

I sat beside her and took a sip of my champagne. Charmaine sipped, too, and waited for me to start the conversation. Already I loved her, loved that she didn't push, loved that she was making me feel comfortable, loved that she was all mine for as long as I needed.

I reached up, untied my scarf, and let it slide from my head. Charmaine did not react, but just held me in her gentle gaze.

Then the tears spilled over my lids and slid down my face. She reached for a box of tissues, placed them on the love seat between us, and took my hand. And she let me cry.

When I showed signs of slowing, she said, "You hair is so beautiful. I know how sad you must be to lose it."

I just shook my head. Yes, I was so sad.

She continued to hold my hand, still giving me her undivided attention, letting me take my time.

Finally, I pulled a tissue from the box, blotted my eyes and face, blew my nose, and said, "Well, it looks like I'm not going to be able to hang on to this beautiful hair, so I guess I'm just going to have to get a wig."

Charmaine smiled and said, "Well, you're in luck because I have a wig for you."

And as sad as I was, her enthusiasm made me smile.

"Do I need to shave my head?" I asked.

"Not if you don't want to. We can tuck your hair inside your wig and just let it come out naturally."

"I'd like that."

"Okay, then, do you have any ideas about what you'd like? Do you want to go short and blonde, long and dark, or shall we stick with red? Some people like a drastic change, just for fun; others like to stick as close to their natural color and cut as they can."

"I think I'd like to stick with long and red."

"Good call, but I have to tell you that I don't have a wig in this shop as beautiful as your hair. But we'll find a pretty good match."

As I sipped my champagne, I watched Charmaine glide from shelf to shelf, pulling down every red wig she could find.

"I know you said long and red, but I thought you might like to try a few different styles, just for kicks. You might find something else you like."

First I tried on a short curly red wig. We both agreed that I looked like Little Orphan Annie, and I decided that wasn't the look I was going for.

Next I tried on a straight wig ending at my shoulders with bangs that hung to the middle of my eyes. I looked like an edgy fashion model.

Charmaine said, "All you need to do is suck in your cheeks, paint your lips black, and smoke one of those skinny brown cigars."

It felt good to laugh.

I settled on a long, red, wavy wig that looked similar to my own hair. I also bought a much shorter red wig, just for a change.

Charmaine pinned my thinning hair up on my head and pulled my new long, red hair into place. She styled it for me and slipped my other purchase in a bag. She hugged me warmly, and, seeing me to the door, said, "This has been such a pleasure, Rowdy. And you look beautiful. Not everyone could pull off that color. You take care, Sweetie. Bye, now."

I took some comfort in Charmaine's kindness, but I left knowing that I was returning to my life of cancer and chemo and nausea. I was just going to face it with new hair.

But the new hair did little to stave off the anger, the isolation, and the grief for the long haul. My time with Charmaine was merely salve, not a fix. Once the reality of wearing fake hair over my thinning real hair set in, my crappy attitude returned. I needed Mark to comfort me and tell me that we'd get through this together. My heart ached because I knew that wasn't going to happen. I took my pain out on everyone and everything. I yelled at Nick Nack, sending her scurrying for safety. I stomped around the house, flinging things in anger and frustration. I even lost patience with Alex, something I vowed I would not do. But I was powerless to the emotions that were part of the illness. I had to be mad. And hurt. And scared. And lonely,

So I took my new hair and my attitude and dragged myself back to the clinic. Holly, the nurse on duty, would always be waiting with a welcoming smile. Only I didn't want to be welcomed. I'd plop into my chair without making eye contact and let her begin the ordeal what would, by the following morning, have me crawling on the bathroom floor, weak and limp and oh, so sick.

And then the chipper chatter would begin. Other patients brought friends, daughters, mothers, sisters to keep them company. They'd knit and crochet, discuss books they were reading, movies they'd seen. They'd laugh and joke, but I couldn't understand what they were finding to laugh and joke about. *Cancer* was no joke. *Chemo* was no joke. This was serious business. How dare they laugh at it. They should be angry. And they should be silent. I wanted all those sick people to shut up and let the treatment do it's magic.

I'd ignore their attempts to draw me into their circles and would glare icily as they talked and laughed. Eventually, they turned their backs on me—just as I'd hoped they would—and talked in hushed tones.

An hour into my treatment—I could set my watch by it— Adrianna, volunteer do-gooder, would twirl into the clinic, smile firmly in place, prepared to bestow cheer on all of us, even those of us who made it clear that we did not want her cheer. Well, one of us made it clear she did not want her cheer. Make-up just so and clothes perfectly coordinated and tailored, she looked as if she were dressed for tea, rather than raining good cheer on cancer patients. Expensive gold jewelry dripped from her ears and jangled on her wrists, and happiness at being the well one in the room oozed from her pores. I resented everything about her: her prosperity, her polished appearance, her joy, her health. Especially her health.

For weeks she attempted to draw me out with her good humor, but I was having none of it. I was still stuck in pissed-off stage.

When she'd approach, I'd turn my head, so as to ignore her. Around week four of my treatment, she made her usual rounds, and when she approached me, I exuded my customary ass-hat attitude. But she wasn't having it.

"Here, Rowdy, I have something for you," she said.

Even at my rudest, I couldn't ignore her.

When I turned to face her, I found her holding a package out to me, a gift wrapped in balloon-festooned paper and tied with curly, red ribbon. I was so shaken by her thoughtfulness that I couldn't even reach to take the present from her. So she gently laid it in my lap.

"It's just socks, my dear. My feet used to get so cold during chemo, and I was always forgetting my socks. Sweet Nurse Holly could always manage to scrounge up a pair for me. I thought your feet might get cold." Then sensing my discomfort, she smiled sweetly and said, "Bye, now," turned, and walked out of the clinic.

I looked up to find all the other patients staring at me as my cheeks flamed with embarrassment. Quickly they returned their attention to their daughters, friends, mothers and allowed me to tend my shame in private.

I had thought that Adrianna was just a bored housewife do-gooder whose husband had made a boatload of money and she felt guilty with all her riches and all her free time. And now she was *giving back*. Isn't that what do-gooders do?

"I give back because *I have been so richly blessed.*"

Adrianna wasn't just a do-gooder, though being kind to a disrespectful, unappreciative lout every Wednesday was a pretty worthy deed. She had once been right where I was sitting, had felt just what I was feeling, had been just as frightened as I.

I fingered the bow on my gift but, for some reason, was not ready to dive in, to fully accept another's kindness. I closed my eyes and held tight to the present, Adrianna's gentle words still fresh. Finally, I pulled the ribbons until they fell away into a curly, red pile in my lap. It reminded me of my lush, red curly hair falling into a pile in my lap.

I usually rip into a present, balling the wrapping and tossing it in the trash, insensitive to the love the giver put into wrapping it. That day I gently pulled back the tape at both ends and smoothed the paper as I unwrapped my gift. They were socks, yes, but they were no ordinary socks. There were three pairs: one pair had colorful stripes and a jagged, pointed cuff like a jester's hat; another pair was orange with black cats and skeletons; the third pair was red with decorated green trees and bells hanging from the cuffs.

And they all had individual toes.

I pushed the afghan away, exposing my cold, bare feet and unpainted toenails. I had lost interest in toenail night, along with just about everything else in my life. We were almost two months away from Halloween, but I wanted to wear my black and orange socks. I pulled them on my feet and all the way up to my knees. They warmed me instantly. And my toes: each had its own little casing. I wiggled them back and forth, and the wiggling made me giggle. I wiggled them faster and laughed out loud. People turned to stare. I lifted my foot and waved it in the air. And I just couldn't stop laughing. I felt like an idiot, but I didn't care. As I laughed loudly, the tears flowed down my cheeks.

"They have toes!" I yelled between giggles and tears.

Everyone must have felt that I had turned a corner because the room erupted in loud laughter.

I had been wearing my victimhood like a shroud, lamenting Mark's abandoning me and absconding with all the friends, leaving me to deal with cancer alone. All it took was silly socks to show me everyone who was waiting patiently for me with laughter and open arms and open hearts. All I needed was to open my own heart and accept their offer of love and friendship.

And my very best friend was waiting for me at home, with the greatest of patience, as she had been since the day she came to live with me over three years before.

When my treatment ended, I removed my silly Halloween socks and wrapped them neatly, along with the others, back in my festive paper. I stood to leave and turned to the other patients.

"Bye, bye. Thanks. Thanks to all of you."

One by one they turned my way and smiled.

As I headed for the door, they called after me, "Bye, Rowdy, see you next Wednesday."

That's when I realized that they all knew my name. Sadly, I didn't know any of theirs.

But I would.

Twenty-one

I had been stuck in anger, angry at everything and everyone. I had become intolerant of Nick Nack's hovering, and she was a perfect target for my rage. As my illness had progressed, I had begun yelling at her again, yet she never cowered. She just smiled up at me with her loving eyes, as if she understood and accepted the cause for my verbal abuse. When she got too close, I'd give her a shove. She always returned to my side. But no matter how sick I got, no matter how angry I got, and no matter how I took my sickness out on her, she never held it against me and continued to love me—a phenomenon that baffled me.

When the fallout of the chemo brought me to my knees on the cold tile of the bathroom floor, Nick Nack hovered in concern. She would lean into my side and wedge her nose into my underarm. Too weak to yell or shove her away, I just had to close the door and shut her out, assuring that I wouldn't have to contend with her attentiveness, as well as the nausea. She would lie on the floor outside the bathroom, breathing into the crack beneath the door. From time to time she would sigh in exasperation because she couldn't tend to me as she thought she should. By the time I would emerge, she'd appear frantic with concern.

The day Adrianna gave me the socks with the toes, I felt I had cleared a hurdle of some kind. I laughed for the first time since— well, I guess I hadn't laughed a great hearty belly laugh since that day Mark walked in the back door and announced that he was leaving me. That's a long time to go without a really good laugh. And to think it took silly socks.

When I got home from my chemo treatment, Nick Nack was waiting for me just as she had done every day since she had come to live with us. This time, though, I didn't brush past her as I usually did or tell her to get out of my way. Instead, I knelt beside her and, for the first time, put my arms cautiously around her neck. She didn't seem surprised but acted as though she knew this moment would eventually arrive. I buried my face in her beautiful, shiny black fluff, knowing that she'd never bite me, never hurt me in any way. Being afraid of dogs was no longer an excuse for avoiding Nick Nack. She had taken my intolerance and abuse since she had come into my life, yet she had always stuck by my side.

I said, "Thank you for never giving up on me, Nick Nack. You're a good girl."

I expected her to be happy that I had finally paid attention to her, had finally given her the cuddling she had earned. But she didn't treat me differently than she ever had. She didn't leap for joy. She didn't slobber on me with gratitude. She just let me hug her for as long as I needed. When I stood to leave, she followed me down the hall to the kitchen, just as she'd always done.

The next Wednesday morning I grabbed my purse, my keys, and my silly toe socks and headed for the door. Nick Nack followed me and sat obediently, as always.

I opened the door wide and said, "Let's go, Girl."

She looked up at me quizzically, and I said, "It's okay, Nick Nack, you can go."

Still she stared at me, confused.

So I said the words that Alex always yelled that would make Nick Nack streak out the door: "Car, Nick Nack, car!"

She loved riding in the car with Mark and Alex; however, I'd never invited her to be my passenger. When she heard the word *car*, she lifted one paw timidly across the threshold and stared up into my face.

She was so accustomed to my screaming, "Stop, Nick Nack! Come back here, Nick Nack! Damn it, Nick Nack, get back in the house!"

This was all new to her; she wasn't quite sure what I expected of her. We were both charting new territory. We'd just have to make up the rules as we went along.

When Nick Nack was certain that I was going to let her ride in the car with me, she padded out of the house and waited while I locked the front door behind us. She followed me down the sidewalk to my car, looking up at me from time to time to gauge my mood. I opened the passenger door of the car and coaxed her in. Like a polite lady, she hopped up onto the seat, sat quietly, and peered out the window, ready to go wherever I'd take her. She rode silently for the twenty-minute trip, craning her neck to see the scenery along the way.

When we arrived at the hospital, she waited patiently as I parked the car, got out, and came around to open her door to free her. She hopped down and trotted along beside me as I headed for the hospital entrance. We were met with curious stares, but no one protested or stopped us until I reached the treatment room.

"Well, Rowdy, I just don't know. No one has ever brought a dog to chemo, and the other patients...," Holly let her voice trail.

"There's nothing about dogs in my long list of instructions. It does say, though, that a friend may accompany me and stay with me during my treatments. Nick Nack is my friend."

I scanned the room to gauge the other patients' reactions to Nick Nack's presence. Since the beginning of my treatments, I had been none too hospitable to any of these people. But last week they had witnessed my silly toe waving and laughter and tears. Perhaps they'd see my bringing Nick Nack to chemo as just another step toward my healing. I hoped they would. Some offered weak smiles before they returned their attention to their friends or their knitting or their reading. Others didn't rouse from their naps. But no one protested.

Holly shrugged and said, "We'll give it a try."

As I settled into my chair and put on my Christmas toe socks, readying myself for my treatment, Nick Nack stood only inches from Holly as she inserted the needle into the back of my hand and made sure the solution was flowing properly. Once she had covered me with an afghan and promised to be nearby if I needed anything, she left Nick Nack to examine all of her handiwork. She sniffed the needle in my hand and followed the tube up to the bag of fluid hanging on the IV stand. When she was certain that everything was in order, she made a quick check of my afghan before settling on the floor by my side.

I reached down and ran my hand through the downy, black fluff on her back. She showed no reaction at all. Nick Nack had always reacted to me the same way, regardless of how I treated her. She was just there for me, to be whatever I needed her to be, if the time ever came that I needed her at all. And I found that stroking her beautiful black coat soothed me and gave me great comfort. I thought of the years she had been by my side, ready to give me comfort, and my stubbornness had not allowed me to accept it. I nodded off, soaking up years of comfort Nick Nack was saving just for me.

After an hour Adrianna breezed in with her usual flourish, skirts rustling, wrists jangling. On that day she didn't annoy me. I roused, stretched, and motioned with a crooked finger for her to come over. She nearly danced to my side and sat on the corner of my chair, facing me.

"Thank you so much for my socks, Adrianna," I said and pulled my foot from under the blanket to show her my tinkling Christmas pair.

"I'm glad you like them, Rowdy."

"Well, Adrianna, it's not the gift I love so much. It's the thought that went into it. Why did you do something so thoughtful when I have been such a bitch?"

Adrianna reached over and clasped my hand. "Oh, Rowdy, you haven't been a bitch. You have been a sick, terrified woman. I've been right where you have been. I understand what you're going through."

Knowing full well Adrianna could never behave as atrociously as I had, I smiled and said, "Were you a bitch?"

Smiling back and standing to leave, she just said, "We all react differently."

When my treatment ended and Holly released me from my tether, I said, "Come on, Nick Nack, time to head on home. You did a great job."

When we left the hospital, a hot blast of air greeted us. Indian Summer had set in. We're accustomed here in the South to a resurgence of summer in mid-September, but the renewed heat and humidity had me wilting and wet with perspiration by the time I reached the car. Nick Nack panted as she trotted along beside me and dragged herself into her seat and melted into a puddle.

I cranked up the air and turned on the radio.

"Summer's back, folks," said Greg Fishel, Raleigh's favorite meteorologist. "Expect temps to reach into the low 90's today and tomorrow and the humidity to do the same."

On the way home I let the air vents blow into Nick Nack's and my faces while Sara Bareilles and I sang Alex's and my favorite song, *Brave*,[7] and Nick Nack kept time with her tail. When we reached home, we raced from the car to the house before the heat could catch up with us.

I had just closed the front door and dropped my purse on the hall table when I heard a knock. Nick Nack sat patiently and ladylike beside the door to greet our guest, whomever that might be. I opened it to find Madge Hummel, head librarian at the library where I volunteered, standing rigidly, clutching a potted plant in her arms.

Madge is the stereotypical librarian of 1940's fiction. Steel gray hair pulled back severely into a bun and cat-eye glasses on a string, she wore long dark skirts and cardigans, paired with lace-up shoes and dark stockings, summer and winter. I had no idea she knew me from Adam, yet there she stood on my porch, looking sharp and crisp in the withering heat.

"Rowdy, I just heard. I am so sorry I didn't know," she said, thrusting her potted plant at me.

I took it from her and stepped back, saying, "Please come in out of the heat, Madge."

When she crossed the threshold and saw my dog, looking like a bear, smiling up at her, she gasped, stepped back, and drew her arms into her chest.

"Don't worry, she's a kitten." And to Nick Nack I said, "Go on, Nick Nack, and lie down."

The smile disappeared from Nick Nack's animated face, so disappointed that she wasn't going to be invited to the party. She hung her head, sighed, turned around, and sauntered pitifully to the kitchen. Nick Nack could be dramatic, but I knew her feelings would soon recover and that she'd forgive me.

I led Madge into the living room, where I placed her plant on the coffee table and said, "Sit down, please. Could I get you something to drink?"

"No, thank you. I'll keep you only a minute."

She sat on the edge of my wing-back chair, ramrod straight, hands in her lap, and said, "Rowdy, we had no idea you were ill. I'm so sorry. Is there anything at all we can do for you?"

Still taken aback by her visit, I just stammered and said, "Thank you for your concern, but I've recovered from the surgery and radiation, and now I'm taking chemo treatments."

"Rowdy, we miss you so much at the library. You are the best volunteer we've ever had. Most volunteers come to the library to socialize and make contacts. You, on the other hand, come to work, not chit-chat. I fear I don't compliment my staff as some feel I should, but that's just not my style. I go to my job to work, and I expect my staff to do the same. But please know that I appreciate what you do and hope you'll be able to return to help us."

I was moved by her candor and pleased to learn that she actually knew me and appreciated my help.

"Thank you, Madge. That means so much to me."

"Everyone sends their best wishes," she said as she reached into her purse, pulled out an envelope, and handed it to me. "We all signed this for you." Clearing her throat self-consciously and avoiding eye contact, she said, "Well, I've kept you long enough." Then she stood abruptly and inched uncomfortably toward the door, adding, "Please know that your position will always be open for you."

When she left, I returned to the living room and opened the card. It was signed by everyone who worked and volunteered at the library. Each wrote a personal note and signed it with much love. They all cared; they all knew me. They just went to the library to work, not to socialize, make contacts, or chit chat.

I was still sitting on the sofa, re-reading all the well wishes from the library staff, when Alex came bounding in from school, her face flushed from the heat, her wet curls stuck to her face.

She threw her backpack down in the hall and exclaimed, "It's so hot out there!"

She dragged herself into the living room and flopped down on the sofa beside me. I could feel the heat rising from her body.

"Whatcha got?"

I held my card to my heart and said, "Friends."

I had missed my work at the library, and I was pleased to learn that the staff did know me, did appreciate my help. I considered, briefly, returning to volunteer but realized I needed more. Along with all its negative side effects, cancer also had positive fall-out. I had come to appreciate time more than I ever had. I didn't know how much of it I had left, and I wanted to cherish ever second, use every moment to its fullest. And though I had once loved taking care of my books, I didn't want to spend my time in solitude. I needed human contact, friends who could chat with me without being *shushed!*

But Madge's visit had touched my heart. It was a wonderful surprise when I least expected it and a kindness when I needed it the most.

Still clutching my card to my heart, I said to Alex, "Want a snack?"

I was way too hot to move and was so hoping she'd say, "No."

But, instead, she said, "Just some juice, I think."

So we dragged our sticky bodies to the kitchen, where Alex filled Nick Nack's water bowl, and I poured us some apple juice.

We ate a light supper, and Alex did her homework at the kitchen table while I washed the dishes and then joined her to lend a hand. After she had finished her math, she voluntarily turned in early, too hot to do much else.

Before closing up for the night, I moved Madge's plant from the coffee table to the kitchen counter, where I pinched off a few brown leaves and gave it a drink of water. I was still so touched, yet surprised by the thoughtfulness.

I said, "Let's go to bed, Nick Nack. We've had an eventful day."

She joined me as I turned out the light and headed down the hall. I trudged up the stairs, the oppressive heat weighing me down, making it difficult to put one foot ahead of the other. The air conditioner had been pumping non-stop, but still the air in the house felt stifling. It was hard for the old system to win the battle with both heat and humidity that hovered near ninety.

I grabbed the banister with my right hand, slowly hoisting myself one challenging step at a time. With my left hand I waved my filmy, cotton nightgown back and forth, in an effort to create a little breeze on my sticky legs. Nick Nack climbed along with me, dragging herself through the thick cloud of heat. When we reached the landing at the top of the stairs, she went straight to her rug by my bed, flopped down, and panted herself into sleep. I paused to catch my breath, still fanning my gown about my thighs.

I peered into Alex's room and found that she had thrown back the sheet and shed her pajama top, tossing it in a puddle on the floor. She lay splayed like a starfish in the center of her double bed, wearing only her ruffled pajama bottoms, the ceiling fan gently stirring the muggy air above her.

I tiptoed into her room and welcomed the semi-cool breeze from the fan. I sat gently on the edge of the bed, so as not to awaken my daughter. Getting back to sleep in the muggy heat would have been a chore.

The almost-full moon shone through the window, bathing the room and my little girl in a comforting blue. I smoothed the wet curls away from Alex's face and watched her smile in her sleep, her dimples coming to life.

I looked at her precious body, budding, curving, and straining to be a woman. Soon she would need a bra, sanitary pads, and someone to understand and help her corral her raging, hormonal emotions.

One day she would erupt when she couldn't find her barrettes. The next day she would stamp her foot because her favorite skirt was in the soiled laundry. Then she would sob because Sarah Jane snubbed her and Scott talked to another girl.

The pain would ease, and soon she would leave her barrettes at a sleep-over and not care; she'd outgrow her skirt or find a much cuter one at The Gap. She and Sarah Jane would hug and cry and pledge their undying friendship. And she would forget Scott as soon as Brian held her hand.

But while the hormones raged, these slights, these losses would seem insurmountable, and she wouldn't be able to deal with the weight of their cruelty alone. She would need someone to understand. She would need her mother.

When my hormones kicked in and dealing with missing barrettes seemed an impossible task that sent me screaming to my room, Mama was my comforter, my understander. As I lay face down on my bed, sobbing over my current tragedy, she would join me in my suffering.

She'd lie beside me, rubbing my back, running her fingers through my hair, always cooing, "I know, I know."

She really didn't have to know the content of the crisis. She just needed to know that her confused daughter needed her comfort until the pain passed. She gave all my tantrums equal weight, treating them all the same. My wonderful mother knew that when you're an emotional teenager, lost barrettes and soiled skirts and girlfriend slights and boyfriend betrayals all hurt, and they all need an "I know, I know."

As I watched my still-smiling child sleep, I prayed, "Oh, please

God, don't let me die and leave her. Please let me live so that I can assure my confused, emotional teenager that 'I know, I know.'"

While I begged God to let me stick around, the smile and its dimples disappeared from Alex's face and were replaced with a quivering lip and a painful little cry. Had someone's thoughtlessness hurt my child? Was she feeling the weight of her parents' separation? Was she frightened by her mother's illness? It didn't matter what was making her cry out in her sleep. Whatever it was, it hurt.

So I lay beside her, and ignoring the stickiness of our skin, I gathered her in my arms, gently rubbed her back, and cooed, "I know, I know."

While Alex watched me lie motionless on the bathroom floor or hover over the toilet, vomiting until I sobbed from pain and exhaustion, there was absolutely nothing I could do to allay her fears. It was what it was. Her mother had breast cancer and was very, very ill. My doctors and I were doing everything in our power to assure that I would survive the ravages of the disease, but, in the meantime, the whole ordeal was damn terrifying—for Alex and for me.

But hovering in the back of my mind, yet years away from invading Alex's brain, was the realization that she was carrying around in her budding breasts the predisposition for breast cancer. The knowledge broke my heart and made me sob with sorrow. I could endure my own breast cancer, but I could not imagine witnessing the child I loved beyond everything having to deal with the same horror.

I'd also learned that women whose mothers have had breast cancer before the age of forty have twice the odds of developing breast cancer themselves. When Alex got older, I'd have to tell her. Her doctor would have to explain about genetic markers and predisposition to the disease and the odds of her suffering the ravages that her mother had endured. How could we break the news to her gently? How could we keep her from falling to pieces under the weight of that terrifying sentence? How could we convince her to be vigilant without being obsessive, cautious without being forever fearful. I wanted her to understand the risks but not let them consume her life.

I knew the time would come. But I also knew that I could buy some time, could deal with my own sentence while I watched her enjoy her childhood innocence for a few more years.

The realization, though, is that all women should be vigilant, cautious, aware. Sure, women with incidents of breast cancer in their families have a greater risk of developing the disease, but the disease has to start somewhere.

It started with me.

As I whispered, "I know, I know," Alex's cries calmed and the dimples returned.

Ignoring the oppressive heat, I held her even closer, kissing her dewy cheek. She turned on her side, facing me, and reached for a handful of my wig hair. She twiddled it with her fingers, just as she had done with my long, natural hair when she was an infant.

"It's hot," she said and jolted me awake.

I had fallen asleep, my wig still on my head but now askew. Alex and I had spent the night holding onto each other. The sun was rising, and I was betting we were going to have another scorcher.

"I know, Sweetie."

"It's okay, though," she said, still holding on, reaching once again for my hair. She closed her eyes and twiddled.

It was suffocating, but I'd hang on as long as Alex wanted, because all crises are important, and my child needed an "I know, I know".

Twenty-two

I was crumpled on the bathroom floor, my head resting on the toilet seat. Nick Nack was by my side. I had decided that I needed her burrowing her nose in my armpit, rather than under the crack of the bathroom door. Trying to get rid of her had been an exhausting job, and I hadn't had the strength to fight both cancer and Nick Nack. Now I cherished her presence and was sorry that I had ever resisted her devotion.

And I knew for certain that she really didn't want to bite me in the neck.

Then the phone rang. My morning of retching had left me too depleted to drag myself to a prone position. So I just let it ring.

When the answering machine kicked in, I heard Mark shouting, "Rowdy, pick up! Rowdy, pick up!"

Had Alex been with her father and Tawni, the urgency in his voice would have given me the adrenalin to propel myself from bathroom floor to kitchen telephone in a single bound. But Alex was safe at school.

I didn't care what Mark had to say; I did *not* want to pick up, did *not* want to talk with him. But he persisted. When the machine clicked off, he called right back.

Same message: "Rowdy, pick up! Rowdy, pick up!" I still let it go. His messages became insistent: "Rowdy, I know you're there. I saw your car in the driveway. Pick up!"

I knew he wasn't going to give up.

But I was exhausted and drenched with perspiration. Those

161

episodes after chemo left me weak and wobbly, in a puddle of sweat. But I willed myself to stand and made my way on rubbery knees to the telephone, clutching the wall all the way. The phone was silent for the moment, but I knew for certain Mark would call back. He did not give up.

Since he had passed up his Paris honeymoon to care for *my* child, he expected us to be buddies. Just like Alex, Mark couldn't understand why we couldn't be just one big happy family. We all loved Alex, didn't we? That should be glue enough to stick us all together and make us real chummy. I just wasn't feeling it.

Just as I expected, the phone rang again as I reached the kitchen. I picked up.

"Oh, Rowdy, thank god!"

"What is it, Mark?"

"Rowdy, the best news: the twins have arrived, a little early, but they are healthy and gorgeous. Anna is a little over five pounds, and Zach is almost six pounds. And Tawni was such a trooper. I'm so proud of her. She's as beautiful as ever—not a hair out of place. And, Rowdy, the babies look just like Alex."

Well, first of all, the babies could *not* have looked like Alex since Alex looked exactly like me, and I hadn't had a damn thing to do with those twins. And, most importantly, I didn't give a crap how beautiful and brave Tawni was. As kind and accommodating as she'd been caring for Alex, Mark made it really easy for me to resent her when he sang her praises. What the hell was he thinking? I had heard of people screwing their brains out, but I believe this was the first case of someone actually doing it. The man was clueless.

"Rowdy, you there?"

"Mark, this isn't a good time."

"Rowdy, how long do you intend to punish me? Isn't it time we buried the hatchet? Can't you just be happy for me on the happiest day of my life?"

The happiest day of his life? I thought the day of Alex's birth had been the happiest day of his life.

I so wanted to say, "Mark, I'm dealing with cancer alone because my husband dumped me for a hottie, and I'm heaving my guts out as a result of a chemo treatment that I also endured alone because my husband left me for a hottie, and, as hard as I'm trying, I'm still angry as hell at you for leaving me and don't give a rat's ass about your new and perfect life!"

Instead, I said, "Mark, I had chemo yesterday, and I'm really, really sick this morning."

So he just said, "Oh, okay, sorry. Let me know when you feel like talking. Bye."

And he hung up.

I threw my phone across the room, lay splayed on the cool kitchen floor and let the tears fill my ears. As far as I'd come, as much as I had endured, Mark and his new perfect life and his cluelessness could still break my heart and make me cry.

As I lay on the floor, Nick Nack clicked across the tile and stood over my lifeless body. She peered into my face, her nose just inches from mine. Sensing that I was too spent to move, she lay down, nestled close beside me, and let me hold onto her while I drifted into sleep.

❧❦

And that's where Alex found me when she came in from school—sound asleep on the cold kitchen floor, clinging to a dog.

"Mommy, are you okay?"

She had been calling me *Mommy* a lot lately. Calling me *Mommy* had become Alex's way of letting me know that she was scared and needed to be comforted. My sickness frightened her so. What child isn't terrified to see her mother weak and ashen and heaving her guts? It's just not something we want our kids to witness. But sometimes we have no choice.

Most mothers prefer to meet their kids with milk and cookies when they arrive home from school. But there I was, weak from my hours on the cold bathroom tile, hugging a dog. No wonder Alex was calling me *Mommy*.

And though I wasn't in the best condition to do it, I had to tell her that she had a new little brother and a new little sister.

And I had to act happy about it.

"Hey, Darlin'," I said, as cheerily as I could manage from the kitchen floor. "Nick Nack and I were just sitting here chatting. Guess I must have drifted off."

She didn't say a word, just stood there wide-eyed. I was certain she wasn't buying my explanation, but it was the best I had to offer.

"Run put your backpack away and wash your hands, and I'll get you some milk and cookies."

Slowly she backed out of the kitchen, still eyeing me suspiciously.

I clutched the edge of the counter and hoisted myself to my feet. I opened the fridge and grabbed a bottle of ginger ale. I needed a quick fix to settle my queasy stomach and get myself pumping again. I took a swig straight from the two-liter bottle and returned it to the shelf. I leaned over the kitchen sink and splashed some cold water in my face and, with my wet hands, tamped down my disheveled wig and straightened it on my head. I mopped my dripping face with a paper towel.

When Alex returned, still looking uneasy, she found a glass of milk and three Oreos on a plate. I thought two cookies constituted the appropriate treat, but the third was my guilt portion: guilt for being sick and not being able to care for my child the way I wanted; guilt for a broken home that was beyond my control; guilt because the cookies were not homemade.

"Thanks, Mommy," said my little girl, as she bit into a cookie and, taking a swig of milk, gave herself a white mustache. The smile was returning to her eyes, and she revealed chocolate teeth.

I sat down beside her and leaned forward till we were eye to eye.

"Would you like to hear some really good news?" I whispered, conspiratorially.

She was anticipating the twins' arrival, had been for months. She surely knew what the good news was, but instead of blurting it, she just clapped her hands and yipped excitedly, "Oh, tell me, tell me, Mama!"

I smiled broadly and stretched my eyes wide, for my child's sake, and said, "You're a big sister."

I didn't need to elaborate. She was up, twirling and shrieking, forgetting all about her after-school snack and, I was hoping, the sight of her mom huddled on the kitchen floor, clinging to a dog.

"When can I see them? When, Mama, when? Oh, I have to see them. I have to go right now. Oh, please, Mama, please!"

"Hold on, Sweetie. Let me call your dad. If he says right now is okay, we'll get you to the hospital to see them."

"Oh, Mama, thank you so much," she cried and sailed into my arms, hugging me close, leaving chocolate smudges on my tee shirt.

Then she said, "I love you, Mommy," and looked up into my face, smiling sweetly.

Somehow she understood this was Mark's joy and Tawni's joy and her joy. But it wasn't my joy. She was my joy, and she wanted me to know that she knew that.

Yes, children *can* be pretty smart at times.

I called Mark, and he was in that jolly, new-daddy mood that lasts until the first time the baby throws up on him and cries through the night.

"I'll be right over. I can't wait for Alex to see the babies. And after I take her to the hospital, we can get a pizza, and then she can stay with me tonight, if that's okay with you."

"That sounds fine, Mark. Will you be able take her to school in the morning?"

"Yeah, sure. Then I'll go pick her up after school for the weekend. She can help me get Tawni and the babies home from the hospital."

I thanked him profusely and hung up quickly, before he had a chance to rethink the plan and back out.

I went to Alex's room to help her pack her bag for her weekend with her daddy. After she threw in her pajamas, her school and weekend clothes, and her toothbrush, she clapped her hand over her mouth and exclaimed, "Oh, I almost forgot!"

As soon as she'd heard of Tawni's pregnancy, she'd begun saving her allowance. When she'd amassed enough, she bought receiving blankets for the babies and wrapped them herself. She retrieved them from the back of her closet and gently placed the presents in her overnight bag.

"All ready," she said, shivering with excitement.

"Well, then, let's go downstairs and wait for Daddy," I chirped, sounding a whole lot cheerier than I actually felt.

Mark strolled in, glowing with excitement, looking much too old to be the father of newborn babies.

"Well, let's go, Alex. Anna and Zach can't wait to meet their big sister."

"Oh, Daddy," she said, "you're so funny. The babies don't know who I am."

"Oh, yes, they do. When I left the hospital, they both said, 'Where's Alex. We want our sister, Alex.'"

Alex just rolled her eyes and said, "Oh, Daaaad."

"Thanks, Rowdy, I'll have her back Sunday afternoon around five, if that's okay with you."

"Sure, that's fine," I said, wrapping my arms around myself, trying to hold myself together, trying not to expose my raw, vulnerable nerves. I had known it was coming, but I still wasn't prepared. It hurt. It just hurt.

Alex shimmied with excitement, oblivious to her mother's anguish, as she ran out of the house screaming over her shoulder, "Come on, Daddy!"

❧❧❧

The weekend was longer and lonelier than most. I couldn't seem to salve those raw nerves, no matter how hard I tried. I just clung to Nick Nack and waited for Alex's return. Nick Nack sensed I needed her more than usual and never left my side. Late Sunday afternoon I was lying on the living room sofa, Nick Nack on the floor beside me. I was waiting there for Alex when she came bursting through the front door, more excited than I'd ever seen her. And I was painfully aware that something about her was different. She seemed older. She looked like a big sister.

"Oh, my gosh, Mama, they are so precious!" she cried, dropping her bag and plopping down on the sofa beside me. "Tawni wrapped them in my receiving blankets, and she let me carry Anna home from the hospital. Can you believe that? And I got to feed them their bottles. And Tawni taught me how to change their diapers. The babies' cribs are in the living room, so I got to sleep right beside them. When they woke up in the middle of the night, Tawni and I got up and took care of them. Oh, Mama, it's just wonderful. I just can't wait to see them again. I just love them so much!"

As sad as I was, I was glad for Alex's joy. She had gone through so much with Mark's and my divorce and my illness. She deserved this happiness. She deserved to be a big sister.

I reached out and pulled her to me. I wrapped my arms around her, kissed her forehead, and said, "I'm so happy for you, Darlin'. I know you are going to be a wonderful big sister."

❧❧❧

"Have you lost your mind, Mark? Surely you could have found another house, another neighborhood in this entire city."

"But, Rowdy, it's convenient. Alex can come and go when she pleases, can see the babies whenever she likes."

I understood that Mark and Tawni needed to find a bigger place. They didn't have room in their toy house with the Easy Bake Oven for two adults, two babies, and a sometimes-there nine-year old.

But a block and a half from my house?

It was just way too close for comfort, and it felt so intrusive. I didn't want Mark popping in whenever he pleased. I didn't want to run the risk of bumping into beautiful, busty, fashionable, fun Tawni at my grocery store. And I especially didn't want to have to see the babies, the physical evidence of Mark's infidelity. I didn't think that was too much to ask, but, then, I hadn't been getting much of what I'd asked for lately.

Despite my protests, Mark, Tawni, and the babies went right ahead with their plans to relocate to my neighborhood. They'd taken everything else. Did they really need to add insult to injury by claiming my neighborhood as their own, as well?

However, once I got over the shock of having my ex and his new family living just around the corner, I had to agree with Mark that it was very convenient. We no longer had to coordinate transportation; when it came time for Alex to go to her dad's, she'd just kiss me good-bye and walk out the door. And since she had a room of her own at their house, she didn't even have to pack a bag. She had clothes, pajamas, tooth brush—all the essentials—at her *other* house. And she handled the transition with such ease, such maturity—with much more maturity than I. I was very proud of her.

And I figured as long as the happy family stayed a block and a half away and I didn't have to interact with them, I'd be just fine. But, of course, the chances of that happening were nil.

⋘⋙

I was boiling the water for our macaroni, waiting for Alex to come from her weekend with the babies, when I heard her at the front door: "Mama, there's somebody here to see you."

I turned the burner down on the stove, rinsed and dried my hands, made sure my wig was on straight, and headed for the front hall. There I found Alex and Tawni wrestling a twin carriage through my front door.

"I'm sorry to barge in unannounced, Rowdy, but we were out strolling the babies, and Alex insisted. She wouldn't take *no* for an answer. I hope we haven't caught you at a bad time."

"No. Sure. Come on in," I said, none too cordially.

The two of them maneuvered the contraption into my living room, and I said, "Please, Tawni, won't you sit down?"

I offered only out of the southern hospitality my mother had taught me but was so hoping she'd decline. She did not.

"Sure, thanks," she said as she perched on a chair, her wonderful legs stretching to the other side of the room.

"Oh, Mama, look! Didn't I tell you they were adorable? Aren't they precious?"

And they were. They looked like duplicate Gerber babies with their big blue eyes, dimpled chins, and downy caps of golden hair, both of them cooing like little angels. They were, indeed, beautiful babies.

But they were no more beautiful than their mother, who was all toned and tanned, with her body returned to pre-baby size-two condition, her long, blonde hair perfectly coifed, her nails perfectly manicured. I was so hoping that she wouldn't open her mouth and say something nice or give me cupcakes because I so wanted to hate her. I wanted to hurt her. I wanted to pinch her, but she had nothing to pinch. I wanted to force feed her Little Debbie snack cakes.

All of a sudden I was so grateful that the babies were there. They gave me something to talk about with this other-worldly Tawni.

"They're so cute, Tawni."

"Thank you, Rowdy. Mama says they look just like I looked when I was a baby."

Tawni had been a baby. I'd seen her only as a sultry, flaxen-haired vixen, as if she had sprung from the earth fully grown and gorgeous. But she had once been a baby, someone's daughter, an innocent child who had grown up to be a mother. And she stared at her children adoringly, the same way I stared at Alex.

Then she looked over at my child and said, "I just pray they turn out like Alex. She's a wonderful little girl. I love her so much."

Damn it! I couldn't pinch her.

I had assumed that once her babies arrived, she'd tire of Alex and push her aside. But as she talked about my daughter, she looked at her with the same love and affection she had for her own infants.

Then she stood abruptly and said, "I hate to run, but Mark is going to keep the babies while I go for my labs."

Labs? What labs? Was Tawni ill? Why hadn't anyone told me? And what kind of lab work would she be having done on a Sunday afternoon?

"Tawni, I don't mean to pry, but are you ill?"

"Ill? No. Why would you think I was ill?"

"Well, you said you had to go for your labs."

She looked at me quizzically and then laughed, "Oh, no, not labs. Laps. I'm going to the University pool to swim laps. Gotta keep these abs toned," she said as she slapped her flat, tighter-than-a-drum stomach, making a sharp thumping sound.

There I stood with my bald head covered in fake hair, hoping the brutal chemo was shrinking my tumor. There Tawni stood with her blonde mane flowing, hoping the laps would shrink her abs.

Different priorities.

Maybe I *could* find something to pinch, after all.

"Well, see ya," Tawni chirped, as she kissed Alex and strolled the babies out my front door and down the steps on her muscled, longer-than-should-be-allowed legs.

Twenty-three

My sidekick and I climbed the stairs to bed. While Nick Nack did her twirling and settling-down ritual, I went to the bathroom to brush my teeth and put on my nightgown. When I returned, I found her lounging at the foot of my bed on my great grandmother's quilt.

It was a nondescript quilt that would have meant nothing to anyone except the young women who took possession generation after generation. My great-great grandmother Ruth made it for her daughter's hope chest. My great grandmother Catie Caroline wanted a scrap quilt, not one of those frilly wedding quilts all those silly girls wanted.

"Well, Darlin', don't you want something pretty for your wedding night?" her mother asked.

"Oh, Mama, don't make me have one of those prissy things like Esther Ann and Bertie. I'd rather die. They're so boring and unoriginal. I want a scrap quilt made from all our discarded clothes."

So great-grandmother Catie Caroline took to her marriage a quilt made from christening dresses, debutante gowns, nightshirts, house smocks, and any other odd mismatched scraps she could find. And the more mismatched the scraps, the better she loved it.

Catie Caroline adored her quilt and loved telling everyone who would listen, much to her husband Hugh's embarrassment, that all of her girls had been conceived under her wonderful mismatched scrap quilt.

"Why, it's because of that wonderful mismatched hodgepodge of a quilt that my girls are all unique, eccentric, and so different from

170

one another."

Hugh would blush and say, "My precious, must you tell everyone the story of our children's conceptions? Don't you consider that a private, personal matter?"

"Oh, no, my dear, the story is so beautiful, it just begs to be told."

My grandmother Emma was the eldest of Catie Caroline and Hugh's four daughters conceived under the quilt and was, therefore, its rightful heir. She cherished memories of winter nights crowded into one large feather bed with her three younger sisters, snuggled under the mismatched quilt. They'd finger the bumpy dotted Swiss and Irish lace and make up stories about each piece of fabric: Great Uncle Arbogast wore this lace at the neck of his linen shirt when he met Beauregard Hermitage at dawn to duel over the honor of Miss Emily Oliver. Great Aunt Bethany tore this piece of sateen from the hem of her cotillion dress and gave it to Mr. Ainsley Watkins the night before he rode into battle.

My mother, Aurelia, had only one sibling, older brother Emmett, so the quilt passed effortlessly to her. Her quilt memory was of Christmas Eve with her brother: their mama would make a pallet in front of the fireplace for the two children to sleep and would cover them with the old quilt that was getting frayed from generations of love and hard use. Aurelia and Emmett would will themselves to stay awake to see Santa but, year after year, would fall asleep before his arrival. Each Christmas morning they would wake in their chilly living room in front of the dying embers, still snuggled under the quilt.

Then the quilt became mine, since I am the only daughter in a family of five children. By the time it reached me, it had been loved to a near thread-bare state. I folded it gently across the foot of my bed and dared my brothers to lay a finger on it. I cherished it and looked toward the day when I would bring my own daughter home from the hospital swaddled in it and pass it into her loving arms.

Trouble is, Alex couldn't stand The Quilt. I was horrified that the fifth generation rightful owner didn't like it, didn't want it, didn't want it touching her. When she was sick, I'd lovingly cover her with The Quilt, only to have her kick it off and whine, "It's hot. Get it off. It's scratching me." So I kept it folded neatly at the foot of my bed, sad that it's loving ownership would end with me—unless Alex matured and decided she wanted to take part in the tradition, after all.

When I found Nick Nack lounging on The Quilt, my instinct was to drop kick her down the stairs. Instead, I screamed like a banshee for her to get the hell off. She didn't cower or run for cover; she just peered up at me with a quizzical look on her face, as if she had no idea why she wouldn't be allowed to lie on the cherished fifth-generation heirloom. My tirades no longer sent her leaping to the corner to shiver in fear. She just yawned in boredom at my immature behavior and dragged herself from the bed to her rug on the floor.

Night after night she'd test me. As I got ready for bed, she'd raise a paw in the direction of The Quilt and turn to look at me.

"Don't you even think about it," I'd tell her, and she'd slowly lower her paw, as if she were insulted that I'd intimate that she'd touch The Quilt.

Then she'd spend several minutes sniffing every square inch of The Quilt that she could reach. I don't know what she found so appealing about it, why she wanted to be near it. Perhaps it was my scent. But I was still baffled that my scent captivated her. Each night, though, she'd go through her ritual: raise paw, look at me, lower paw, sniff quilt, settle into a sleepy puddle by the side of the bed. I didn't understand her infatuation, but as long as she refrained from lounging on it, I didn't care how much she admired The Quilt.

In addition to sniffing The Quilt each night, Nick Nack also nuzzled me beneath my chin. Guess she figured we'd become BFF's and that I could handle it. And she was right. I was stunned that I could allow a dog to get that close to my neck without my freaking out, but this was no ordinary dog. Nick Nack had truly become my BFF.

She and I had just endured a tiring day of chemo, my being treated, her being caregiver. After she went through her sniffing and nuzzling ritual, I gave her a big hug, and she settled into her usual ball on the floor. We slept well until the alarm sounded for me to rouse myself and get Alex off to school.

She hopped up when she heard Nick Nack and me stirring and was already dressing when I dragged myself across the hall to say good morning before heading downstairs to fix her breakfast.

"Morning, Precious, what do you want for breakfast?"

"Cheerios sound good. And maybe a banana."

"You got it, Kiddo."

By now she was dressed and pulling up the covers on her bed. I hadn't asked her to make her bed; she just took on the responsibility on her own when she knew how sick I was. She also knew that today was Thursday, Bad Day. That's what she named it when she first saw what happened to me on Thursday, the day after chemo. She hated Bad Day, as did I, and was particularly agitated on Thursdays. Even her teacher noticed. I tried downplaying the effects of my treatments, but there was just no hiding it.

Fortunately, on this Thursday I was able to feed Alex and send her off to school with a smile before the nausea kicked in. But by mid-morning I was weak, shivering, and bathed in perspiration, crouched on the bathroom tile floor, my head resting on the toilet seat. Nick Nack stayed by my side, and I clung to her and took comfort in having her with me.

About noon, though, she left the bathroom, but I was too weak and nauseated to wonder or care where she was going. If she needed to go outside, she'd just have to figure it out for herself. Soon, though, she returned, dragging my great-grandmother's quilt in her mouth. Too sick to protest or even care, I let her painstakingly cover me, pulling here, tugging there, until she had me covered just the way she wanted. Then she nestled down beside me.

By mid-afternoon when Alex returned home from school, the nausea had subsided. I firmly believed that Nick Nack's care had hastened my recovery. I was so grateful Alex didn't have to find me sprawled on the bathroom floor as she often had. I'd even been able to eat a few saltines and drink some ginger ale to revive myself before her arrival.

"How was Bad Day, Mama?"

"Not awful, Sweetie. Nick Nack took really good care of me."

"I know," she said, dropping to her knees beside the dog she still considered hers, though Nick Nack and I knew better. "You're a good girl. Thank you for taking care of Mama for me."

Nick Nack nuzzled her lovingly, wallowing in the adoration.

The following day, though I was still quite weak, I felt human again. I began thinking about all that I had missed since Mark had left me, and I realized that every bit of the missing was of my own doing. I had stopped living and had simply begun reacting to the life that came hurtling at me. But I wanted to make a change, to start living life again, instead of just going through the motions. I had already faced my biggest fear: I had embraced a dog—a snarling, menacing, neck-biting beast. Of course, Nick Nack was none of those things, but I was certain that if I could hug a dog and let it nuzzle my neck, I could tackle anything.

Mark would be picking up Alex from school that afternoon for their weekend together. Today would be the perfect time to tackle my next challenge: Emerald Isle.

So I said to my shadow, "Nick Nack, how would you like to go play on the beach?"

Her ears perked, then she smiled her great big doggie smile and trotted for the door. I swear the dog understood every word I said. Or maybe my tone of voice just said, "Let's go bye-bye." Well, whatever I was offering, she was taking.

It was December, a little cool for the usual beach-goers. I wouldn't see happy, sunburned vacationers, smell Coppertone lotion, and hear beach music wafting from radios. But I would have crashing surf, waving sea oats, soaring gulls and pelicans, and plenty of salt air. So I grabbed some jeans and sweatshirts and my toothbrush and stuffed them in a bag, and Nick Nack and I set off for the coast.

She loved our adventure from the start. Usually a quiet passenger, during our drive to Emerald Isle, she sat up front in the passenger seat and barked to every dog, every person, every mailbox she passed. It was as if she were bragging, "Look at me. I'm going to the beach, and you're not." Had she been able to sing, "Nah nah nah nah nah," she would have.

Three hours, two potty breaks, and lots of excited barking later, we crossed the bridge to Emerald Isle. They don't call the place Emerald Isle for nothing. Bogue Sound, the stretch of crystal blue water that separates the mainland from the island is dotted with small, grassy green mini-islands for as far as you can see. Beautiful, slender white egrets tiptoe in slow motion through the marshes, searching for their dinner. During the summer months ski and pleasure boats race up and down the sound, but on this mild but cool December day only a few small fishing boats bobbed in the water.

Shortly after exiting the bridge I made a right onto Coast Guard Road and was surprised to find that I still got that spine-tingling excitement I always had as a child when I knew we were getting close. As I traveled the narrow road lined with scrub pines, live oaks, and low, dense yaupons, I could hear my brothers in the back of the station wagon, arguing over whose turn it was on the top bunks. As Coast Guard Road curved to the left, groves of trees opened to small beach cottages dotting the way. When the road ended at Inlet Drive, I took a left and drove until I reached the sandy drive that brought me Home. The place hadn't changed much: the siding still needed a coat of paint, the oleander bushes flanking the front stairs were growing out of control, and the great live oak, tilting precariously toward the cottage as it had all my life, made a huge umbrella over the porch, shielding it from the afternoon sun.

I could hear the surf crashing beyond the dunes, a sound I have always loved, one that still makes me want to wiggle into my bathing suit. I opened the car door for Nick Nack, expecting her to hop down and hover nearby, waiting for me to lead the way. Wrong! She leapt from the car and took off like a rocket in the direction of the ocean, as if she knew exactly where she was going. Past the house, over the dunes, and across the sand, she ran straight for the surf. She acted as though she had been going to the beach all her life and was so happy to be back. I left my purse and bag in the car and chased after her. By the time I crested the dunes, she was already riding the waves. She'd get whacked and sent tumbling to shore, only to jump up and run back for another pummeling. She had never seen the ocean, yet I wasn't frightened by her daring. I knew she could take care of herself. When she tired of surfing, she loped out of the water and ran up and down the beach, chasing sand pipers and digging for sand crabs, yipping and shivering with excitement. She caught neither piper nor crab, but that didn't prevent her trying. I sat on the beach, watching her play, laughing at her antics, sorry I'd never given her this adventure and grateful that she was with me as I faced this challenge. Periodically, she'd run to me, just to make sure she had my full attention before romping off to tackle more waves.

She reminded me of a child who screams, "Watch me, Mommy, watch me!"

As I gave her my undivided attention, a flock of sea gulls appeared out of nowhere, soaring overhead and dive bombing all around me. My brother Will hated gulls, calling them rats with wings. As majestic as they look soaring overhead, their graceful wings stretched wide, up close they are nothing but scavengers who can annoy the hell out of you, begging like starving orphans for any crumb you might toss their way.

Will would say, "You can't even get your Cheese Doodle bag open before the rats with wings attack you for a hand-out."

So I shooed them with flailing arms and screamed, "Go away; I don't have any Cheese Doodles for you!"

When Nick Nack saw that I had diverted my attention from her frolicking to the rats with wings, she came bounding out of the waves to give those intruders a piece of her mind. They chased up and down the beach, like children playing tag, Nick Nack doing the chasing for a while, then the gulls doing the chasing for a while.

After an hour or so of flinging herself from one new activity to another, Nick Nack dragged herself to me and collapsed from exhaustion by my side. I knew I had to open the house and air the furniture, but I wasn't ready to let the moment go. I was finally feeling that comfort I had been seeking. And for all the companionship Nick Nack had given me and I had *finally* accepted, she deserved this joy. I wanted to live in the moment, let my reunion with My Ocean last a little longer. Nick Nack drifted into sleep, and I let her relax.

I stretched my legs in front of me, leaned back to rest on my elbows, and let the sun warm my face. The pounding surf had turned gray, no longer the azure blue of summer, the blue that lured me like a siren's song. I could feel the rush of the waves on my body, could hear my little brothers giggling and galloping up and down the beach, as Mama breathlessly chased in all directions, panting, "Come back here, you little rascals."

The boys had each other for companionship and entertainment as they romped along the shore and, later, played video games perched on their bunk beds. I, on the other hand, spent the summers alone in the surf. I didn't mind. My Ocean was all the companionship I needed.

But when I became a teenager, Mama said, "Rowdy, how'd you like to have a house party? You know, invite the girls down from Raleigh for a week?"

And so we started a tradition: summer after summer one of the girls' daddies would haul the four of them—Patty, Stephanie, Katherine, and Sue Ellen—down to Emerald Isle for a week of teenage joy and sheer abandon.

During the days we'd lie on the beach in the sun, listening to Mariah Carey and Whitney Houston and Bon Jovi on Patty's boom box, talking about boys. We'd spend hours in the surf, shrieking as the mountainous waves pounded and pounded us. At the end of the day, we'd drag our salt-sticky, sunburned bodies back to the house, where Daddy would grill hot dogs and hamburgers for all of us.

After supper we'd shower and put on our cutest, shortest outfits and our neon-colored Jelly sandals. Then we'd anchor our bigger-than-life hair to our heads with god-awful-tacky bows. After coating our mouths with glittery lip gloss, we'd head down the beach, in search of boys. Our first stop would be the Surf Shop, knowing that was our best bet for finding guys. We'd pretend to be looking at bikinis, all the while giggling a little too much, talking a little too loudly. The guys would pretend to be sizing up the surfboards, shaking their shaggy, sun-bleached surfer hair and cutting their hooded eyes our way.

Finally, one of them would muster enough courage to approach us.

"Hey, what y'all doing?"

"Nothing."

"Wanna do some'pm? Me'n my friends are just hanging out. Wanna hang out?"

"Sure," we'd say, still perusing the bikinis, acting sort of half interested in his proposal.

"Lemme go talk with the guys. Be right back."

While he was gone to talk with his guys, we'd continue to act like we were looking at the bathing suits, all the while whisper-yelling, "Oh, my gahd, oh, my gahd! He's so cute! I *love* his hair! I get dibs on him!"

Patty, our leader—she would wear the tiara if leaders wore tiaras—always got the cute one with the cool hair and the sexy swagger. It was just the unwritten law. We all knew it and abided by it.

Their leader would return with enough guys to go around, and we'd engage in pseudo foreplay that we all knew was going nowhere. After a reasonable amount of posturing, we'd pair off for the evening.

We'd walk to the putt-putt golf course or the water slide or the snow-cone stand, each guy casually draping an arm across our shoulders, claiming possession of *his girl*, if only for just one night. We might end the evening in the dunes, making out, not even knowing our partners' names.

If the making out became more heated than propriety permitted, we'd blame curfew, not morals, and ease away from our clumsy paramours. We'd stagger to our feet, straighten our clothes, dust off the sand, and take our swollen lips back down the beach where all five of us would crash in my small bedroom and giggle about our daring.

But it didn't matter that we dared. It was summer. We were free. We'd never cross paths with our one-night guys again. We'd just enjoy the moment and carry the memories back to Raleigh to drag out at sleepovers or lunches at Hardee's.

As I sat there on the beach, stroking Nick Nack's soft coat as she snoozed, I thought back on those times with such delight and accepted the memories for what they were: just memories. I felt blessed for the joy my friends had brought into my life and so fortunate to have been able to share My Ocean with them. We had all grown up and grown apart and grown away. But that was all right. That's the way life works. I could accept that they had moved on and was relieved to find that I was finally able to let go and move on, as well.

I looked at my watch. It was getting on to mid-afternoon. I hadn't eaten since I'd had a piece of dry toast and tea for breakfast. I wasn't really hungry, but I knew that I had to eat something to keep up my strength. But another one of the side effects of chemo is a loss of appetite and taste buds that are shot all to hell. As much as I tried to eat, everything tasted like a tin can. Cancer is the gift that just keeps on giving. But you never know what surprise awaits you at the next corner. There were two foods that I found palatable, foods that didn't taste like tin: macaroni and cheese and applesauce. Cancer sometimes has a sense of humor.

But being on Emerald Isle, sharing My Ocean with Nick Nack, suddenly I had a hankering for shrimp, good old boiled shrimp. You just can't go to the beach and not eat shrimp. And I knew just where to get the best shrimp on the Island. And, maybe, just maybe they wouldn't taste like tin.

"Nick Nack," I said, as I gently shook her awake. She rolled onto her back, stretched her full length, and yawned loudly. Looking over at me, sheer contentment on her face, she smiled her sweetest doggie smile and wagged her tail.

I stood and stretched out the kinks. As I brushed the sand off my butt and elbows, I said, "Come on, Girl, we're going to go get us some shrimp."

With great reluctance she hoisted herself and followed me slowly up the sand to the house, looking back from time to time at the crashing waves.

"It's not going anywhere, Nick Nack. And neither are we. We'll be back tomorrow, I promise."

She must have believed me because she fell in beside me and trotted to the cottage.

She was none too pleased with the cold shower I gave her with the hose, but I couldn't have her dragging her sand-laden coat all over the house. She stood on the porch and shook herself dry as I threw open the windows to air the house.

Once I had the place straightened and looking like home, I said, "Come on, Nick Nack, we're going visiting."

Twenty-four

As soon as she heard *go*, Nick Nack was down the stairs and in her passenger seat, barking her approval before I could start the engine. I backed out of the drive and headed toward Coast Guard Road, on our way to Town. Well, the locals call it Town, but it's little more than a small strip mall with a grocery store, a book store, a restaurant, and a few ever-changing seasonal souvenir shops. Several more local businesses and restaurants dot the main drag, and there is even a stop light. But that's the extent of Town.

Just before reaching the mall, I turned left down a narrow, sandy path, headed in the direction of Bogue Sound. Strangers to the island wouldn't notice the lane, covered with kudzu and yaupon, but I knew it well, having taken many a trip down this overgrown trail. As the bushes scraped the sides of my car, sounding like chalk on a blackboard, I came upon the familiar sign staked in the ground beside the path:

DO NOT ENTER!
THIS MEANS YOU!
UNLESS YOU'RE WANTING
SHRIMPS, OYSTERS OR FIREWOOD

The sign, weathered since my last visit, the sandy road, the property all belonged to Gatewood Purdy. Gatewood's family had owned the land since recorded history. On our very first trip to the island, Daddy had gone looking for some fresh oysters. A local directed him to Gatewood. We've never bought our shrimp or oysters from anyone else.

"Should I call you Woody?" Daddy asked.

"No sir," he replied. "Gatewood's always worked for me."

"Well, Gatewood, it's a pleasure to meet you. I'm Will Alexander, and this is my wife, Aurelia, and our children, Rowdy, Will, Greg, Kevin, and Sam."

Gatewood shook Daddy's hand and said, "Mighty good to meet you, sir. That's a fine-looking family you got there."

"They are fine, Gatewood, really fine."

When we met him, he was a relatively young man—probably in his late thirties. Never married, I figured by now he'd reached his seventies. His skin resembled tanned, crinkled leather from his life in the sun, but he had thick, white hair and the most beautiful, sparkling blue eyes I've ever seen. And he owned some of the most precious property on the Island, property he refused to let go.

"Croachers," Gatewood's name for *encroachers*, "been after me for just about forever to let 'em have my propitty. Say they give me a fair price. They take me for a old fool? Ain't nothin' fair about any price they could offer. Ain't for sale. Never will be."

And as the *croachers* bought up the waterfront property on either side of Gatewood and developed neighborhoods with high-rise condo complexes and multi-million dollar estates, there he sat in his two-room cottage on one of the prettiest pieces of land God ever created.

The place hadn't changed one bit. Gatewood had given his home its yearly whitewash and had put a fresh coat of Carolina Blue paint on the shutters and door. And his favorite saying was still posted on a sign to the right of his front steps:

IF GOD AIN'T A TARHEEL,
WHY IS THE SKY
CAROLINA BLUE?

A die-hard Tarheel basketball fan, Gatewood had never stepped foot on the University of North Carolina campus. He just knew that watching Tarheel basketball on his little black and white portable television with the rabbit ears covered with aluminum foil was about as close to heaven as a body could get. He and Daddy, a North

Carolina State University alum, had a good-natured rivalry over their favorite teams, Daddy true to his Wolfpack and Gatewood swearing by his Tarheels. Every season Daddy would make the trip from Raleigh to Emerald Isle to watch the two State-Carolina basketball games with Gatewood on his little black and white TV. Daddy had season tickets to watch all the home games in his beloved Reynolds Coliseum on the State campus in Raleigh, but he preferred to watch the two State-Carolina games in black and white with his good friend Gatewood. The two men competed each season for a trophy: an old, beat-up, barnacle-ridden conch shell. The Tarheels had won the last game just before Daddy died, so the trophy would live for eternity on Gatewood's mantle. He had a small blue plastic ram, Carolina's mascot, and a red wolf, State's mascot. If Carolina were the reigning champion of the two-team rivalry, he'd stand the ram inside the shell; if State had won the last game, he'd stand that Wolf in the shell, in honor of Daddy.

When I pulled up in Gatewood's front yard, I found him sitting on his front porch, shucking oysters with his pocket knife, eating them right out of the shell. He'd pry one open, stab it with his knife blade, tilt his head back, and drop the oyster into his mouth.

I used to sit on the porch by his chair with my head thrown back and my mouth wide open like a starving baby bird as he pried and stabbed, saying, "One for me; one for Rowdy Doody."

That's what Gatewood called me: Rowdy Doody. The first time he saw me, he said, "Rowdy, huh? That's a mighty fine name. And look at all them freckles and curly, red hair. Looks like Howdy Doody, don't she? I b'lieve I'll call you Rowdy Doody. That a'right with you?"

I had heard of Howdy Doody but wasn't sure who he was, but having Gatewood give me a nickname was more than all right with me. I was taken with this sweet man from the minute he smiled his kind smile, crinkled his sparkly blue eyes, and made me feel special by giving me a nickname. Seeing him sitting there as I'd seen him since I was a small child touched my heart and made me so very glad that I had returned to Emerald Isle.

I pulled my car right up to the front steps, stopped, and opened the door. I stepped out, and Nick Nack crawled across the driver's seat and hopped down to the ground beside me, wiggling with excitement. Gatewood stopped his oyster shucking, leaned forward in his chair, and squinted his eyes, I guess to determine if I were a 'croacher or a shrimps buyer.

"You know where I can find me some shrimp?" I called.

"I just might. Who's asking?"

"Rowdy Doody."

As soon as I said my name, a huge grin spread across his face, making his blue eyes sparkle. He laid his pocket knife on the table, wiped his hands on the thighs of his jeans and hoisted himself out of his rocker. I was on the porch and in his arms before he could move. He gave me a long, gentle hug then held me at arm's length.

"Let me look at you, Girl. Lord, you're still a pretty thing. Where you been, Sweetie? I looked for you all summer, but you just never showed up. I'd 'bout give up on you. And here you are, my Rowdy Doody."

I needed another hug, so I walked back into his embrace and said, "It's been a rough year, Gatewood, but things are looking up."

"Well, sorry 'bout that rough year, Rowdy Doody, but I'm glad to hear you talking positive. Lord can't work his magic if we don't stay positive and let Him in."

Once again, he freed himself from my embrace and reached down to scratch Nick Nack on the head, saying, "And who is this beautiful woman?"

Nick Nack shimmied with enthusiasm as I told Gatewood, "This is my best friend, Nick Nack."

"You mean like *nick nack paddy whack give a dog a bone?*"

"One and the same."

"Well, she's a beaut. Y'all come on in and let's make us some iced tea. Sound good?"

"Sounds excellent." And we walked arm in arm into his cottage, Nick Nack close behind.

The first thing I noticed was the little red plastic Wolf standing in the conch shell on the mantle. I had lost track of basketball and hadn't realized that the Wolfpack was the reigning champ of the State-Carolina rivalry.

I made the sign of the Wolf with both hands, as all avid Wolfpack fans do, and yelled, "GO PACK!"

"Now, don't you go getting carried away, young lady. That little wolf is in honor of your daddy, and he was the only person I've ever allowed to yell 'GO PACK!' in my home."

I knew that the State-Carolina rivalry was reserved just for Daddy and Gatewood, but it had ended when Daddy and Mama had been killed by that drunk driver. I'd leave Gatewood to celebrate the rivalry in his own private way.

I followed our host into his tiny one-person kitchen where he and I had bumped into each other on many occasions while we made a pitcher of tea. I knew he kept his sugar bowl in the refrigerator to avoid ant infestations, so I reached in and grabbed it, along with a lemon. While Gatewood put the tea bags on the old two-burner gas range to brew, I tiptoed and pulled from the overhead cupboard his glass pitcher festooned with apples that were faded to pale pink from years of use.

First I dumped about a half cup of sugar into the pitcher, about enough to make our sweet tea real sweet, just like all southerners like it. As I was slicing the lemon on the cutting board by the sink, Gatewood turned to me and said, "Is it worth telling?"

"You mean my year of hell?" I said over my shoulder.

"S'pose that's what I mean."

"If you'll listen," I said, wiping my hands on the red-checked dish towel and turning to face him.

He let me talk, tell it all, without reacting. He didn't judge Mark, didn't pity me my cancer. He just offered a thoughtful ear and a strong shoulder. I didn't realize until that moment that that was exactly what I needed. I needed to hear myself say It out loud, every detail, to get It out of my system.

"Mark left me, Gatewood. He left me for a young student. It blindsided me and left me a withered husk. Just as I was trying to come to terms with the separation, Mark and the girl—her name is Tawni—found out that she was pregnant with his twins. So he filed for a quickie divorce from me, and shortly after that they married. During all of this Alex was in a perfect glee, as if they were having a party and she was an invited guest. She loved being with her father. But who could have blamed her? Mark and Tawni were giddy with their new-found love, and they gladly shared their fun life with her."

Gatewood turned the flame off under the tea to let it steep. He returned his attention to me, crossing his arms and narrowing his eyes. He nodded his head for me to continue.

"Just days before they married, I found a lump in my breast. Cancer. So I've been dealing with that since June. Surgery. Radiation.

Chemo treatments. Nausea. Lost my appetite. Lost my hair. These beautiful curls are a wig."

The tears welled in my eyes, but I shook them off.

He closed his eyes, pinched his lips tight, and moved his head slowly from side to side.

Then I laughed and said, "And, Gatewood, on top of all that, Mark left me with a damn dog, a dog I never wanted and certainly never planned to take care of."

"You know," he said, "I was surprised when I seen you with that dog. Ain't you scared of dogs? Didn't one bite you in the neck that one summer you was down here?"

Gatewood was right. Right here on Emerald Isle was where my fear of dogs began. My family was on the beach out in front of our cottage. I was nine that summer. My brothers were all little, and they were running in all directions, Mama trying to keep an eye on them. She said it was like herding kittens. Daddy was standing at the edge of the surf, fishing for our supper. I had just finished an hour of surf tumbling and was digging a hole in the sand, making myself a fort. I was about waist-deep in my excavation.

I looked up when I heard a dog barking and saw it loping down the beach, a young couple chasing after it. The dog was headed in my direction, to play, I assumed. As it approached, I reached from my sand hole to pet it's wavy, yellow coat; and when I did, it snarled at me and bit me in the neck. It was over before I realized what had happened, and the dog took off, racing down the beach.

When I saw the blood and reality set in, I began screaming. Daddy and the dog's owners were at my side in an instant. The couple showed concern but were soon off to capture their unfettered dog before it could wreak more havoc. In the confusion my father failed to get the dog owners' names or find out where they were staying. Unable to determine if the dog were rabid, I was subjected to two weeks of daily shots in my stomach. Of course, the episode left me paralyzed with fear every time I saw a dog. Recalling the experience made me shudder, but I chose not to relay the details to Gatewood.

"Sure did," was all I could say. "I wore a big bandage on my wound, and at the end of the summer, I had a white square on my neck that hadn't tanned."

Gatewood chuckled and said, "Yeah, I remember that."

Nick Nack had been sitting quietly by my side as I told my story.

I crouched down and wrapped my arms around her neck and said, "But I have nothing to be afraid of with Nick Nack. She loves me and would never hurt me. And, you know, she's instrumental in my being here on Emerald Isle again. She also helped me start smiling again."

Gatewood pulled a metal ice tray from his freezer, ran a little warm water over its bottom and gave the handle a yank, making the ice cubes screech and hop out of their shells. He filled the pitcher with ice and poured in the tea. As the ice crackled and popped when the warm tea hit it, I stirred the sugar from the bottom with a big plastic spoon. I reached into the cupboard and grabbed two faded Flintstone jelly glasses, the same Flintstone jelly glasses I had drunk from as a child. Gatewood handed me the pitcher as he filled a bowl of water for Nick Nack, and we headed out back to sit in the frayed lawn chairs and gaze out over the sound.

Gatewood gave Nick Nack her bowl of water and scratched her behind her ear. She lapped loudly and thirstily, as I poured the tea. I handed Gatewood the Fred and Barney glass, saving my favorite Pebbles and Bamm-Bamm glass for myself. I settled back and took a long swig, and the super-sweet tea made my jaw ache in a good, familiar sort of way.

Once we were settled, I said, "What's been going on with you?"

"Not much. Same old, same old."

I knew that was about all I was going to get out of him. As long as I had known him, I had never heard him say anything personal about his life. All I knew was that he lived on Bogue Sound, sold shrimps and oysters and firewood, and was an avid Tarheel fan. I also knew that I was special to him, special enough for him to give me a special nickname.

So we just sat in the afternoon sun, watching the gulls soar overhead and listening to the water lap against the seawall. And we sipped our jaw-aching sweet tea.

As the sun made diamonds on the choppy water of the sound, I said, "Do you think you could come over tonight and share some shrimp with me?"

Gatewood hesitated for a bit, but I gave him all the time he needed to think about it.

"B'lieve I can do that," he said, still looking out over the Sound.

"Seven sounds good, don't you think?"

"Seven sounds good," he agreed.

We sat, sipping our tea for another good hour or so, neither of us saying much. The near-quiet felt right.

Finally I said, "Well, how about selling me a pound of your best shrimp."

We carried our glasses and pitcher and Nick Nack's bowl back to the kitchen, and Gatewood placed them in his small sink.

"I'll wash 'em up later."

He walked me back to the front porch where he kept a huge cooler full of shrimp and oysters, packed in ice.

He reached in and grabbed a bag of jumbo shrimp, shook off the ice, and handed them to me. I shoved my hand deep into my jeans pocket, pulled out a wad of bills, and tried to pay him, but he just closed his eyes and waved my money away.

I knew that pressing him would insult him, so I just said, "Thanks, Gatewood." And to Nick Nack I said, "Well, let's go, Girl. We've got some shrimp to boil."

I let Nick Nack into the car and followed. After I revved the engine and turned the car around, I looked in the rearview mirror to find Gatewood still standing, hands in his pockets, shoulders hunched. He watched me until I disappeared into the brush that covered the narrow, sandy path.

I stopped by the Food Lion, just down the road. The day was warm for a late fall day but cool enough for Nick Nack to wait in the car for a few minutes, so I told her, "Nick Nack, you lie down and rest, and I'll be right back."

She did as I told her, such a good girl, and I cracked the windows so she could get a nice breeze. I was in the store just long enough to grab cocktail sauce for the shrimp, some shrimp spice, two baking potatoes, a pound of butter, salt and pepper, and a tub of cole slaw. I considered fixings for hush puppies but felt my taste buds and queasy stomach weren't ready for deep-fried food.

When I came out of the Food Lion, I found Nick Nack watching the door, anticipating my return. When she saw me, she broke into a huge grin and began wriggling with excitement. I'd never elicited that much enthusiasm from my own human family. By the time I reached the car, she was flinging her tail merrily, beating out a drum solo on the dashboard and the seat back.

When I got home, I pulled out Mama's big seafood pot, filled it halfway with water, threw in some spices, and set it over the flame on the old gas stove. When the water came to a boil, I dumped in the shrimp. Within minutes they were turning pink; it doesn't take long for shrimp. I transferred them to the big colander in the sink, waiting for them to cool so that I could shuck and de-vein them. While I waited, I washed the potatoes, wrapped them in foil I'd found in a drawer, and popped them into the oven.

The shrimp were cooled, cleaned, and ready to eat when Gatewood knocked on the door at seven on the dot. He'd showered and shaved and had changed into clean jeans and sweatshirt. For a tanned-and-weathered seventy-plus year old, he was an elegant looking gentlemen.

He handed me a bottle of grocery-store wine, still in its brown paper bag, and a bunch of yellow mums wrapped in a cellophane sleeve.

"They're beautiful, Gatewood. Thanks so much."

While he and Nick Nack tussled on the living room floor, I stuck the flowers in a tall, chipped blue earthenware pitcher and placed the bouquet in the center of the dining table. The wine was red, but who cared if red is for beef and white is for poultry and fish?

I finished setting the table, pulled the potatoes from the oven, and poured a glass of Gatewood's wine for each of us.

I said, "If you kids can stop playing for a while, we can eat these delicious shrimp."

We sat, Nick Nack settled beside her new friend, and I reached for my fork. Before I could dig in, Gatewood took my hand. He held it tight and bowed his head.

"Dear Lord Jesus, I thank you for bringing my friend Rowdy home. Please be with her and hold her in your loving hand, Father, as she fights this cancer. We love you, Lord, and believe in your great goodness. All things are possible for those who believe in your Holy Name. And, Heavenly Father, we thank you for this bountiful feast that you have laid before us. Guide, guard, and direct us, Lord God, today and all our days to come. We ask this blessing in the name of your Son and our Savior, Jesus Christ. Amen."

Touched by his heartfelt blessing, I said, "Thank you, Gatewood."

Without looking my way, he picked up his fork and said, "Well, okay, then, let's dig in."

Although Gatewood was a man of many words when he prayed,

he ate in silence. I prattled a bit, until I realized that I was a one-woman show. So I got up and shuffled through my father's collection of old vinyl records until I found one by his and Gatewood's favorite group, General Johnson and The Chairmen of the Board. I pulled the record gently from its aged and battered cardboard sleeve, adorned with three pompadoured soul singers decked out in lime green tuxedoes with ruffled white shirts, dropped it on the stereo turntable, and lowered the needle.

The General began singing, "Carolina girls, best in the world,"[8] in his raspy, plaintive wail, as Gatewood tapped his foot and smiled.

"Now, that's what I'm talking about," was all he said.

For the rest of the meal.

Though I found that our supper wasn't as yummy as I'd hoped, that my taste buds hadn't suddenly sprung to life with renewed vitality, the evening was perfect: fresh flowers in a chipped earthenware pitcher, dinner with Gatewood after a long absence, my best friend, Nick Nack, by my side, the General insisting that Carolina girls are, without a doubt, the very best in the world.

I was beginning to believe that we are, indeed.

After dinner I shooed Gatewood and Nick Nack to the back porch while I washed the dishes and tidied the kitchen. Once I was finished, I grabbed two afghans from the sofa and joined them. I handed one to Gatewood and wrapped the other around my shoulders. The sun had set, and the night air was rather chilly. As I sat in the rocker, Nick Nack clicked across the wooden planks, plopped beside me, and rested her head against my knee. We sat quietly, listening to the waves rumble to shore and watching the outlines of the few beachcombers who had bundled in hooded sweatshirts to brave the brisk sea breeze for one more walk along the strand.

Then Gatewood said, "I loved William."

Gatewood was the only person I know who ever called my father by his given name. Daddy went by Will, just as my brother does, but I believe Gatewood felt that calling him William was a sign of respect.

"I know, Gatewood. He was easy to love."

"I ain't never said that about another man. Oh, I loved my own daddy, but I ain't never told nobody that in words. But I did love your daddy, and his dying near 'bout broke my heart."

"He loved you, too, Gatewood. He considered you one of his dearest friends."

"I know that. That's one of the things that made me love him so much. He was a smart man, a educated man, and he'd been places and saw things I ain't never dreamed of seeing. I'm just a simple man, but he took me as his friend just the same. He didn't never look down on me or talk down to me. He always treated me as his equal."

For once I let Gatewood do all the talking.

"We sorta, you know, clicked that first day he come to buy some oysters, back when you was just a little thing. Don't know what it was, but I just felt it. I think he did, too. That's the day he started ribbing me 'bout being a Tarheel fan. That didn't never stop. And I'm glad it didn't. We had our most fun when it was just the two of us, talking basketball-rivalry fool."

"Daddy loved that, too, Gatewood."

Then he fell silent again, but I could tell by the twinkle in his eye, the purse of his lips that he had something more to say on the subject and was just trying to muster the courage to say it.

"You know, Rowdy Doody, me and your daddy drank a six-pack ever' time we watched a game."

His admission surprised me since neither Gatewood nor my daddy, to my knowledge, were drinkers. In fact, I'd been surprised that Gatewood had brought a bottle of wine for supper that night. I was not surprised, however, when he didn't touch the glass I'd poured for him and, instead, excused himself from the dinner table to draw a glass of tap water at the kitchen sink.

So I said, "Gatewood, you don't drink. Neither did my daddy."

"I know that, but some'pm 'bout them basketball games made us feel like we needed to drink beer. We'd walk up to the Food Lion and get us our six-pack, a big bag of greasy old Wise potato chips, and some Pemmican beef jerky. William said only Pemmican would do. We'd eat that whole bag of potato chips, gnaw on some beef jerky, and get a little tipsy. Then we'd holler and shout and cut the fool and talk trash about each other's team. Lord, we'd laugh so hard we'd cry like crazy old fools. After them games your daddy didn't go back to y'all's house. Said he didn't think it would be wise to get behind the wheel of a car in his condition. He'd just sleep right yonder on my sofa."

I laughed and said, "And Daddy'd come back to Raleigh all

proper, like he'd just watched a simple basketball game with a friend."

"Ha! Wudn't nothin' simple 'bout it," Gatewood nearly shouted. "There was a trophy at stake!"

Again I laughed, and so did Gatewood, until we were crying like crazy people over that silly conch-shell trophy. And maybe about that daddy we both loved so much.

When we'd composed ourselves, Gatewood said, "Wudn't a mean or ornery bone in your daddy's body. Never met a kinder, nicer man. You're one lucky daughter, Rowdy Doody. Don't everybody get a daddy like that."

"Oh, Gatewood, I know how lucky I am. He was the best father ever."

"And, boy, was he ever proud of you when you decided to go to State. Now, I was fit to be tied 'cause you didn't pick Carolina, but what could I do?" and he just chuckled. "And then them sorry brothers of yours all up and went to Duke. What in god's name was they thinking?"

"Well, Gatewood, they were all so smart, and they were thinking they just couldn't turn down the offer of a scholarship to Duke."

"Well, yeah, I guess that makes sense, but I just couldn't believe they wanted to be Dookies."

And he and I laughed again as we watched the full moon rise high over My Ocean.

Nick Nack snuggled in closer and sighed as I scratched her head.

"Yeah, I know, Girl. This is the life, isn't it? Thanks for helping me find my way back."

And I leaned down and kissed her between her pointy ears.

Twenty-five

It was only a matter of time before the other chemo patients warmed to Nick Nack. One by one they beckoned her to them. She'd look at me to get my approval before leaving my side.

I'd say, "Go say, 'Hi,' Nick Nack," and she'd click across the tiled room to offer her paw or her nose.

She'd wait for a pat on her back or a scratch on her head or a smooch between her eyes before leaving to greet another. She could, somehow, intuit what each patient needed and how long to hang around, so as not to overstay her welcome. Sometimes she'd settle in for a lengthy visit; other times she'd just yip a greeting and move on. After she had made her rounds, she'd return to me, still her favorite patient, once again check my IV and blanket, and settle down by my side with a long sigh as she drifted off to sleep.

Word traveled through the hospital about the big, fluffy black dog who tended to the chemo patients every Wednesday. Nurses, doctors, and even patients' visitors came by to meet her. Loving the attention, she greeted them all with a warm smile.

One morning a young woman dressed in a brightly printed pink smock came into the chemo room. As she whispered to Holly, she turned and pointed at Nick Nack.

The two women approached, and Holly said, "Rowdy, this is Melody Upchurch, a nurse from Pediatric Oncology. She has come to ask a favor of you."

"A favor of me?"

Melody said, "Yes, we'd like to borrow your dog?"

"Borrow my dog? You mean Nick Nack? What for?"

"Until last week we had a dog, Chocolate, that entertained the children in Pedes. But she'd gotten old and arthritic and just couldn't handle the kids anymore. Now our department is dog-less, and the children are so sad. I'd heard about Nick Nack and how she cares for chemo patients. She sounds like just the kind of medicine our kids need."

"Well, you're welcomed to borrow her, but wouldn't she need some kind of training before she could be around the kids?" I asked.

"Well, when the program started, the regulations were pretty stringent, but over time the rules have relaxed considerably. Now we just observe pets with the children to make sure they are a good fit. And from what we hear, she's great with patients. Do you think we could give it a try?"

"Why, sure. She's very gentle and loves kids. Actually she loves everybody. She's never met a stranger. When would you like to audition her?"

Melody smiled and said, "How about today, when you finish your treatment. We could introduce her to the kids and see how it goes."

"Sure, that sounds fine," I said. "Where do we go?"

"We're on this floor in the other wing of the hospital. Just pass the lobby and keep going. You can't miss us. We'll be waiting for you."

When my treatment ended, I gathered my belongings and my dog and headed to the children's ward to introduce Nick Nack to her new friends. I don't know what I was expecting: sick little children lined up in hospital beds? Stark white walls? Monitors beeping? Nurses passing silently? Instead, I was blasted by an onslaught of color and flashing animation coming from a large TV. There were vibrant patchwork carpets and colorful beanbag chairs scattered throughout the room. Children's artwork covered the walls. There were some children too weak to leave their beds, but others sat on the carpets, reading and playing games, while others sang along with Dora.

Nick Nack didn't hesitate. She left my side and trotted across the floor to a group of kids sitting around a table, coloring and playing games. She sat quietly between two children, peering over the edge of the table as they played. She didn't approach any of the patients but let them come to her, just as she had done with me. One by one the children noticed her and came close. Once they were comfortable with her, they petted and hugged and kissed her. Within an hour she had met all of the children and was smiling and wearing a party hat.

The following week Nick Nack accompanied me to chemo, and then I followed her to Pedes. I sat in a small child's chair and watched as she took care of her little charges, letting them dress her in silly outfits, watching them play games, allowing them to hug her and lounge on her.

After several weeks I said to Melody, "Why don't I just drop Nick Nack off before I go to my treatment, let her spend some time with the children, and pick her up when my treatment ends?"

"Are you sure, Rowdy? Don't you need her with you during chemo?"

Sure, I loved having Nick Nack with me, but once she greeted the other patients and checked to make sure I was settled, she just slept. And, in all honesty, I was exhausted and ready to head home after my treatment, not sit in a ward of children and watch them play with my dog.

So I said, "Nick Nack is with me all the time. I can share her with the children for a few hours a week."

"Well, if that will work for you, that would be great."

The following week I dropped her at Pedes before heading for my treatment. She went to work immediately, taking care of her children, and didn't even notice when I turned to leave.

All of the chemo patients asked about Nick Nack. They said they'd miss her but agreed that she belonged in Pedes with her gentle spirit and winning smile. I missed having her around, but I also agreed that the children deserved a few hours with her.

Following my treatment I went to collect Nick Nack before heading home. I looked around the room at the children playing games, coloring, watching TV. Then I spied her. She was sitting beside a little girl in a bright pink beanbag chair. They seemed deep in friendship, so I approached quietly so as not to disturb them. The little girl was dressed in pink, frilly baby doll pajamas, and she wore fluffy, pink bunny slippers. She had a string of pink beads hanging around her neck, and on her bald head she wore a pink plastic head band with a large pink flower sprouting from it. Nick Nack also sported a pink plastic head band with a large pink flower, as if it were just part of her normal, everyday attire.

Nick Nack's little friend had an oxygen tube leading from a tank to her nose, and I could see her small chest heaving as she labored to breathe. Her frail arms and legs protruded from the openings in her pajamas, and her skin appeared purple and translucent. She was, apparently, a very sick child, but today she was just an ordinary, happy little girl who loved pink, playing with a new friend.

She was reading Goodnight Moon to Nick Nack. I had read Goodnight Moon to Alex every night for—how many?—maybe three years. But I had never thought to read it to Nick Nack, which is a shame since she seemed to be enjoying it just as much as Alex ever had. She'd stare into the little girl's face as she read and occasionally would turn her focus to the book, as if checking out the pictures, then back to the little girl again, the pink flower on her headband waving as she moved. They were in a world of their own, these new friends.

When they finished their reading, I tiptoed over and crouched by the two of them.

"Hi, Nick Nack, I see you have a new friend," I whispered.

When Nick Nack saw me, she flapped her big tail on the floor and grinned up at me.

The little girl reached out a frail, weak hand and said, "Hi, I'm Olivia. You must be Nick Nack's mommy. Thanks for letting her come and play. I don't get visitors often. Only my mommy and daddy. I love Nick Nack. She is my friend."

"Hi, Olivia. I'm Rowdy. And I guess I am Nick Nack's mommy, and I love her, too. I'm sure she has enjoyed her visit with you, but it's time for us to get on home."

Olivia said, "Can she come play tomorrow?"

"Well, maybe not tomorrow, but I'll make sure she comes back next Wednesday."

"Why can't Nick Nack come back till next Wednesday?"

"Well, that's the day I come to the hospital for my treatment."

"What treatment?"

Should I tell her? Would it scare her? But how could I scare this little girl any more than she had already been scared? Perhaps she'd be able to relate to me better if she knew we were going through the same thing.

"Chemo," I said. "I have cancer."

"You do? Me, too!" she cried, as if she had just discovered that we were sorority sisters.

"Are you sick?" she asked.

"Well, yes, but not all the time. The chemo is killing my cancer, but the treatment makes me feel awfully yucky for a while."

"Yucky," she giggled. "I like that word."

I laughed and said, "Well, I like the word, too, but I don't like feeling yucky."

"You have hair. Why do you have hair? My treatment made my hair all fall out. Why didn't yours fall out?"

I never took off my wig and revealed my bald head to anyone—except Nick Nack, who showed no judgment or pity. But I was self-conscious around others, even Alex. I felt naked without my hair and sad for my loss. I still did not wear my baldness as a badge of honor, and I didn't want to be pitied.

But without even thinking, I reached up and lifted my red wig from my shiny bald head. Olivia broke into a broad smile and reached out her slender hand. I bent toward her and let her caress my head. I wouldn't have allowed anyone else to do that, but, somehow, I felt safe letting Nick Nack's little friend touch my baldness.

As Olivia gently caressed my head, she whispered, "You're beautiful, Rowdy, just like me."

Twenty-six

Since Nick Nack had a new job, there was no one to greet the chemo patients, to make sure they were all settled in.

I thought, "What about me?"

Sure, I wasn't loppy and fuzzy, and I couldn't smile and wag my tail cunningly. But having watched Nick Nack make her rounds, I knew that most patients just liked a little attention, someone to show them some compassion. I was a patient, too. Once I had allowed myself to accept others' caring, I realized that a little kindness went a long way. And if the patients wanted to scratch me on the head or kiss me between my eyes, that was okay. I could give it a try.

The following Wednesday I showed up at the hospital a little early so I could drop Nick Nack off in Pedes and take over her rounds in the chemo unit. As I breezed through the door, waving and giving a cheery, "Hello," all the nurses stared quizzically. I just winked and headed for the patients who were already plugged it, waiting for their cocktails to do their stuff.

"Hey, Miss Maudie, how you doin' this morning?" I said, as I crouched beside her chair.

This was the doctor's third attempt to bring Maudie's cancer to its knees. Her pale, blue watery eyes crinkled around the edges as she managed a wan smile from her weary, ashen face. A Christmas-red stocking cap covered her baldness. She reached bruised, arthritic hands toward me and cupped my face. They were shaking and frigid but so very gentle.

"Much better, Sweetie," she said, in a halting, raspy voice. "You're so kind to ask. You look wonderful, my dear. You must be getting along splendidly."

"Yes, I am, Miss Maudie."

"Well, that's excellent news. I'm sure Nick Nack is glad to hear that," she said with a chuckle. "Now, you give that precious pooch a kiss for me, and tell her I miss her."

"I will, Miss Maudie."

I moved from patient to patient, all of whom I had shunned or treated with disrespect at the beginning of my chemo. They didn't hold it against me, but, rather, welcomed me with kindness and open arms. They, too, had walked the same path.

Eliza had been a long-distance runner, and bone cancer had taken her leg. Talk about cancer kicking you in the ass. But she hadn't been daunted by her disease, just slowed down a bit.

"Hey, Rowdy, how's it going? God, you look gorgeous. Who is he?" And she threw back her head and laughed her raucous laugh.

"Why do you assume it's a man?" I said, slapping her playfully on the arm. "I just figured laughing is better for me than bitching."

"You got that right, Girl. You show 'em!"

I hugged her and crossed the room to talk with Beth. Her story broke my heart. She and her husband, Chip, had been childhood sweethearts and had married right out of college. They couldn't wait to start a family. On their honeymoon Beth had become ill. The diagnosis: ovarian cancer. Three weeks after their wedding Beth underwent a hysterectomy and began chemotherapy.

"Hey, Rowdy," cried Beth, arms open for a hug as she flashed her dazzling smile. She wore a stunning teal flowered scarf, folded around her bald head like an origami swan, ending in a huge bow drooping over her right eye.

Beth and Chip could have been bitter, could have whined, "Why us?"

But, instead, they loved each other unconditionally and cherished each moment they had together with a maturity far beyond their twenty-three years.

Before Beth's first chemo treatment, Chip presented her with a beautiful silk scarf. He followed that with a book on scarf-tying art and a new scarf each week.

"How do you like my new scarf?" Beth chirped.

"It's gorgeous. Is that Hermes?"

"Sure is. Chip had to go to New York on business, and he got it for me while he was there. Can you imagine his taking the time out of his busy trip to find me a Hermes scarf? Oh, Rowdy, I'm so blessed."

If cancer's ass could be kicked, Beth and Chip could do it.

Then I came to a young woman whom I had not met but guessed was no more than thirty years old, though it's sometime hard to tell with a very ill cancer patient. She still had some of her hair, but she was going through the clumps-in-the-shower-drain stage, a very emotional time. I also guessed from her appearance that she was experiencing the worst kind of nausea.

I approached quietly, laid my hand gently on her arm and said, "Hi, I'm Rowdy Murphy. I've come for my treatment and thought I'd say 'Hey' before they strapped me in."

She pulled her blanket up to her chin, turned her gaunt face from me and said, "Thanks, but I'm not interested."

I understood her so well. I knew her fear and pain and anger.

Though she didn't see my smile, I hoped she heard it in my voice as I touched her shoulder and said, "I know."

I crossed the room and climbed into my chair.

"All set. Hook me up," I said to Andrea, the nurse on duty, as I closed my eyes and delighted in my new job.

When my treatment ended, I waved good-bye and headed for Pedes to collect Nick Nack. As usual, she was hard at work, this time wearing a bonnet and watching television. Two children were straddling her and two were leaning against her. When she saw me, she stood and shook off her wards and pleaded with her eyes for me to take the silly bonnet off her head. And she did look silly. Large brims and bows tied under her chin were just not her style. She was better suited for pointed party hats and flowered head bands.

After telling everyone good-bye, Nick Nack headed for the door. Once we were in the car, she sat at attention in her seat, anxious to get home. But today I was planning to make a stop along the way. When we got to the mall, I made a turn into the parking lot.

Nick Nack looked at me with confusion, as if to say, "No, this isn't right! This isn't home! Go straight! Don't turn!"

"Don't worry, Girl, we'll only be a minute," I told her, as I pulled into a parking space right at the door to Belk's Department Store. "Just lie down and take a nap, and I'll be right back."

As if she understood, she curled into a ball and closed her eyes, weary from her day's work with her children. It was chilly outside, but I cracked the window just a bit so Nick Nack would have a little fresh air and locked her in safely.

I rushed through the door and headed for the hosiery department. "Socks, socks," I said under my breath, as I rushed from rack to rack. I was looking for socks with toes, preferably Christmas and Halloween socks. I did not see exactly what I was looking for, but I did find a pair of red and blue striped and a pair of black with pink and green polka dots. Most importantly, they had toes. Once I'd paid the clerk, I was back in the car, headed for home, with Nick Nack still dozing.

The following Wednesday before leaving for the hospital, I found a big pink ribbon and tied a bow around the two pairs of socks. Once I'd delivered Nick Nack to her job, I headed for the treatment room. I saw her the minute I entered. Still gaunt and pale, she had lost more hair but had not yet cut it or covered her head with a scarf, hat, or wig. I approached quietly.

"My feet get so cold in here, and a friend gave me some of these silly socks. I thought maybe you could use some, too."

She didn't look my way, but a big tear rolled down her cheek. She pulled her blanket closer and turned away from me. I laid the socks next to her, and after making my rounds, moved to my chair to begin my treatment, settling in to read Pat Conroy's latest book. Occasionally, I'd look her way. Her way. I didn't even know her name. I was hopeful she'd soon tell me, but I was not going to pressure her. She lay motionless for a good while but finally pulled one hand from the covers and picked up the socks. She turned them over and over, examining them. She drew them under the blanket, curled into a ball, and cried silently. When her treatment ended, she stood, raked her sleeve across her wet face, and left the room without looking my way. She was clutching her socks to her chest.

The nausea that week was not so bad. Either I was getting used to it or I was getting better. I had regained my strength, and I was feeling fit. Most of all, my attitude had changed. I looked in the mirror and didn't see a victim. I saw a woman who was determined, grateful to be alive, and moving on with her life. I didn't know what I was going to do with that life; I would figure it out in time. But for now I was going to be glad for each day. And I had Nick Nack to thank for that.

Much to my surprise, I was anxious for Wednesday to arrive. I'd never relished treatment day, but I was looking forward to getting back to my patients. Since Nick Nack had taken her new job, her former friends had become my responsibility, even if I were the only one who was aware of that.

I rushed Nick Nack into Pedes, gave her a quick hug and was out the door, dispensing hellos over my shoulder as I ran to the treatment room. When I breezed through the door, all eyes turned to me, and everyone smiled and greeted me with, "Hey, Rowdy!" All except one patient. The young woman I'd given the socks to lay motionless with her eyes closed. She didn't look as though she were sleeping, just shutting herself off from the rest of us.

Miss Maudie's treatments were not going well, but she was still upbeat.

"Why, Darlin', I'm an old lady who has been blessed with a glorious life." And in a conspiratorial whisper she said, "Did I ever tell you that I once danced with the Rockettes? Yes, I was quite the cutie in my day. But Herb whisked me off my feet, transplanted me to North Carolina, and made me the luckiest woman in the world. We've had four children and eleven grands. And just last week I got to meet my first great-grandchild. I'd say my life is complete. My precious Herb left me ten years ago, and I have missed him every day. I'm ready to join him."

I had to swallow the lump that was growing in my throat, but I knew there was no need for tears. Miss Maudie was a happy woman and was resigned to leaving us so she could see her Herb.

"Rowdy, I can't wait for you to see my new leg," Eliza told me, as she scooted over and made room for me to sit beside her. "It's one of those cool titanium running legs. It should be here next week, and I'll be back on the track in no time."

How could I have ever whined when she had so much courage?

"Oh, Rowdy," cried Beth, as she grabbed my hands, "I'm so glad you're here. I just couldn't wait to tell you. As soon as my treatments end, Chip and I are going to start looking into adoption. I know I can't be a mom till I'm out of the woods, but nothing says we can't start thinking about adoption soon. Chip is just over the moon with excitement, and I can't wait to be a mommy."

She grinned from ear to ear and kicked her heels with excitement.

I hugged Beth and headed toward Andrea, who was waiting to begin my treatment.

Then I heard someone call my name: "Rowdy."

I turned to find a foot waving in the air. It was wearing a black sock with green and pink polka dots—and toes. I walked toward the foot and grabbed it. It's owner stuck out her hand and said, "Peg. I'm Peg."

I took her hand and sat down beside her.

"Thank you," she said. "I love my socks, but mostly I love you for not giving up on me. Please forgive me for being so rude."

I remember uttering those exact words.

"Peg, I've been right where you've been. I know what you've gone through and what you have ahead of you. It's a hard road. We all handle it differently, but it's a bitch for all of us. And, trust me, no one has behaved more rudely than I."

"One more thing," said Peg. "Where can I get a wig like that? It's gorgeous. I've always wanted long, red hair."

"Why don't I pick you up so we can go wig shopping. We can do lunch and make a day of it. Sound like a plan?"

"Sounds like a plan," she said.

I pulled my cell phone from my purse and said, "Give me your number, and I'll give you a call."

Once I'd taken her info, I headed for my chair where Andrea was now tapping her foot impatiently. As I sat down, I looked over at Peg. I made a telephone out of my hand and placed it to my ear, mouthing, "I'll call you."

She nodded, leaned back, and looked down at her feet. Then she wiggled her toes and smiled broadly.

Twenty-seven

Nick Nack sensed Wednesdays. She must have had an internal calendar. After her Wednesday morning breakfast, I'd let her out into the back yard. Once she had finished her private time, I'd let her back in. She'd head straight to the front door where she would sit until I was ready to leave for my treatment.

She rode silently in the passenger seat, eager to get to her little patients. Once she and I arrived at the hospital, she was on her own. She no longer needed to be led to her job. She'd just trot across the lobby and down the hall to the pediatric wing. When she reached Pedes, she'd scratch on the door until someone heard her and let her in.

As she made her journey, people would call out to her, "Hey, Nick Nack, come here, Girl," but she'd never stop.

She was a dog on a mission. She had children who were depending on her.

And I never knew what I'd find when I went to get her. She seemed to love being read to most of all, but these visits weren't about Nick Nack. She was there for the kids. If a child were so sick he couldn't play, she'd crawl onto his bed and snuggle quietly by his side. She'd also agreeably lie in front of the TV while children lounged all over her. If the kids just needed for her to watch them while they played in modeling clay, she'd happily oblige, sitting quietly, peering over their table as they pounded, rolled, and molded.

For some reason, the children loved dressing Nick Nack in costume. One day I'd find her wearing a party hat on her head and a lei around her neck; another day she'd be wearing clown-size sunglasses. Nothing was too silly for Nick Nack. She'd just grin and bear it if it made her little friends feel better.

She was born to do this job.

Nick Nack's job, though, was dependent upon my continued treatments. But my chemo couldn't last forever. When, after eight months, my treatments ended, I, much to my surprise, had mixed emotions. As sick as the chemo had made me, it had also given me hope—hope that I would live, live to enjoy this new life that I was forging for myself. Mostly, though, it gave me hope that I would live to mother Alex through her raging teens, those years when she would need so many "I knows."

And the hospital, its staff, and the other patients had become very special to me. I had found the kind of friendship I didn't know existed—that kind of friendship that comes from the heart, from compassion, from understanding. I had also learned how to be that friend—that friend who understands. I'd never been that kind of friend. It was a wonderful feeling.

As I stood to leave on my last day of treatment, I burst into tears. Holly was on duty that day and came to me and wrapped me in her loving arms.

As she handed me a tissue from her pocket, she rubbed by back and said, "I know, I know."

How was she aware that I needed an "I know, I know?"

Her tenderness just made me weep harder. She held me and stroked my back. When I'd composed myself, I mopped my face and gave her a kiss on the cheek. Then I turned to my friends. One by one, I said my goodbyes to them.

Eliza refused to let me cry. "Go kick some ass, Girl!"

I was sure she was going to kick some racing ass with that new titanium leg of hers.

Beth looked beautiful, as ever. She was wearing a new coral scarf with a geometric print, tied around her head, turban style. She smiled and said, "I believe we're getting closer to finding that baby, Rowdy."

I didn't doubt for a minute that she and Chip would be parents.

Peg, sporting her new long, red wig, gave me a hug and said, "Thanks, thanks so much for everything."

I loved the way she had turned the corner. And all it had taken was silly socks. And a long, red wig.

But I couldn't contain my tears as I approached Miss Maudie. I sat by her and took her frail body in my arms. I knew I was seeing her for the last time.

"Don't cry, my dear," she said, as she wiped my tears with her gnarled, shaking hand. She had lost so much weight that the only thing that kept her jangling wedding rings on her finger was her swollen, arthritis knuckle. I held her cold hands in mine as she said to me, "Life is too precious to spend one second crying. I will cherish our chats. Now, you take care, and tell Nick Nack I love her."

I left the treatment room, still sniffling, and headed for Pedes to collect Nick Nack for the last time.

"We'll miss her," all the nurses said. "We love her just as much as the children do."

"I know, but it's time for us to move on. My chemo is complete, and I won't have to be coming back, I hope."

"That's great news," they all said and hugged me.

⊸⥿⥽⊸

But Nick Nack did not understand that my chemo had ended. So the following Wednesday she planted herself at the front door, ready to leave for work. How do you explain to a dog that you no longer need chemo treatments and that you won't be going to the hospital anymore? Nick Nack was smart, but there were just some things even she couldn't grasp. She'd wait and wait—so patiently. Occasionally, she'd let out a whimper or an exasperated sigh. Throughout the day she would look longingly up at me and whine, trying to tell me that she was late for work.

After several weeks of Nick Nack's waiting and my realizing that she wasn't going to forget about Wednesdays, I called the hospital and asked to be transferred to the Pediatric Oncology Department.

"Good morning, this is Rowdy Murphy."

"Well, hi, Nick Nack's mommy," said the nurse who answered the phone. "We sure do miss our girl."

"Looks like she misses you, too. She just doesn't seem ready to give up her job. Is there still an opening?"

"Oh, yes. She is welcomed to come play as long as she wants."

So it was settled: on Wednesdays after Nick Nack finished her morning ritual and made her way to the front door, I'd be waiting for her, ready to take her to work. When we got to the hospital, she seemed to brighten. We were on her turf. I'd follow her as she trotted down the sidewalk to the lobby door. Once inside, she'd click across the marble entry, take a sharp left to the pediatric wing, stopping to scratch on the oncology room door. There she'd be greeted with hugs and laughter, and she always seemed to sense exactly where she was needed each work day.

I'd wait to make sure she was settled with the children before leaving for home or errands. I'd return after several hours to find her entertaining the children. Nick Nack was back on the job, and she was one happy girl.

One Wednesday I stopped by to pick up Nick Nack and found her sitting in a circle of children. A volunteer was reading a story to the group, and Nick Nack was sitting attentively, dressed in costume, of course, a bright red bandana around her neck. Rather than interrupt the reading, I took a seat in a small child's chair off to one side and waited.

A frail little girl with huge, hollow hazel eyes and wispy straw-colored hair toddled over and, without speaking or taking her thumb from her mouth, climbed into my lap, leaned against my chest, and sighed from the effort. I was taken aback by her trust but moved by her vulnerability. I instinctively wrapped by arms around her and touched my lips to her downy little head.

"Hi, Precious. I'm glad you came to visit me. My name is Rowdy."

Without moving her body, she tilted her head back, smiled a weak smile, and said around her thumb, "Rowy."

"And what's your name, Cutie?"

Still refusing to take her thumb from her mouth, she managed, "Natalie."

"Well, hi, Natalie. You just rest right there, and we'll listen to the lady read the book. Okay?"

Head still tilted back, she closed her eyes and melted into me. I had forgotten how sweet a little body can be when it clings to you and trusts you to take care. I stroked her back and breathed in her little-girl smell, and soon she was purring in sleep. When reading circle was over, Nick Nack noticed that I was there, and she came to greet me, smiling happily but tired from her day's work.

"Ready to go, Nick Nack?" I whispered, so as not to wake Natalie.

I rose and handed my sleeping bundle to Mary Helen, the head nurse on duty, and said quietly, "Nick Nack and I will see you next week."

Wednesday after Wednesday we returned for Nick Nack's job, but I found myself coming to pick her up earlier each time. I'd so enjoyed holding Natalie, and I was hoping I'd get to cuddle another little child. Alex had gotten so big that it was uncool to cuddle anymore. I'd get a peck on the cheek, a brisk embrace with a pat on the back, and a perky "Love ya!"

As the children became accustomed to me and knew that I was their darling Nick Nack's mommy, one by one they approached me. Some wanted to sit in my lap; others just wanted to hold my hand or stand nearby. Some brought books for me to read or toys to share. I loved it all. I found that whatever the children needed was what I needed, as well. I was beginning to understand Nick Nack's approach to child care.

One Wednesday morning I walked Nick Nack to Pedes and waited for her to scratch on the door, as she always did. But she didn't scratch. She just stared at the door and then stared up at me.

"Well, Nick Nack, it isn't going to open itself."

Still she just stared. Then I realized she was waiting for me to open the door for her. When I did, she moved halfway through and looked up at me. She wouldn't budge.

"Don't you feel like going to work today, Nick Nack?"

Still she stood and stared at me. Finally, I went into the unit to tell the nurses it appeared that Nick Nack didn't feel like staying. But I was wrong. As soon as I was in the ward, Nick Nack led me to a circle of children playing and stood staring at an empty chair.

Then it hit me: Nick Nack wanted me to stay and play.

As soon as I took a seat in the chair, she left me to tend to her patients. From time to time she'd come to check on me, but, for the most part, she just took care of her children.

All morning I cuddled, rocked, and played with the tiny patients. I couldn't remember ever being so content, so needed. It only takes a little love and attention to please a child, especially a sick one. And I found that attending to the children was amazingly comforting.

Around noon Mary Helen pulled up a little chair and sat next to me.

"Treat you to lunch?"

"Lunch?"

It was lunch time. Nick Nack and I had been playing for three hours.

"Let's let Nick Nack play with the children, and you and I can go down to the cafeteria for a bite. The food's not great—you know what they say about hospital food—but it's filling and pretty healthy."

"Yeah, thanks, I'd like that."

I stood, stretched my cramped legs, and extracted myself from my cadre of mini-friends and said, "Gotta run for a sec, but I'll be back. Save my place."

They all whined and held onto me, much to my delight, but finally let me go.

Mary Helen had been right: the food was not that great, but how much damage can you do to a salad? But the food didn't really matter. I was having lunch with a new friend. The invitation felt so good. Sitting across from Mary Helen reminded me how much I had missed the camaraderie of a girlfriend. I hoped this wouldn't be a one-time deal.

"You're great with the kids, Rowdy," said Mary Helen, between bites. "They all just love you."

"Well, much to my surprise, I love them all, too. I have just one child and she is my heart, but she's gotten to be such a big girl, too big and too cool to cuddle. My affinity for these little ones surprises me."

"Rowdy, have you ever thought of going into nursing?"

I let out a guffaw, so loud that other diners turned to look, and I snorted, "Good lord, no!"

Mary Helen said, "You make it sound as though I've asked if you'd ever considered drinking battery acid. It's actually not that distasteful. It's really a wonderful, rewarding profession. And we try not to torture too many of our patients."

"Oh, I'm so sorry, Mary Helen. I didn't mean to offend you. It's just that it never entered my mind that nursing was a profession for me."

"Well, what is your profession?"

"I don't have a profession," I confessed sheepishly. "I used to teach school, high school English. I majored in English because I loved to read, and I'd wanted to be a teacher since I was a little girl."

"Did you enjoy teaching?"

"Well, I did for a while, until I realized that my students didn't want to learn. And unlike you, I *did* torture many a student with

Chaucer and Shakespeare."

Mary Helen laughed and said, "Yeah, I remember being tortured with Chaucer and Shakespeare. That's probably about the time I decided to become a nurse." Then she asked, "How long ago did you quit teaching?"

"Long ago. I taught for just two years. Then I volunteered at the library, but mostly, I've been a stay-at-home mom. Problem is, I have little to stay at home for anymore. Alex is ten now, and she's growing up and away from me fast."

"Doesn't sound very rewarding, Rowdy."

It was true. Sure, I'd committed to living my life, rather than just reacting to the life that had come hurtling at me. I felt that I was making progress, but did I really have a plan? What was my future?

"Rowdy, I see how you are with the children. You would make a wonderful nurse. You're a natural. I wish you'd consider it. And it seems like you've got the time to devote to it."

I was optimistic about my treatment, but I had to be realistic, as well. There were no guarantees that I would be cancer free. Did I dare commit to schooling and a new career when there was so much uncertainty about my chances of a complete recovery?

"But, Mary Helen, I have cancer. What if my treatment doesn't work? What if I have just six months left?"

She reached over and took my hand. "Rowdy, maybe you do have just six months left. But you also may have six years. Or sixty years. We have no way of knowing."

I smiled weakly, considering that I may have only six months but, all of a sudden, wishing for sixty years. Until then I hadn't allowed myself to ponder a time frame.

I squeezed her hand and said, "Thanks, Mary Helen," but refused to commit to anything.

"Rowdy, do you think that nursing is something you might enjoy?"

The notion was so new, so unexpected. I still couldn't respond.

Sensing I wasn't ready to jump in, Mary Helen went on: "I graduated from Carolina Nursing School and have stayed active in the Alumni Association. I've even served on the Alumni Board. I know people, *lots* of people. I'd love to help."

I told her I'd think about it, but I wasn't very convincing, even to myself.

She looked at her watch and said, "Well, I guess I'd better get back to the ward. Grace and Susan need to take their break."

I'm certain she didn't want to belabor the point, just wanted to give me time to consider her proposal.

When we returned to Pedes, we found Nick Nack standing by the door. When she saw Mary Helen and me, she looked at each of us expectantly, as if she had been part of the nursing conspiracy and was just waiting to hear what I'd had to say.

"Hey, Girl, ready to go?"

She turned to give her charges a little yip goodbye, then headed for the door, confident I'd trail after her.

I reached out and touched Mary Helen's arm and said, "I'll give it some thought. And thanks so much for lunch. It was nice."

"Sure, Rowdy. I'm very serious. I won't pester, but I'm here to help if I can."

Twenty-eight

S he didn't pester, just as she had promised, so I pushed her offer to the back of my mind. It kept slipping forward, though, piquing my interest. No one had ever told me that I was good at something—not even at teaching, my chosen profession. Mark had never told me I was a good wife, a good mother, a good housekeeper. But Mary Helen had seen something in me, something that told her I'd be good at *her* profession. After several more weeks of accompanying Nick Nack to her job while still trying to ignore the idea of my becoming a nurse, I clicked on the computer and surfed for the UNC School of Nursing website.

I liked what I saw. There were testimonials from current and former students, all eager about their studies and their jobs, all proud to be Carolina nurses. I read about the work they did, the gratification they derived from helping others. It made me feel guilty. I didn't help a soul. I just lived from day to day, focused on myself: my illness, my loneliness, Mark's new life. I wanted to feel what those nurses felt. I wanted to feel as though I made a difference.

I checked out the requirements and found that I exceeded the minimum. I had taken all of the compulsory science courses, and I had graduated from NC State summa cum laude, with a 3.8 GPA. My only B's had been in some of those science courses.

The more I discovered about the program, the more excited I became. There was even opportunity for service abroad. I could already envision myself helping sick children in third-world countries. My enthusiasm must have shown because Nick Nack pulled herself up from her puddle on the floor and trotted over to see what was so exhilarating.

"I think I'm going to be a nurse, Nick Nack. What do you think about that?"

In her usual show of support, she flipped her plumy tail in a circle and gave me a sincere doggie grin.

"I know, Girl, it's exciting, isn't it? But you and Mary Helen have been planning this all along, haven't you?"

She let out a cheerful yip before spinning in circles.

Leaving Nick Nack dancing, I reached for the phone. Remembering the hospital number by heart, I dialed.

"Hi, would you please connect me to Pediatric Oncology?"

"Sure thing, Hon, hold on jus' a sec," replied the operator in her honey-sweet accent.

While I waited, my stomach did flip-flops. Was I rushing into this? Was I making a smart choice, or was I letting my emotions make this decision for me? Well, I wasn't signing in blood. It wouldn't hurt to check it out.

"Pediatric Oncology, may I help you?"

"May I speak with Mary Helen, please?"

"She's with patients right now. May I take your number and have her call you?"

"Yes, that would be fine. This is Rowdy Murphy calling."

"Oh, hey, Rowdy, this is Melody."

"Hi, Melody. If you'd just have Mary Helen call me at 919-828-9979, that would be great."

"Sure thing, Rowdy. I'll give her the message."

In fifteen minutes the phone rang.

"Hey, Rowdy, what's up."

"I've been thinking…"

"About?"

"Nursing. I've been thinking about your offer, and I believe I'd like to check it out. Now, I've perused the UNC Nursing School website, and it really looks like something I'd like to take a look at. But, you understand, I'm not committing to anything just yet."

"No commitment, no promises. I understand. It's a big step to take, but it won't hurt to look."

"Good," I said, letting out my breath in relief.

"Why don't I make an appointment with the Dean, and then I'll call you back. We can go talk with her and some of the professors, check out the classrooms, get a bite of lunch, do a little shopping on Franklin Street. We'll just make a girls' day of it. Does that sound good?"

"That sounds perfect. Any day but Wednesday will do because, you know, that's the day I have to take Nick Nack to work."

Mary Helen laughed and said, "Don't I know that. We can't have Nick Nack missing a day of work."

✂✄

The following Monday Mary Helen pulled into the driveway at nine sharp. I was waiting with purse in hand, eager to write the next chapter of my life. I knew that chapter just might not include nursing, but I was confident that it would hold more than endless days of nothingness. This trip was just the beginning.

Nick Nack stood eagerly by the front door. I crouched and put my arm around her neck and gave her a kiss between her ears.

"Not today, Nick Nack. You'll have to stay home this time and take care of things for me."

She tilted her head and looked quizzically at me as I stood and reached for the door. But she didn't whine or protest or try to follow me as I let myself out, leaving her standing alone. As I walked down the sidewalk, a motion in the living room window caught my attention. Nick Nack had made her way there and had perched on her hind legs so she could watch my departure. I waved at her, and I could tell that she had barked me a "Goodbye" when the window fogged and obscured her snout.

"Morning, you ready for this?" asked Mary Helen as I hopped into her passenger seat.

"Think so. I didn't sleep much last night. I know I said I wasn't making promises, but just checking this out is a big step for me."

Mary Helen smiled, reached over, and patted my arm. "No promises, just a girls' day out. Right?"

"Right."

Thirty minutes later we were on the beautiful University of North Carolina campus. The spring semester was underway, and the grounds were lively with smiling, bustling students, all of them looking as if they had some important place to be. I wanted to look as if I had some important place to be. We strolled the campus, Mary Helen pointing out landmarks, explaining interesting facts about this building or that monument. Like the students, Mary Helen looked energized just by being on the University campus, a place she loved passionately.

We had a 10:30 appointment with the Dean of the School of Nursing, so we made our way to her office, Mary Helen happily skipping and chatting along the way. I don't know what I was expecting in a dean of nurses, but what I found was a lovely woman, warm and welcoming.

She stood and shook my hand firmly, saying, "Please call me Evelyn," and smiled sincerely as she told me how delighted she was that I had taken *my* time to visit with *her*.

"Mary Helen has told me so much about you, Rowdy. I've been quite eager to meet you."

I was taken aback by her kindness.

"Thank you so much. And I'm grateful that you were willing to make time to talk with me."

"Well, when Mary Helen recommends a potential student, we know we have a winner."

I looked at Mary Helen, and she grinned and winked at me.

Then the Dean folded her hands on her desk, leaned toward me, and said, "And why do you want to be a nurse, Rowdy?"

I went hot all over. I wasn't expecting that, but why wasn't I? By all appearances I was here looking into nursing school. Why wouldn't the Dean assume that I wanted to be a nurse? But as frightened as the Dean's question made me, a calm came over me, and I really felt like a woman who did want to be a nurse. Someone had told me I was good with sick children, and I knew that I loved comforting and caring for young patients. And at that moment I knew, for sure, that I did want to be a nurse. I also knew why I wanted to be a nurse.

"I've been sick, sick with breast cancer. It has been a difficult journey, a journey I could not have made without the help of my caregivers."

I didn't mention that my favorite caretaker was a dog, but she didn't need to know that.

"I want to make people feel the way they have made me feel. I want to let people know that I care and understand and have walked in their shoes. And I want UNC School of Nursing to teach me how to do that."

Evelyn smiled and said, "Rowdy, we can teach you how to do

that."

❧❧

The following weeks were a whirlwind of transcript gathering, interviews, and scheduling. With Mary Helen and the Dean's help and a lot of string pulling, the UNC School of Nursing admitted me in time to begin classes the first summer semester.

When my acceptance letter arrived, I screamed, jumped up and down, and danced around the kitchen with Nick Nack. Then I called Mary Helen.

"Oh, Rowdy, I knew you could do it."

"Me? Mary Helen, you did this. And I can never repay you, never thank you for your kindness."

"Well, I helped get you there. You're going to do the work to stay there and show that you were meant to be a nurse."

"I won't disappoint you, Mary Helen."

"I know you won't, Rowdy."

Then I made another call.

"Gatewood, this is Rowdy. You're not going to believe this."

"Uh oh, what have you done now?"

"Rowdy Doody is going to Carolina!"

"Get out of town!"

"No lie, Gatewood. I'm going to study nursing. I'll start classes in June."

"Well, dang, I believe you're gonna make this old man cry, Sweetie. I'm just proud as I can be. Couldn't be prouder if you was my own. And as much as your sweet daddy loved that Wolfpack, he'd be busting with pride for his little girl."

"Thanks, Gatewood. I just wanted you to know."

"Well, I'm touched, Rowdy. Now you keep me posted, you hear?"

And I hung up, glad that Gatewood was proud of me and knowing that my sweet daddy would be proud, too. But, mostly, I was proud of myself.

But what about Alex? What would she think about her mom returning to school? I hadn't wanted to tell her until I got my acceptance. I felt she didn't need to know until it was a done deal. Also, my cancer had distanced me from her, not by choice, but it had happened just the same. Would she feel that I was abandoning her if I embarked on this new commitment?

I planted myself in front of the living room window, waiting for her to come home from school. When I saw her round the corner with Conner and Everette, giggling and skipping, I prayed I was making the right decision, not only for me, but for Alex, too.

When they reached Conner and Everette's house, Alex hugged them both good-bye and ran the rest of the way home.

"Mama, I'm home," she yelled as she burst through the front door.

"I'm in here, Darlin'," I called from the living room.

"Geesh, I'm hungry. We had fish sticks for lunch. Blech!"

"Well, let's go get a snack," I said, linking my arm in hers and skipping toward the kitchen.

I poured her a glass of milk and said, "What do you want?"

"Oreos, please. Can I have three?"

It's *may* I have three, but I no longer corrected her grammar. I'd leave that to her teachers and hope they did their jobs.

"Sure. Three it is."

I put her Oreos on a napkin and placed them on the kitchen table in front of her and sat down next to her.

"Alex, what would you think about my going back to school?"

"Huh? What school?" she said, her mouth full of cookie.

"I've decided to become a nurse. I want to go to nursing school."

Her eyes grew wide, and she said, "Oh, Mama, that's soooo *awesome*."

Awesome. The height of a ten-year old's compliment.

"You mean like a nurse in a hospital?"

"Yeah, maybe in a hospital."

"That is so neat."

"I'm glad you think so 'cause I've already been accepted at Carolina. I'll start classes in June.

"Oh, Mama, that's great!" she screamed and reached over and hugged me. Then grabbing her last two cookies, she said, "I gotta go tell Conner and Everette. They're gonna freak!"

She reached the kitchen door but turned around and said, "Mama, you rock!"

And she went pounding out the front door to tell her friends.

I looked at Nick Nack and said, "And I was worried. I'm not only cool and awesome, I also rock."

Twenty-nine

It happened so fast. I just turned around and there I was, sitting in my first nursing class, as if I'd planned to be a nurse all along.

The courses were fascinating. Having come from a liberal arts background, I was surprised to discover how much I enjoyed the sciences. But I did. The first semester I took Disciplines of Nursing, Nursing Role in Nutrition, Pathophysiology, and Health Assessment. And I proved to myself, and anyone else who cared to know, that I really belonged in the program, that I deserved to be a nurse. I aced my subjects and finished my first semester with a 4.0 average. Can't get any better than that.

Mary Helen was wonderfully supportive, calling regularly to check on me and to see if I had any questions or needed any help. Alex, too, was so proud of me and continued to think I was so cool, but she was growing up and had school and friends and interests of her own. Nick Nack, though, was the most supportive of all. She'd meet me at the door every afternoon, shivering with excitement over my return. She'd follow me down the hall to the kitchen, staring up into my face, eager to hear about my day. Once we got to the kitchen, I'd grab a bottle of water and sink to the floor, my first relaxation since early morning. Nick Nack would plop beside me, and I'd tell her every detail about my classes, my new friends, my professors. And she rewarded me with her undivided attention. Every once in a while, she'd slap her tail on the floor or give me an excited yip, as if she were following every word I was saying. I was beginning to think she was.

I rewarded Nick Nack by continuing to take her to the hospital each Wednesday morning. I'd get up extra early and go ten miles out of my way so she could continue to keep her job. Each Wednesday afternoon I'd battle the east-bound traffic to pick her up from work. She was always happy to see me, showering me with kisses, but she hated leaving her little patients. Guess we were both meant to be nurses.

❧❧

I overslept one Wednesday and had to rush to grab Alex a Pop Tart and get her off to school. I had just enough time to choose between taking Nick Nack to work or packing my lunch. I figured I could find something to eat on campus and rushed to get Nick Nack to the hospital.

I arrived on campus just in time for my eight o'clock class and wasn't able to get even a cup of coffee. Throughout my morning classes my stomach rumbled from hunger. By noon I was ravenous, and my stomach sounded volcanic. I rushed to the snack bar, finding a line of students snaking from the lunch counter out the door. I grabbed a pack of Nabs and a Coke and headed straight for the express check-out. I figured that would fill the growling pit and tide me over until I got back to Raleigh.

Open Coke and Nabs in one hand, Nutrition textbook in the other, I walked across campus to my next class, re-reading the day's assignment.

"Oomph!"

My Coke hit the pavement, spewing its contents across the jeans of the person with whom I'd collided.

"Oh, I'm so sorry!" I gasped as I looked up into the face of a man who looked somewhat familiar.

"Hey, that's okay. They needed washing anyway," he said with a smile. "Are you all right?"

"Of course, I'm all right. My Coke ruined *your* jeans, not *mine*. I really am so sorry. I'd offer to wash them for you, but I'm assuming you don't have an extra pair in your backpack. So I guess you'll have to wash them yourself, and I'll just be embarrassed for my clumsiness."

As mortified as I was, I was quite taken aback by the way I was bantering with this stranger. I hadn't bantered with a man since Mark had admired my hair and eyes and I'd told him he had great taste. It actually felt like flirting, and I blanched at the very notion.

He continued to smile and extended his hand. "Hi, I'm Kent Southerland."

"Oh, sure, you're in my Nutrition class. I'm Rowdy Murphy," I said, tucking my book under my arm and reaching to shake his hand.

Taking my hand in both of his, he said, "I know you're Rowdy Murphy, and I'm in *all* of your classes. And, by the way, cool name."

Blushing with embarrassment and, I'm guessing, because I hadn't held a man's hand in god-knows-how-long, I stammered, "Oh, I'm sorry...again, and...glad you like my name."

"Hey," Kent said, checking his watch, "we have about thirty minutes till class. How about we grab a cup of coffee and sit in the sun so my pants can dry?"

Still blushing, I smiled and said, "Sure. Maybe if I'd had my breakfast coffee, none of this would have happened."

"That would have been sad," was all he said, as we walked toward Starbucks on Franklin Street.

As we drank our coffee and I shared my Nabs with Kent, the sun dried the Coke on his pants to a nice brown stain. We chatted comfortably, lost track of time, and were late getting to class.

That accidental meeting had gone so well that we'd decided to try again—minus the Coke.

◈◈◈

"Your dog is what?"

"A nurse. Well, I guess she's a nurse's aide since she doesn't give shots. But she could if she wanted to."

We had just begun our second week of daily coffee meet-ups. We'd discovered right away that we had the same silly sense of humor, and we'd spent that first week trading jokes and superficialities. That was enough to get our friendship off the ground.

"She's really quite brilliant. It was her idea that I go to nursing school—well, hers and Mary Helen's, a nurse who works in her department."

"*Her* department?"

"Yes. Pediatric Oncology. Nick Nack is in charge of patient morale."

"Nick Nack! Love it! How do y'all come up with these cool names?"

I marveled at how comfortable I felt with Kent from the start. I was confident he felt comfortable, as well. But there comes a time in a friendship when you have to move beyond the superficial and offer up some truth—if, in fact, you want that friendship to flourish. And I think we both wanted that. But I wasn't sure I was ready for self-disclosure, so I was grateful when he chose to take the lead.

"I grew up in Raleigh, but I went away to school, to MIT."

"Wow, I'm impressed."

He blushed but said, "Well, I guess you should be. I am awesomely smart."

I could tell that even when we were serious, we'd still manage to be silly. I liked that.

"Before graduation I interviewed with IBM, they offered me a job, and I moved right back to Raleigh the day I graduated. I've been in the area ever since. It's home. There's no place else I'd rather be."

"Me, too," I said, "but I've *never* left. I went from Broughton High to State and settled down in Raleigh after graduation."

He continued, "I went to Sanderson High. I was in the tenth grade when my mom died. It was just my dad and me after that. He was my best friend."

"You said 'was.' Is your dad still living?"

"No. He had a heart attack," Kent said and looked off wistfully. He paused and took a sip of coffee before looking back at me. "We were fishing out on Falls Lake. I didn't know what to do, Rowdy. I felt completely helpless as I watched my dad die."

"Oh, Kent, that's so sad. I'm sorry."

He took a deep breath and continued, "If I'd known CPR, I probably could have saved his life. But it never dawned on me until then that I was going to need to save my dad's life. I'll never get over that," he said and looked sadly into his coffee cup.

I wanted to tell him, "Oh, no, you shouldn't feel that way," but that wasn't for me to say. He had every right to feel remorseful, sad, and it wasn't my place to negate his feelings. So I just let him talk.

"I learned CPR and became an EMT. Rowdy, I started saving lives. It was incredible. The day I saved a man who was having a heart attack, I felt like my dad was forgiving me. That's when I decided that caring for people, not their computers, was my calling. I quit my well-paying job and used my savings and my inheritance from my dad to enroll in nursing school." And spreading his arms wide, he smiled broadly and said, "And here I am. Best decision of my life."

Then he leaned across the table and took my hand for the first time. I thought I was going to cry. A man hadn't touched me in nearly two years, and his tenderness tugged at my heart.

"And what's your story, Rowdy?" he asked. "Your smile is beautiful, and you are so incredibly funny, but there's a sadness behind those gorgeous emerald eyes."

Where should I start? And was I really ready to share the details of my life? To pour out all the sadness that lurked behind my emerald eyes? He knew that I lived in Raleigh with my ten-year-old daughter and my dog who was a nurse at Rex Hospital. What else did he need to know? Well, if we were going to be friends—and, apparently, we were—and if he were going to share the intimate details of his life—and he had—I guessed I owed him a glimpse into mine.

So I said, very matter-of-factly, "I have cancer."

I don't know what I expected his response to be. Shock? Pity? Retreat?

"Well, that sucks all to hell!" he exclaimed, and slapped his hand on the table, causing our coffee to slosh.

I smiled wanly and said, "There's more."

He reached for my hand once more and said, "Okay." That's all he needed to say. That *okay* meant "I'm all ears, and I'm going to hold on to you while you tell me, and I'll be right here if you need me."

At least I was hoping that's what it meant.

"Well," I said, taking a deep breath, "I discovered the lump in my breast just days before my ex-husband married his pregnant-with-twins girlfriend."

"Holy cow! You're making this up, right?"

I laughed, because as painful as it had been, hearing it out loud sounded absurd. "I'm just not that creative, Kent. I could not have made it up."

His gaze softened as he said, "So that's the pain lurking behind those gorgeous eyes."

"Well, yes, it has been very painful. But I am doing quite well, thanks to my nurse."

"And that nurse would be Nick Nack?"

"Right. She gave me a swift kick in the butt and insisted I start living again. She and my nurse friend, Mary Helen, are the reason I'm in nursing school."

Thirty

I could easily get bogged down in my studies. I would forget to eat, resist sleep, and find myself face-down on the kitchen table in a puddle of drool at three in the morning, my pencil still poised over my notes.

From time to time, Nick Nack would hoist herself from her pallet in the corner and click across the linoleum to check on me. I'd scruff her thick coat, give her a kiss, and chuck a biscuit onto the floor. She'd chase her treat, sliding across the slick tile, and sling it in the air a time or two for my entertainment. Then she'd settle down to crunch on her snack and drift back to sleep.

"How'd you like to go for a walk, Nick Nack? We haven't been to Shelley Lake for a long time."

At the mention of Shelley Lake, Nick Nack's ears perked. She and I hadn't visited since our early-morning trek the week I learned that I had cancer and Mark remarried. Lots had happened since then, and I'd come a long way.

I unfolded myself from my chair, my joints creaking. I rubbed my sore back as I headed for my bedroom to shed my pajamas and put on my shorts, tank top, and tennis shoes. I brushed my teeth, washed my face, and crammed my short wig on my head. My hair was growing back, but I wasn't quite ready to bare my stubble-laden head. I skipped down the stairs and returned to the kitchen to collect Nick Nack and a bottle of water.

The day was beyond beautiful: mid 80's, moderate humidity—unseasonably mild for summer in central North Carolina. I was so glad Nick Nack and I weren't wasting this precious gift as we hopped into our car and headed for the lake.

We weren't the only ones anticipating enjoying the weather; the parking lot was crammed to overflowing. We circled around and around till a jogger called it a day and backed his Prius out of a coveted spot. Other circlers shot me angry looks or envious stares as I slid into the empty space.

Nick Nack and I were halfway around the two-mile trail when I heard a breathless voice behind me.

"Come here often?"

I turned to see Kent jogging in place, his blue Carolina tee shirt soaked with perspiration, his welcoming smile stretched wide. I normally prefer my men blond with blue eyes, but this guy with the dark hair and playful black eyes was looking mighty fine.

"Who wants to know?" I said coyly.

"That guy who just passed asked me to find out."

"Well, maybe that guy should speak for himself."

Kent's and my relationship had progressed past friendship to that silly, flirty stage. It was fun, but, for the time being, I needed to keep it just fun and flirty—nothing more serious. School and cancer were just about all I could handle at one time. But who knew where it might lead? I pushed that thought to the back of my mind and filed it under *Things to Think About Way Down the Road.*

Nick Nack had been romping, stealing some other dog's Frisbee—she swore she was just borrowing it—but all her romping and stealing came to an abrupt halt when she discovered that I was sharing my attention with someone else. She dropped her buddy's Frisbee and sailed to my side. She leaned into me and peered suspiciously at Kent.

"It's Nick Nack!" he yelled and dropped to his knees to ruffle her thick fur.

And all was forgiven.

It was love at first hug. She licked his hand and smiled excitedly, as if they were long-lost buddies.

"She's gorgeous and wonderful. I love her!"

"Of course you do. What's not to love? She's a fellow nurse."

After a five-minute love fest that excluded me, Kent pried himself from Nick Nack's adoration and said, "I need to get a move-on. My air conditioner is on the fritz, and the repairman is coming this afternoon."

"This afternoon, meaning between noon and nine p.m., right?"

"Yeah, something like that. So I'd better get on home and start the waiting game."

He gave Nick Nack one more scratch on her head and, before turning to leave, said, "You live near here?"

"Not far. I live off of Bridgeport in Salisbury Park."

"No way!" he exclaimed. "I'm on Dresden Lane in Valley Estates."

We couldn't have lived much more than a mile apart.

"Do you ever have coffee at Starbucks in Stonehenge?"

"All the time," I offered.

"How about tomorrow morning?"

"Sounds good. Nine-ish?"

"Nine-ish sounds perfect. But Nick Nack has to come, too."

"I don't think Starbucks allows dogs."

"We'll have our coffee outside."

Backing away at a slow jog, he pointed at me and yelled, "You, me, Nick Nack, Starbucks, Stonehenge, tomorrow, nine-ish."

And he turned and jogged away at full speed. That's when I noticed, for the first time, what a nice tush Kent had. Then I filed that in my *Things to Think About Way Down the Road* folder.

❧❦❧

At the last minute I kicked my shorts and tennis shoes into the corner of my bedroom and went to my closet. I pulled out my blue-and-white striped sundress, stepped in, and zipped it up the back. Then I slipped on my strappy, yellow sandals and picked up my purse.

I clattered down the stairs and yelled, "Let's go, Nick Nack!"

Within seconds she came flying out of the kitchen and galloped down the hall to find out where we were going. As soon as I opened the front door, she raced across the porch, down the stairs, and up the sidewalk. She was standing by the car before I could lock my front door. When I reached the car, I found her prancing impatiently for me to open the door so that she could hop up onto her perch. All the way to Starbucks she shimmied with excitement of the unknown.

As soon as we pulled into the parking lot, I spied Kent. I was so glad I had changed out of my shorts and tennis shoes. He was dressed in khakis, a blue Polo, and deck shoes. I had seen him in only

225

jeans or sweaty jogging shorts, so I was taken aback by his put-together appearance, his stunning good looks.

Nick Nack was in a perfect glee when she discovered that Kent was waiting for us.

She looked at me with such delight, as if to say, "Well, if I had known he was a member of this club, I'd have joined long ago."

She greeted him with a huge smile, a flinging tail, and excited shimmying. Kent returned her greeting with a warm hug and two doggie biscuits. Nick Nack looked from the biscuits up at me. I swear she had stars in her eyes.

"I know, I know. He's just wonderful. But, remember, I'm the one who scoops your poop and keeps your dishes full. Don't be swayed by slick talk and tasty treats."

But she was having none of my rationale. She was loving this new friend. I really couldn't blame her.

Chuckling at our antics, Kent said, "Nick Nack, find us a table, and I'll go get coffee for Rowdy and me." Then to me he said, "Black with one-half packet of the pink stuff, right?"

"You've been paying attention."

"'Course I have," he said with a shy grin, as he left to place our order.

Nick Nack was beside herself with excitement and let out two loud barks, a surprise to me since she was typically quite docile.

"Calm down. I know he's cute."

Strutting around, she yipped at me.

"I know, but we just can't afford to get distracted from our studies right now."

When she whined, I said, "We'll see, Nick Nack, but for the time being, we'll just have to settle for coffee dates."

Nick Nack huffed, and I said, "Well, I don't expect you to understand, but it'll all work out. If it's meant to be, it'll be."

I was chatting and Nick Nack was sighing when Kent returned.

"What are y'all talking about?"

"Oh, just girl stuff," I said and scratched my BFF between her ears.

Kent handed me my coffee, doctored with half packet of pink stuff, and joined Nick Nack and me at our table.

Some say that dogs are chick magnets. Nick Nack was just a people magnet. Folks couldn't resist approaching this big black dog that looked like a bear, yet could smile cunningly and was as gentle as a kitten. Kent and I made countless friends because of my people magnet. Sure, they were drawn to her, but I like to think they stayed because of Kent's and my charm and sense of humor.

That first Saturday five or six people stopped to greet and pet Nick Nack. She welcomed each into our party, like an amiable hostess. Two biker guys, Jon and Roy, pulled up chairs, sat, and became permanent members of our group. Over time we added tables as the assemblage grew. We invited our fellow nursing students, and soon they, too, joined and fell in love with Nick Nack.

The last Saturday we took roll there were twenty-two of us.

Thirty-one

I could always tell when Pedes had lost a child. When I'd pick up Nick Nack, she wouldn't be her usual sassy, happy self. Her head would droop, she'd saunter rather than sashay, and she'd sigh, as if the grief were just more than she could bear. I'd open the car door for her, and she'd climb in with none of her usual gusto. Instead of sitting up, looking out the window at all the interesting things passing by, she'd lie beside me in the seat, staring at the floor. My heart would break for her. There were just some things her joy couldn't fix, and she took it hard.

One day I went to pick her up, and she was particularly droopy. She ambled to the car, head down, and when I opened the door, she jumped, lost her balance, and banged her chest into the side of the seat. She let out a loud yelp. I figured she must have been distracted by the loss and had not been paying close attention. On the second try, she dragged herself into her seat and lay motionless all the way home. For two days she moped around the house. She would drink her water, but she showed little interest in eating. She would sigh as if her heart were breaking, and when she did move around, she actually appeared to be limping. Most alarming, though, was her lack of interest in being my shadow. Though she loved attending to her children, she considered being my protector her most important job. But instead of following my every move, she spent her days curled in a ball in the corner of the kitchen. I was so worried that I called the children's ward.

"Mary Helen, did you lose a child this week?"

"No, Rowdy, everyone is hanging on."

"Well, did something happen when Nick Nack was with you Wednesday?"

"No, the children were holding their own, but we noticed that Nick Nack wasn't acting herself. She seemed to be dragging, limping around the ward. Is something wrong?"

"She's been moping around since Wednesday and isn't eating well. I thought it might have something to do with one of the children. Guess I'd better have the vet take a look at her."

As soon as I hung up, I called the vet's office.

"Dr. Reneker's office. Trisha speaking. May I help you?"

"Trisha, this is Rowdy Murphy."

"Oh, hey, Ms. Murphy. How you doin'?"

"Well, Trisha, I'm fine, but Nick Nack is under the weather. She isn't eating, and I'm really worried. Can Dr. Reneker see her today?"

"You're in luck, Ms. Murphy. He has a three o'clock cancellation. If you rush, it can be yours."

"Thanks, Trisha. We'll be there as quickly as we can."

I knew it would be tight, but I felt we couldn't wait for another opening.

"Come on, Nick Nack, let's go bye-bye."

She opened her eyes and tried hard to smile. With great effort she stood on wobbly legs, huffing all the way. She limped slowly to the front door and stood with her beautiful head down until I could collect my purse and keys. I opened the door for her, and she trudged across the porch and hobbled down the stairs. She followed me down the sidewalk but just stared up at me when I opened the car door and tried to coax her into her seat. She just couldn't do it. I flung my purse and keys onto the driver's side and reached down to lift Nick Nack into the car. Expecting it to be difficult to hoist her, I was shocked to find her so light. She'd lost weight in just the past couple of days. She winced and whimpered when I lifted her but settled quietly in her seat, shut her eyes, and slept through the twenty-minute trip to the vet's office.

. When we got there, I had to wake her. She wasn't able to get out of the car by herself, so, once again, I gave her a hand. I lifted her, easily, and carried her as gently as I could into Dr. Reneker's office. We arrived at the stroke of three.

Trisha said, "Good timing. Come on back," as she led us down the hall to an examining room.

Nick Nack was a clinic favorite since she was a happy dog and had such a good disposition. And she loved her vet visits because Dr. Reneker and the nurses showered her with hugs and attention and doggie treats. Today, though, she didn't have the energy to be sociable. She just let me cradle her in my arms until her doctor came into the examining room.

"Just put my girlfriend right there on the table, and we'll take a look. Hey, Nick Nack! How's my favorite girl?" Dr. Reneker said as he stroked her downy fur.

Normally Nick Nack would greet her doctor with smiles and wags, but on this visit she just didn't have the energy for either.

The vet listened to Nick Nack's heart, peered into her ears and nose and mouth, poked and probed her from top to bottom. Nick Nack lay motionless, looking up at me with eyes that were full of pain, eyes that begged me to make it stop. She couldn't tell me what was wrong, but I knew that she hurt and didn't understand why. It was my job to take care of her and keep her comfortable, but I was doing a lousy job.

"I can't find anything from my exam that would make her so listless. I'm going to draw some blood and send it to the lab. We should have the results of our tests in about two days. Then we'll know what's going on and where to go from here."

"What do you think the problem is?"

"Rowdy, I just don't know. That's why I'm ordering some tests. I'll let you know just as soon as I have answers."

The next two days lasted an eternity. Nick Nack didn't improve, and there was nothing I could do to help her. I couldn't entice her to eat, and she drank very little water. I tried to coax her outside, thinking the fresh air would lift her spirits. She tried, but she just didn't have the energy to move far from her pallet in the corner of the kitchen. I knew that something was seriously wrong.

True to his word, Dr. Reneker called in two days with the lab results.

"What do you mean? That can't be!"

"I'm so, so sorry, Rowdy."

"But Dr. Reneker, she's only five. She's too young to have cancer."

"I know, Rowdy, but you have to remember that's dog years. A five-year-old dog is the equivalent of a thirty-five year old human."

Thirty-five. The very same age I was when I was diagnosed with cancer.

And I buried my face in my great black dog—yes, she was mine, all mine—and sobbed. My darling Nick Nack had cancer. How could that be? That wonderful creature was put on earth to care for and cheer cancer patients. How could life have played such a dirty trick on her? And on me?

What caused this and how could I have missed such a thing? The guilt ate me alive, and I cried in anguish as Dr. Reneker told me that there was no known cause and that cancer in dogs can sometimes go undetected—especially if a dog is a giver and not a complainer.

A giver and not a complainer: that was my Nick Nack. She had given all her life and had never asked for a thing in return.

"What can you do for her?"

"Well, Rowdy, there are lots of treatments but no cure. They might put Nick Nack in remission, but she will relapse, probably sooner rather than later. Considering her advanced stage, my advice is to love her and keep her as comfortable as you can. I will send you something for her pain, but her best medicine will be the comfort she gets from being with you."

Dr. Reneker knew my Nick Nack so well.

My days were spent hovering over Nick Nack, trying to anticipate her needs and make her as comfortable as possible. I wanted to return the love and comfort she had given me and all her little sick friends. I was so immersed in Nick Nack's care, that, for the first time in two years, I almost forgot that I, too, was a cancer patient.

As I was filling Nick Nack's bowl with fresh water, the phone rang. I put the bowl in front of her, hoping she'd be interested, dried my hands on my jeans, and answered the phone.

"Yo, Rowdy!" yelled Dr. Easterling. "Get out those dancing shoes, baby. Your last tests are clear, not a sign of cancer. If I were there, I'd kiss you smack dab on the lips."

I didn't know what to say, so I just let the tears flow. My emotions were hovering right on the surface anyway, and I needed a good cry. I felt so blessed to be hearing such great news. I just wished that Nick Nack and I could be celebrating together.

"Thanks, Dr. Easterling. I'm really happy, honest I am," I said with a nervous, self-conscious laugh.

I couldn't tell the doctor who was trying to save my life that I was crying because my dog was sick.

"Well, I know this is an emotional time for you. You deserve a good cry. Now, take care, and I want to see you in my office in six months."

I hung up the phone, grabbed a wad of tissues and mopped my eyes and blew my nose.

I so wanted to share my good news with someone, but no one was around. Alex was at camp, and Mary Helen was at a nursing conference in New Orleans. Then there came a knock at my front door. That meant a human—a human with ears.

"Thank you, God. Someone to share my good news. I don't care if it's the meter reader, he's going to hear that I'm in remission."

I raced down the hall and flung open the front door, where my joy instantly evaporated. There stood Mark with his head bowed, his shoulders shaking.

Lifting his head, he wailed, "She left me, Rowdy!"

And he didn't see that coming? Just as I had been anticipating My Cure, I had also anticipated Tawni's leaving Mark. How could she not? Mark was sixteen years older than she, and he looked it and acted it. I had known all along that it was only a matter of time before Tawni would tire of Mark's sedentary lifestyle and his pompous, scholarly, know-it-all attitude. I also felt it was only a matter of time before Tawni would find someone new and young and beautiful, just like she was. It had actually taken longer than I had imagined, but the inevitable had finally happened.

Mark was weeping in anguish, but I had a hard time sympathizing with him. Hadn't he once made me feel just as he was feeling. Had he forgotten? I could have mentioned that, but even I couldn't kick him while he was so low.

Instead, I opened the door, stepped aside, and let him pass. He made a bee-line for the kitchen. He took a chair—the one he had occupied at meals for nearly six years—rested his face in his hands, and ramped up his weeping.

Through racking sobs he bellowed, "What am I going to do?"

I clenched my jaw to keep from screaming, "You can be abandoned by your spouse and get breast cancer and suffer through surgery and painful treatments and lose all your hair and think you're going to die and sometimes hope you do die and be scared shitless!"

Mark didn't even notice my clenched jaw or angry, slitted eyes. He just kept crying, "I love her. I miss her. She's my one and only soul mate."

Now, that stabbed a dagger through my heart, but I just let the rantings of a mad, wounded man pass.

I had just heard that I was cancer free. All Mark could do was whine about himself. As he continued to weep in his world of self-absorption, I remembered that excruciating pain when Mark told me he was leaving me. I wouldn't wish that pain on my worst enemy, but Mark, the only man I had ever loved, was feeling that same pain and unashamedly exposing his raw nerves to me. Yet, even after all I'd been through, I still harbored so much anger and resentment for the way he had dismissed me, tossed me aside like used goods. Now that he was back, weeping for my compassion, I just couldn't find it in me.

Then I heard Nick Nack stir in the corner of the kitchen. She moaned as she stood for the first time in days. I watched as she moved slowly on shaky legs. When she reached my side, she looked over at Mark and then up at me. Then she sighed and rested her head in my lap.

Great tears rolled down my cheeks as I thought, "Oh, my wonderful Nick Nack, you're teaching me lessons right to the end."

I stroked my big old dog that I loved with all my heart, and with my free hand I reached out and clasped Mark's trembling hand. And I held it tight while he cried. When Nick Nack was certain her job was done, she crept back across the kitchen floor and groaned as she eased herself down on her palette.

I handed Mark a paper napkin, and as he mopped his face, I said, "You and Tawni are going to have to break this news to Alex, you know."

With that, he started crying again. "Oh, Rowdy, what will we tell her?"

"Well, Mark, you'll just tell her the truth, and only you and Tawni know the truth."

Mark was looking at me with his begging eyes, those eyes that said he wanted me to do his dirty work for him. But he was on his own. This was his life, a life he had chosen to live without me. He had to tell our daughter.

"She loves you and Tawni and your children, and this is going to break her heart. You have to convince her that you all still love her and that she will be able to continue seeing all four of you."

"Where is Alex?" Mark asked, realizing, for the first time, that she was not at home. That was so like Mark.

"She's at camp. Don't you remember that I took her to the mountains last weekend?"

"Oh, yes, yes I remember," and his voice trailed off, as if he weren't too sure about that after all.

"Well, I'm just not ready to talk with her yet," he said, his voice trailing away.

When there was just nothing at all left to say, he wiped his face with the napkin and stood to leave. I followed him to the front door and watched him shuffle down the sidewalk. He looked like an old man, an old, beaten man. His shoulders were hunched, he looked disheveled, and his hair was beginning to thin at the crown. He didn't remotely resemble the guy who had hooked a hottie, lost twenty pounds, and had babies.

As soon as I closed the door, the phone rang. I was certain Mark was calling from his car, to see if I'd changed my mind about breaking the news to Alex when she returned from camp.

I rushed to pick up the phone to tell him, "Absolutely not!"

But it wasn't Mark. It was Kent.

"Ready to head back to class?"

I had been so busy getting Alex ready for camp and tending to Nick Nack, that I'd almost forgotten that semester break was about to come to an end. The fall semester would start the following Monday.

"Hadn't thought much about it, but I'm so glad you called. I have some good news, and I'm dying to tell someone. And I can't think of anyone I'd rather tell than you."

He said, "Well, thanks, Rowdy. What's the news?"

"I just got a call from my doctor. My tests just came back. I'm cancer free."

And he screamed, "Oh, my god, that's incredible! I'll be right over. We need to celebrate."

And before I could tell him that I was worn out from dealing with Mark and just wanted to take care of Nick Nack, the line went dead.

I was sitting on the kitchen floor stroking Nick Nack when Kent came charging through the front door, shouting with glee.

"It's party time!"

He rushed into the kitchen, cradling a Krispy Kreme box.

"Hurry, they're right off the conveyor belt, and nothing is better than Krispy Kremes right off the conveyor belt. I came as fast as I could so they'd still be hot."

This guy just got more perfect by the minute. He knew what was important: HOT Krispy Kremes.

I stood to greet him with a hug, glad I hadn't told him not to come over, and said, "Thanks for coming. I really need a friend about now."

He smiled, pulled me close, and said, "That's what you've got."

"Thanks, friend," I said, breaking away. "Sit down. I'll fix us some coffee."

Then Kent saw Nick Nack lying on her pallet in the corner. He looked at me, his brow knitted.

"It's bad, Kent," I said, my voice breaking. "Just a matter of time. She's gone down fast."

While I made a pot of coffee and dabbed my leaking eyes with a paper towel, Kent stretched out on his belly on the floor close to Nick Nack, his face just inches from her head.

As he stroked her, he whispered, "Hi, sweet girl. Not feeling so good, are you? I'm so sorry. You're a good girl."

Kent was just one more person who had fallen in love with my precious Nick Nack, and he was heartbroken that she was slipping away from us. He laid his head on her side, wrapping his arm around her. I could hear him sniffing back the tears.

As I filled our mugs with coffee, he sat up and wiped his shirt sleeve across his eyes. We sat cross-legged, the Krispy Kreme box between us. What started as a celebration had quickly turned into a somber occasion. Beyond telling me how happy he was about my news, we ate our hot-off-the-conveyor-belt donuts in silence.

But I finally found some comfort in Krispy Kremes. All that had been missing was a friend to share them.

❧❦❧

Days dragged, and Nick Nack's condition deteriorated. I was grateful Alex was still at camp. She didn't need to be around at a time like this. She had already lost so much.

235

I left Nick Nack's side only to shower and change into my pajamas. Then I'd haul my blanket and pillow down to the kitchen so I could rest by her side.

I'd forget to eat, and when I'd remember, I'd find that I had no interest. One night, though, I had a taste for parmigiano reggiano. I reached in the fridge and pulled out an almost-new brick. I recalled the time Nick Nack ate my expensive cheese and sent me into a rage. But today was different. I cut two slivers and placed the block back in the cheese drawer. Then I returned to Nick Nack's side. I popped one piece of the cheese into my mouth and offered the other to Nick Nack. She hadn't eaten in so long, but I was hoping she'd join me for one last treat. As she smelled the cheese, she willed her eyes open, but I knew that she wouldn't be joining me. So I put her piece in my mouth and lay close to her side and wrapped by arms around her, burying my face in her beautiful, black coat. As I held her, I felt her begin to tremble. Holding her close could not make the shaking subside.

I trudged upstairs and lifted The Quilt from the foot of my bed. When I returned to the kitchen, I spread it across Nick Nack and tucked it gently around her body. She forced her eyes open, sniffed the edge of The Quilt and looked into my face. Too weak to smile or wag her tail, I got her message of love and gratitude.

"I know, Girl," I said and kissed her on the top of her head.

I lay close and held her as I listened to her breathing get shallower and shallower. I knew around two o'clock in the morning that she was gone. I couldn't let her go. I held her close until I saw the sun.

Then I released her and laid her on her pallet. In my pajamas I slipped out the back door and went to the garage to find a shovel. Once I'd located it behind the lawn mower and weed eater, I headed for the willow oak. A tree that afforded little shade when Mark, Alex, and I had moved into the house eight years before, it was now so enormous it canopied half the back yard. Though it was a naked skeleton in winter, in spring and summer it cooled the lawn with its umbrella of green. And in autumn that umbrella was so golden that it appeared to create its own light. Nick Nack had always loved that tree. After romping to the point of exhaustion, she would lie beneath its canopy in the cool grass and nap.

I was saddened that she would miss autumn's golden canopy.

When I reached the base of the willow oak, I began to dig. By mid-morning I was drenched in perspiration and standing knee deep in a hole.

I returned to the kitchen, where I wrapped Nick Nack in Her Quilt, as she was its rightful fifth-generation heir. I carried her to the back yard and climbed into the hole, leaned against the cool earth, and held her in my arms.

For hours I wept for the love and companionship that had always been there for the taking and I had missed. But I knew that Nick Nack's and my friendship had unfolded just the way it was intended. I'm convinced that she had never been Alex and Mark's dog. She came into our lives to be mine, all mine. She knew that from the beginning, even if all the humans were clueless. She knew that I was the one who would need her, and, with great patience and unconditional love, my wonderful Nick Nack had waited for me to claim her as my own.

Epilogue

Autumn in central North Carolina is take-your-breath-away beautiful: balmy, shirt-sleeve days and skies so clear and cloudless they can only be called Carolina blue. But the heart-stopping beauty comes from the autumn leaves. The maples are so red and so orange that you swear they just *have* to be on fire. And the oaks, those majestic oaks for which our area is so well known, wear golden leaves that glow from the inside.

But I had allowed the past few autumns to slip by without notice. My victimhood had clouded my vision. Once the scales sloughed from my eyes, I saw it once again and cried that I had wasted autumns that I could never reclaim.

I was deep into the joy of my second year of nursing school, still missing Nick Nack but at my happiest since Mark's departure. *Everything* was beautiful. And along came autumn.

I had shuttled Alex out the front door to the bus stop, watching her skip happily away under the arch of brightly-colored fall leaves that canopied our street. When Conner and Everette emerged from their house and the three friends disappeared, arm in arm in arm, around the corner, I turned my attention to packing my backpack for school.

I'd just slipped a bottle of water and a granola bar into my pack when the phone rang.

"Rowdy?"

"This is she."

"Rowdy, it's Greg."

My pendulous emotions immediately swung between elation at hearing my brother's voice and sorrow that I hadn't recognized it. My emotions came to rest on elation.

"Hi, Greg, I'm so happy you called."

"I know it's been a long time," he said, his words drifting away.

"But it's never too late. Honest, I'm *so* glad to hear your voice."

"Rowdy, I'm so sorry I haven't been there for you. Can you ever forgive me?"

"Greg, I understand," I said, though I really didn't. But I was not going to do anything to strain this tenuous reconciliation. I wanted my little brother under any circumstance.

"Are you up for a beach trip?" he asked.

I was taken aback by his abrupt change in mood, but I jumped on board and said, "You know I'm always up for a beach trip. Are you saying that you are?"

"I think I am. I'm not sure. But I want to give it a try. So do the guys."

Greg didn't identify the guys, but I assumed he was referring to our brothers.

"The guys? You mean Will, Kevin, and Sam?"

"Those are the ones. I've already talked to them. They're not sure about opening the wounds either, but they've agreed to try, with no promises for the future."

"I understand, Greg, but we have to start—well, restart—somewhere."

"You're right, Rowdy."

"By the way, why the sudden change of heart?"

"Not sudden, Rowdy. It's been a long time coming. I've missed y'all so much. But every time I'd try to reconnect, I'd think of Mama and Daddy and lose it."

"I know what you mean, Greg. I still have a huge hole in my heart. I don't think I'll ever be able to fill it, but that's no reason we can't still love one another and spend time together."

"I agree. And, Rowdy, there's another thing."

"What's that, Greg?"

"I want my son to know his aunt and uncles."

"Your son?" I screamed.

"Yeah, surprise, huh? Sandy and I were as surprised as you. But we're five months along. Sandy was dying to tell you, but we waited till we were sure the baby was fine and that she was going to be able to carry him to term. The doctor says it's all systems go."

"Oh, Greg, that's just so wonderful."

"His name is William Rowdy, after, you, Will, and Daddy.

"Oh, Greg, I'm so happy for you, happy for all of us."

"It's amazing how a child can change everything, isn't it?"

"Yes, Greg, amazing."

"Hey, Sis, I've gotta get to work. Okay if I call you tonight so we can make a plan?"

"That's fine, Greg," I beamed. "Tonight will be just fine. And we'll make a plan."

"One more thing, do you still have the bunk beds at the beach house?"

"Nothing has changed, Greg. The bunk beds are waiting for you, Will, Kevin, and Sam."

"I get the top," he said.

"Well, you four will have to settle that. Just leave me out of it."

Greg laughed, a laugh I hadn't heard in so long. He sounded just like Daddy.

"Tonight, Rowdy," he said, the joy in his voice apparent.

The thirty-minute ride from Raleigh to Chapel Hill had me whooping with joy and oohing and aahing at every red maple, every golden oak. As I parked my car, I looked up at the canopy of fall colors casting a red-gold-orange glow over the campus; and I squinted at the blinding sun shining through the tree branches, shooting golden rays of light.

I slipped from my car and onto the trail that would take me to my morning coffee meet-up with Kent. Straight ahead on my path was an enormous, perfectly-shaped willow oak, heavy with gold-coin leaves. A gentle breeze fluttered the leaves, making them sound like so many wind chimes.

As I watched the leaves sway and shimmer gold in the sunlight, a single warm gust of wind passed, rattling those coin-leaves. In one moment *every* leaf on that huge tree loosed its tenuous grip on its branch and twirled to earth, spinning and glistening in the sunlight. As the leaves hit the pavement, they made a concert of popping sounds. I stood speechless, breathless until each leaf was nestled on the ground and silent, creating a beautiful, golden carpet around the naked tree.

Once the tingling up my spine came to rest, I spun around and screamed, "Did you see that?"

But there was no one there. I was completely alone. Not another soul had seen that golden miracle. It was all mine.

And as I stood there alone, marveling at my miracle, I thought of Nick Nack. Did she have something to do with this? I chuckled at the notion but thought, "Why not?" She had seen me through cancer, but that wasn't all she'd done for me. She had taught me to face my fears; had showed me how to embrace friendships; had taught me patience and unconditional love; had helped me forgive. She had even been instrumental in my pursuing a degree in nursing. Why couldn't she be responsible for sending me a golden miracle to show me that she was still watching out for me?

I couldn't wait to share my experience with Kent as I ran the last two blocks to meet him. He greeted me with a warm embrace, one that said *I want to be more than friends.* I returned his hug because I was beginning to consult that *Things to Think About Way Down the Road* file, and Kent was at the top of that list. I chatted animatedly, trying desperately to describe my miracle tree, the leaves falling all at once, the coins of gold spinning through the air, the chorus they played as they hit the pavement. But I wasn't able to do it justice. I just couldn't find fitting words to describe the beauty, the implausibility of what I'd witnessed.

And as I try to recount it here, I realize I *still* can't find fitting words. The splendor of that moment remains all mine.

When classes ended for the day, I again passed the naked willow oak, its golden leaves still carpeting the ground beneath it. And, once again, I thought that maybe, just maybe, I'd witnessed Nick Nack's magic. And what about Greg's call on this magical day? Could Nick Nack have had a hand—well, a paw—in that? Probably not, but who knows? Maybe, just maybe...

I got into my car, smiling, and reversed my journey, still in awe of the splendor between Chapel Hill and Raleigh.

When, thirty minutes later, I pulled into my drive, I was tired—tired but content. I had a half-hour to decompress and regroup before Alex would arrive home from school. Then my second job of after-school carpooling, meal preparing, and homework helping would begin. I decided to use that half-hour to relax, something I'd rarely done since my return to school. I went into the house and dropped my backpack in the hall, still missing my furry, smiling, tail-wagging greeter. I went to the kitchen and grabbed the iced tea pitcher from the fridge and poured myself a glass. I headed for the back porch to sit in the swing and enjoy the sunshine and the majesty of autumn a little longer while I anticipated the reunion with my little brothers.

Then I saw it: the willow oak. Nick Nack's tree. That morning before I left for campus, I had stood at my kitchen window, sipping my coffee, awestruck by its beauty and its glorious golden branches canopying the lawn. But the canopy was gone. Its branches were bare. Not one leaf remained. They all rested neatly in a circle on the ground, creating a magnificent golden quilt where Nick Nack lay.

That's when I knew for sure.

End Notes

[1]Cooke, Sam. "You Send Me." *The Best of Sam Cooke*. RCA, 1962, p.11

[2]Mathis, Johnny. "Wonderful, Wonderful." *Misty*. Columbia, 1957, p.15

[3]Wilson, Jackie. "Lonely Teardrops." *Lonely Teardrops*. Brunswick Records, 1959, p.16

[4]Durante, Jimmy. "Make Someone Happy." *Sleepless In Seattle (Original Motion Picture Score)*. Sony Music Entertainment, 1993, p.21

[5]The Platters. "I'm Sorry." *Golden Hits*. Mercury, 1959, p.52

[6]The Platters. "Only You." *Golden Hits*. Mercury, 1959, p.56

[7]Bareilles, Sara. "Brave." *The Blessed Unrest*. Epic Records, 2013, p.153

[8]General Johnson and The Chairmen of the Board. "Carolina Girls." *Carolina Girls*. Surfside Records, 1980, p.18

About the Author

Padgett Gerler was born on the coast of South Carolina but grew up in the Shenandoah Valley of Virginia. In the 1980's she relocated to Raleigh, North Carolina to attend North Carolina State University. Upon graduating with a BA in accounting, she passed the CPA exam and began her career as a certified public accountant, first in public accounting and then as a CFO in corporate accounting. In 2010 she left accounting to pursue a career in writing. Prior to LESSONS I LEARNED FROM NICK NACK, Padgett published her novel GETTING THE IMPORTANT THINGS RIGHT. She is also the author of the short story "I Know This Happened 'Cause Somebody Seen It" which was published in the anthology SELF-RISING FLOWERS. She is the recipient of the Southwest Manuscripters Short Story Award for her story "The Art of Dying." Her next novel, PELICAN ISLE, is scheduled for release in 2015. Padgett and her husband, Ed, reside on pastoral and inspirational Winchester Lake in Raleigh, North Carolina.

61962037R00141

Made in the USA
Middletown, DE
17 January 2018